Skin Deep

Desiree Holt
Lynne Connolly
Shoshanna Evers

ELLORA'S CAVE
ROMANTICA®
ELLORASCAVE.COM

BEDROOM EYES
Desiree Holt

Bridget Reilly has lived her entire life using dark glasses to hide her deformed eyelids. But she also hides her real self, working a dead-end job and locking herself away from any social life. In secret she lusts for her next-door neighbor, Navy SEAL Clay Randall, a lust unexpectedly fed during an electrical blackout.

When a masked ball provides the opportunity for her to have an entire night of glorious, unrestrained, erotic sex with Clay, how can she ignore it? The night more than exceeds all her expectations and now she wants to find a way to have a real relationship with him, without the mask. She applies to the Durban Trust, a fund set up by a former movie star to provide plastic surgery, and the surgery is successful. But what she hadn't counted on was Clay's reaction when she revealed all to him—and the wedge it would drive between them.

STRANGERS NO MORE
Lynne Connolly

Strangers in the dark, meeting for anonymous, hot and dirty sex. That was the way it was meant to be. But Whitney is increasingly drawn to her Stranger, more than she should be. Even if once he sees her face, he'll run screaming. Then Whitney receives an offer from the Durban Trust for cosmetic surgery. Although she knows looks don't matter, they've cost her too many promotions. She has to change her face to change her life.

Her colleague Jay—reporter and thriller writer—has a secret to match Whitney's. He's her Stranger. He doesn't give a damn about her face, but how does he tell her? Now Jay has two secrets. He put her forward for the surgery. Once he tells her, she'll kick him out of her life, but he has to take that chance. He only wants her to get the job. Because she already has him. Hook, line and sinker.

BEDHEAD
Shoshanna Evers

Michele Peterson is young, pretty, healthy...and bald. Being a woman with alopecia isn't easy—not only do strangers treat her as if she's a cancer patient, but hiding her bald head under a wig is hard on her sex life. Michele can't shower with a lover or feel his hands tangled in her hair in the throes of passion. So at the age of twenty-six, she remains a virgin. Then a generous benefactor agrees to finance hair transplant surgery. Just in time too, because Michele thinks she's met The One.

Andrew Calhoun doesn't understand why the incredible woman he's falling for is so distant—pulling away just as he thinks they're making a connection. When he discovers her secret, he'll have to make her realize that bald really is beautiful—before she goes through a potentially dangerous cosmetic surgery just for his sake. And the best way to make her feel desirable...is in bed.

An Ellora's Cave Publication

www.ellorascave.com

Skin Deep

ISBN 9781419966484
ALL RIGHTS RESERVED.
Bedroom Eyes Copyright © 2011 Desiree Holt
Strangers No More Copyright © 2011 Lynne Connolly
Bedhead Copyright © 2011 Shoshanna Evers
Edited by Helen Woodall and Jillian Bell.
Design by Syneca.
Photography by Fotolis.com.

Trade paperback publication 2012

SKIN DEEP

BEDROOM EYES
Desiree Holt
~9~

STRANGERS NO MORE
Lynne Connelly
~121~

BEDHEAD
Shoshanna Evers
~229~

BEDROOM EYES

Desiree Holt

෪

Dedication

જી

*To my very own personal hero, who dared me to be
myself. And to all my readers — know that real beauty
comes from the inside.*

Chapter One

๛

*Darren tightened his arms around her, his gaze locked with
hers. He didn't think he'd ever get enough of looking into those
slumberous bedroom eyes. Eyes that he could get lost in.*

Bridget Reilly made a sound of disgust, selected the text
she'd just written and hit the Delete key. Eyes, eyes, eyes. She
was fixated on them. Why couldn't she focus on breasts? Or
hips? Or even thighs? There was nothing wrong with those
parts of her body. It was her eyes that were the problem. No
doubt the reason she kept giving her heroines the kind that
were so totally opposite from hers.

*Darren showered kisses along Maggie's jawline and down the
column of her neck. He thought he could spend hours just tasting
every inch of her, drinking in her essence. He'd never met a woman
who could make him come undone the way she did just by looking at
him with those eyes that captivated him...*

Damn! Again with the freakin' eyes. Talk about being
obsessed.

Once more she highlighted the text and hit Delete then
stared at the page. Why was it tonight she was more obsessed
than usual about the deformity she lived with on a daily basis?

*Because today yet another jerk had rudely asked why I had such
fat eyelids.*

She picked up her coffee mug and took a sip. Made a face
when she realized the liquid had cooled and put the mug back
down on her desk. Reading romance fiction had long ago
become her alternate universe, a place where she could
vicariously experience all the things she missed in real life. She
had a boring job that paid her bills and gave her a place to hide

from public view. Rushing home after work she'd curl up with the latest hot romance and lose herself in the pages of a book.

One night, on impulse, she'd decided to try writing a story that was dancing around in her head and had discovered she could actually *become* her heroines. She wrote another story. And another. In page after page of her stories she could live out every one of her fantasies. Give her heroines the thing she lacked—sexy, inviting, appealing eyes. And hotter-than-sin men like the kind she dreamed about. It soon became a wonderful escape for her from the realities of her pitiful sex life.

Again on impulse she'd decided to submit a manuscript to a publisher. She loved the anonymity of the internet. They couldn't see her so she could be any image to them she chose. Seven rejections had come her way before the first contract. Now the fact that someone was actually publishing what she wrote and she was making a little money from it was the frosting on the cake.

No one knew about her little secret. Not even her friend Joni. She wrote under a pen name, deliciously shocked when an epublisher had actually offered her a contract, and stashed the growing royalty checks in a separate account. No, they weren't huge amounts at the moment but each one showed increasing sales. One of these days she'd have enough for her special project. She just hoped it was before she was too old to get any benefit from it.

Her dream—her very, very secret dream—was to have that surgery, come out of her writing closet and attend some important writers' conferences. Maybe even, after a while, be able to conduct a workshop. Have the opportunity to get her out of her dead-end job and into the career she dreamed about.

But none of that would be possible unless she had the surgery on her eyelids. She knew she'd never be able to stand the humiliation of people staring at her. Even her tinted glasses might not be sufficient protection. What if they slipped in public? Or someone saw her when she had them off for some reason? Her talent would be submerged beneath the ugliness of her face.

Meanwhile she'd keep on writing. One of these days she'd have the money for the surgery. Hopefully by that time she wouldn't be too old to really launch her career.

Sighing, she pushed back from her computer desk and did something she'd done far too many times lately. She walked into her bedroom, opened the closet door and stared at herself in the mirror, assessing herself.

Okay, physical assets aside she was smart, could carry on a good conversation and make a mean martini. She had a decent body that she took care of, a figure not too bad. Maybe a tad too wide in the hips but her breasts balanced it off. Nice legs. Her face had good bone structure and she took very good care of her skin. And her hair fell like a shiny curtain of honey-colored silk to her shoulders thanks to an expert cut.

Then she looked at her eyes. Oh, god. She hated seeing them yet was obsessed with constantly checking them, as if by some miracle they would have changed since the last time she looked.

But no, there they were, the eyes themselves peering out at her through narrowed slits, her lids dragged down by the heavy folds of skin over the upper eyelids. Pressing her forefingers on the skin and bracing her thumbs on her cheekbones she dragged the lids upward. Yup. Two perfectly good cornflower blue eyes that she was sure some men might look into and find enticing. If only they could see more than a tiny portion of them.

Oh, they looked at them all right. Stared was more like it, as if she was some kind of freak. If she removed the tinted glasses she'd taken to wearing years ago and the man she was with looked at her eyelids, that was all she wrote.

She could identify the look in seconds by now — stunned, shocked, in some cases horrified. Then the overly polite excuses. The haste to depart. She still couldn't erase the humiliating memory of the man she'd thought was an exception. A man who left her high and dry when she accidentally discovered he'd asked her out on a dare. Like the unpopular girl in high school.

The worst was the lab scientist she'd had one date with who told her they reminded her of the frogs in his lab when their lids were lowered. To make matters worse he hadn't even realized how badly he'd hurt her.

Maybe she should just put a paper bag over her head. The tinted glasses that she wore like a lifeline disguised what she thought of as her deformity. They saved her from the curious looks of her coworkers and people when she was out in public. But some places were so dark she had to take them off to see and then the staring began in earnest.

Dr. Richards, the plastic surgeon she'd consulted with, had carefully explained to her that it was merely an accident of development in the womb. As if that made it all okay. For most people, he told her, the fold disappeared after three to six months of gestation. For some, however, it never changed. How did she happen to be one of those unlucky ones?

As she left the bedroom and walked back to her desk the lights flickered. Once. Twice. Were they about to have a power surge for some reason? Her stomach clenched. Ever since she was a child she'd had an unreasoning fear of the dark.

You'd think someone who looked like me would welcome it.

But no, for some unexplained reason it always terrified her. She still remembered the nights she'd climbed into bed with her sister, huddling under the covers with her, afraid to be alone.

The ringing of her phone cut through the air and broke into her little pity party. She glanced at her watch. Nine thirty. There weren't too many people who'd be calling her at this hour. Or actually any hour. Her unenviable social life was the envy of none.

14

She checked the caller ID. Joni. Now what? Joni, bless her, always had some new idea to pester her about. She couldn't seem to get it through her head that Bridget didn't want to go to parties, be fixed up on blind dates or anything remotely resembling those two things.

"Hey," she said, after picking up the phone.

"Hey yourself."

Bridget dropped into her desk chair. "What's up?"

"Marnie heard about this new place called The Hot Spot," she began. "Three people told her it's *the* place to see and be seen now. We want to hit happy hour after work tomorrow. You on?"

No. No, no, no.

"Um, I don't think so." She twirled a strand of hair around her finger. "I've got...stuff to do. But thanks anyway."

Go to yet another bar to be humiliated? Not in this lifetime.

"Bridget." She heard the exasperation in Joni's voice. "You can't hide in your house forever."

"I don't," she protested. "I go out every day, as a matter of fact."

"Oh, right." Joni snorted. "To work. Big whoop. Honey, you gotta get out and mingle a little. You haven't been out with us in ages."

Bridget and Joni had been friends for a long time but she'd really gotten tired of Joni constantly trying to act as if there wasn't a problem here.

"I'm fine," she snapped. "Thanks for asking but I have to go. I'm right in the middle of something."

Right in the middle of creating a life for myself in the pages of a book that I'll never have anywhere else.

"Don't think you're going to shut me out," her friend told her. "I won't let you hide forever."

"If you were a real friend you wouldn't insist on taking me places where I get insulted," she said with bitterness. "Isn't it enough already?"

"Bridget." She could hear the sound of long-suffering patience in Joni's voice. "I keep trying to tell you that the only person your eyes bother is you."

"Yeah? I don't think so. You aren't the one guys look at as if you're on a microscope slide or ask you embarrassing questions like 'What's wrong with your eyelids? Why do they look so weird?' Thanks, anyway, but I'll pass."

"Oh, honey, listen—"

"I'll talk to you tomorrow," Bridget said firmly and disconnected the call, done with the conversation.

She scraped her hair back from her face, leaned her head back and closed her eyes.

Why me?

She'd been asking herself that question for years but no one seemed to have answers for her. She had done so much research on her condition that by this time she figured she could write a book about it. She also knew that surgery was a possibility but that had created even more problems for her. No doctor would touch it when she was still young because her particular case was extreme and could be complicated.

The operation would still be complex because the fold was unusually large and involved a lot of nerves and blood vessels, and was therefore very expensive. The damn insurance companies classified it as elective cosmetic surgery and paying for it herself was out of the question. Even with the money she earned from her books she was a long way from having sufficient finances.

Pulling her hair back into a ponytail and fastening it in place with a clip she turned her attention back to her computer.

Maggie's heart was racing, her pulse pounding madly. Heat poured from Darren's body, his skin hot against hers. The curled hair

16

on his chest abraded her nipples, already taut with need, and brushed the sensitive skin of her breasts. His cock pressed against the inside of her thigh, a vivid reminder of his intense state of arousal.

The throbbing deep in her cunt accelerated, vibrating through her body.

Darren cupped her head with his lean fingers, his face barely an inch from hers.

"Look at me," he commanded. "Open your eyes and look at me." His dark eyes were now as black as onyx, desire a golden flame dancing in them.

"Darren," she breathed.

"I could get lost in your eyes." His voice was rough with need. "Bedroom eyes. Look at me while I fuck you, Maggie. Let me fall into those eyes while I pump into your body."

He thrust inside her, his gaze holding her in place while he...

Eyes, eyes, eyes. Hell.

Bridget hit Save and pushed back from her desk. Damn it to hell, anyway. No man was ever going to say that to her, that was for damn sure. Why did people have to be so hung up on looks, anyway?

Making a face at the dregs of her coffee, she carried the mug into the kitchen and dumped what was left into the sink. Might as well set up the coffeepot for tomorrow while she was at it, she thought. But when she pitched the used filter and grounds into her trash she sighed at the amount of garbage, pulled the sack out and tied it off. Tomorrow was trash pickup day, which meant she ought to take the big garbage can out to the curb now.

Bother.

She detoured on her way to the garage to get her tinted glasses from the bedroom. She knew she looked stupid wearing them at night but there was always the chance she'd run into her neighbor, Mr. Sexy-and-Good-Looking himself. The ultimate fantasy come to life. Ever since he'd moved in next door she'd lusted after him. Yup, that was the only word.

17

Lusted. If she admitted it, reluctantly, by now it had morphed into something else. If you reached for the impossible, might as well make it as unattainable as you can, right? The image of him was the one always dancing in her brain when she wrote her erotic heroes and every contact with him only reinforced it.

They'd actually had many conversations, on her back porch or his. About his life as a SEAL. About politics, books and movies. Even about sports.

"You're one of the few women I've ever met who's as addicted as I am," he told her once during a heated debate about Super Bowl contenders. They'd even indulged in some casual flirting, scattered episodes that she hugged to her heart and pulled out at night to relive over and over.

The conversations were relaxed and easy, even the flirting, and always—*always*—in the daylight hours so she could hide behind her big, dark sunglasses. Of course he'd never seen her without the glasses and she didn't intend to start now.

If only Clay Randall could fall in love with her as she was falling for him.

If only.

Sure enough, as she wheeled the can out of her narrow one-car garage to the curb there he was, setting out his own trash. Just the sight of him with his muscular body outlined by the soft light of the street lamps was enough to start her heart pounding. She couldn't stop looking at the way his t-shirt stretched taut across well-muscled shoulders and a broad chest that tapered to a narrow waist. Worn jeans clung to narrow hips and long legs.

His sun-streaked brown hair just brushed the top of his t-shirt, framing a face with high cheekbones and a square jaw. Bridget was sure she had his features memorized by this time. Every hero in her books bore an uncanny resemblance to Clay Randall. If she could just keep him in her head and out of her heart. He was so far out of her league.

"Hey, Bridget." His grin was enough to heat her blood and set the pulse in her cunt to beating harder than a jungle drum.

"Hey yourself, Clay." She placed her garbage can very carefully at the curb, making sure the lid was tight. And making doubly sure she stayed out of touching distance from Mr. Hottie.

"What's with the sunglasses?" he asked.

"Sunglasses?" Damn. Bridget felt the familiar knot of tension grab her in the pit of her stomach.

"Maybe nobody told you, sugar, but there's no sun out right now." He made a show of looking up at the sky. "Actually, I think it's pretty dark."

"I, uh, have a problem with my eyes. That's why I always keep the glasses on."

Why didn't I wait and make sure he wasn't out here? I've always avoided him at night just for this reason.

"Oh." His face sobered instantly. "I'm sorry. I didn't mean—"

"It's okay." She waved it off. "No problem."

"So, how's life treating you these days?" he asked, leaning one hip against his can.

"Not bad." *Terrible.* "How about you?"

"You know." He shrugged. "Same old, same old."

"How long you home for this time?"

Bridget knew Clay was a SEAL, often deployed on missions for weeks at a time. He'd bought the house for the same reason she'd purchased hers—to have some permanence and stability in his life. Bridget figured she'd probably never have a home of her own otherwise and apartment living had just gotten too old for her. Clay said he wanted a place to unwind that was all his. A place where he could put down roots. Do whatever he wanted.

19

Every so often she'd see a woman in the backyard with him, or sitting beside him in his car as he backed out of the driveway. Tall, leggy brunettes and redheads, with typically classic good looks. The sound of their intimate laughter was a knife straight to her heart, because she knew she'd never share those kinds of moments with him. She dreaded the day he brought a wife home with him and she was forced to watch them wrapped in a haze of happiness and sexual satisfaction.

"Well." She wiped her suddenly damp palms on her shorts. "I'd better go in."

"Me too. Big night tomorrow night." But he made a faced as he said it.

"You don't look like it's too big. Or that you're too happy about it."

He shrugged. "My team captain happens to live in San Antonio too, just by coincidence, and his wife is involved in some big charitable ball that's going down tomorrow night. The one that kicks off Fiesta. He made everyone on the team who lives around here buy a ticket. Not only that, he insists that we have to go."

And of course he'll be going with a gorgeous piece of arm candy.

"Surely your date will keep you from being too miserable." There. That was the right casual tone, wasn't it?

"No date." He ran a palm over his hair. "No one I could ask to rent a costume and dress up for a masquerade. Bad enough I have to do it myself."

"No gorgeous babe hanging around these days?" She hated herself for asking the question, no matter how casual she tried to make it.

His laugh was humorless. "Not lately. Must be losing my charm. Or maybe it's just that I'm starting to lose interest in all show and no go. I'll just guts it out."

Bridget nodded but both her mind and her heart were racing. She knew all about the masquerade. Joni's boss was also on the committee and Joni had been pestering Bridget for weeks to buy a ticket. The cheapest ones were a hundred bucks, though, and not something Bridget wanted to dig into her stash to buy.

But Clay was going without a date. Well, well, well. An outrageous idea was percolating wildly in her brain.

"So I guess you've got your costume then?"

"Yeah." Lines of displeasure grooved his cheeks. "Thank god at least most of my face will be covered so there's no chance anyone will recognize me."

Bridget cocked her head, all kinds of possibilities suddenly speed-racing through her brain. "You have a full face mask?"

He nodded. "In a manner of speaking. I'm going as a pirate. Figured that wasn't too embarrassing. Got a scarf thing to wrap over my head and a big black mask that matches it over my eyes."

A pirate. Bridget filed that piece of information away in her mind.

"Women love pirates." She hoped her tone was casual enough. "They'll probably be hanging all over you."

Clay snorted. "I doubt it. The women who show up at these things seldom come alone and the ones that do aren't worth the price of a drink."

"Maybe tomorrow night you'll be surprised." She wet her lips. "Tell you what. I'll make a bet with you."

"A bet?"

"Uh-huh. I predict you'll meet a mysterious woman. She won't even tell you her real name. She'll tempt you and tease you and make you want to sweep her off her feet."

Clay's mouth kicked up in a grin. "That right? You guaranteeing it?"

"I said I'd bet with you, didn't I?" She shoved her hands in the pockets of her shorts, waiting tensely for his answer. "Well? You gonna put your money where your mouth is?"

He laughed. "Okay. A bet. Loser buys dinner."

"You're on." She held out her hand.

Clay's grip was firm and warm. Bridget had expected that, but she hadn't been prepared for the jolt of electricity that sizzled up her arm and through her body. She pulled her hand back quickly, doing her best to ignore the gleam of mischief in Clay's eyes.

"I certainly hope so," he teased.

Bridget's cheeks turned hot. This was just harmless flirting, something Clay probably did as naturally as he breathed. But for her this was a scarce commodity. Once men got a look at her eyes all flirting was off the table.

"I-I have to go." She hurried up the driveway, calling over her shoulder, "Good luck. And I expect a full report."

"If it turns out the way you predict," he answered, "don't look for *too* many details."

If only this works.

"Confession time day after tomorrow, okay? We'll meet over the fence."

"Only long enough so I can tell you where I want you to take me for dinner. Get ready for an expensive meal."

"We'll see. Night, now."

She nearly ran into the house, her mind racing. She might never realize her goal of introducing herself in public as a published author but she at least had the possibility of one night with the man who filled her dreams. And one night was better than none.

Joni would surely still be awake. It hadn't been that long ago that she'd called. Bridget's hand was shaking so much as her plan took shape she had to make two tries at dialing the number. Then she nearly stumbled over her words telling her friend why she was calling.

"You want to do what?" Joni's voice sounded shocked at Bridget's request.

"You heard me. I want to buy a ticket to the masquerade ball. Do you still have any left?"

"Masquerade ball?" Joni sounded stupefied. "The one tomorrow night?"

"Yes." Bridget almost shouted the word. "What's the problem? You've been pestering the shit out of me to spend my hard-earned money on this for days. Now that I'm saying yes you act like I'm out of my mind."

"Yes. No. I mean..."Joni's voice trailed off. "It's just that this is definitely not your usual thing. I know I asked you about buying a ticket but honestly, Bridget. Don't take this the wrong way but I really didn't expect you to say yes. And if you did, I didn't think you'd go."

"Of course not. Why would I?" Bridget swallowed the automatic resentment. This was no time to get testy. "So can I meet you for breakfast and get a ticket? I'll even buy."

"Is something going on here I don't know about?" Joni demanded.

"Listen," Bridget pleaded. "Just this one time can you do something for me without the third degree? Do you have a ticket left and can I get it from you in the morning?"

Joni's sigh echoed all the way through the connection. "Sure. Okay. Bennie's Bagels at eight? That'll still give us time to get to work."

Bridget paused. "I'm a taking a personal day tomorrow."

"You're not going into work?" Joni was nearly shrieking. "Something's definitely up. Give me details in the morning and you can have the ticket for free."

"We'll see. Just be there at eight."

She hung up before Joni could pester her with anything else. Back at her computer she pulled up the yellow pages for the city and did a search for costume houses and costume stores. Printing out the list, she circled the most accessible ones, folded the sheet and tucked it into her purse. No one would be open until at least nine but by then for sure she'd be rid of Joni. Tomorrow would be a busy, busy day.

She closed her eyes and ran over her mental list.

Costume.

Hair.

Mani-pedi.

Wax job.

And then the ball.

This was going to cost her a fortune, but if it worked out it would be so worth it. She'd have one wonderful night of memories to hug tightly for a long time.

Bridget knew this could all blow up in her face but she had to do it. No question about it. She tried to tamp down the thrill of excitement wriggling through her. But if she was very, very careful, she could end up with the night of her life.

Chapter Two

ଈଠ

Bridget was desperately trying to control the worst case of nerves she'd had in her entire life. She'd decided to take a taxi rather than drive herself. But when the cab pulled up in front of her house she almost sent it away.

Coward.

Okay, yes. She was definitely that. But then she took one last look at herself in the mirror. Blonde hair piled artfully on top of her head and secured with rhinestone-studded sticks. Makeup flawlessly applied, although ninety percent of her face was concealed behind a red satin mask with wings at the eyes and decorated with sequins. Her body, waxed in all the important places, was laced into a red satin ball gown that flowed from her hips in a wide circle. And beneath it the most sinfully sexy red lingerie she'd ever worn in her life. All of it sprayed discreetly with Decadence, a new scent she'd purchased.

She'd had a couple of moments of hesitation, the first one at breakfast that morning when Joni insisted on filling out a form and giving her a receipt for the ticket.

"Can't I just give you the cash and you give me the ticket?" she asked. No way did she want her name listed anywhere if she could avoid it.

Joni shook her head. "That's not the way they do it. The rules of the ball say everyone gets a receipt because it's a charitable deduction and it also helps compile a master list. One the committee can use each year to get repeat attendees." When she saw Bridget frown she quickly added, "You don't have to go again. Really. I'm not even sure why you're going now. And if they contact you next year just toss the reminder. But my mother will kill me if I break the rules."

The second stumbling block came when she made her appointment at the salon. Everyone would be looking at her. She'd finally insisted she had to keep the tinted glasses on and despite the curiosity she'd managed to get through it all.

Because in the end she'd had little choice if she wanted to go through with this. One night of hot sex with Clay Randall. *If* she could find the right pirate in the crowd. *If* her seduction worked. And *if* — big if here — she could get away without losing herself completely.

So here she was, about to attend the first event like this in her thirty-one years. No one could see her face. No one could mock her. She'd be a mysterious woman who looked beautiful behind her disguise. For one night he would be hers. She could even delude herself into thinking he was in love with her. A memory to cherish for a lot of years, even as she watched him with the ever-changing parade of eye candy.

Okay. Deep breath. Now or never, kiddo.

Still, all the way to the hotel her heart beat erratically and she kept wiping her palms with the lace-edged hankie she was holding. Of course there was a traffic jam at entrance to the hotel and the cab had to wait its turn to pull into place. A uniformed valet attendant opened the cab door for her and helped her out. Which was a good thing because she wasn't used to moving in this kind of voluminous skirt.

Reaching into a deep pocket of the dress she pulled out a tiny purse and fished out money for the driver. Then she drew a deep breath, let it out slowly and pushed through the glass door into the immense lobby.

People in costume were everywhere, a steady flow heading toward the elevators and escalators. Including a fair number of pirates. Oh, lord. How was she supposed to recognize Clay? She should have gotten a better description of his particular costume. Moving carefully she made her way to the escalator, too impatient for the long wait at the elevator. In the wide gallery in front of the ballroom the crowd was even more jammed together, the noise level rising. And from behind the closed doors of the ballroom she could hear the strains of the orchestra.

Men in tuxedos were stationed at each door and when she approached one he smiled and said, "Ticket please."

Nervously she pulled the small square of rich cardboard from her pocket and handed it to him.

"Enjoy yourself, madame. There are several bars set up around the room and you may sit at any table that does not have a reservation sign."

Sit. At a table. Bridget hadn't even thought about that. It wasn't a dinner, just dessert and drinks, so she'd just figured everyone would be standing around drinking or dancing. Well, no worries. She'd be spending most of her time looking for Clay.

But looking around she realized just how difficult that might be. The huge ballroom was jammed but not too many people were sitting. They were either lined up at the bar, gathered in small groups or on the dance floor. The music was something Latin and people were throwing their hips into it.

Bridget managed to squeak up to one bar and finally get a glass of wine, gulping half of it to bolster her flagging courage. How on earth had she imagined she'd be able to find Clay in this mob, much less set out to seduce him?

Then she turned and bumped squarely into a tall, muscular pirate. He might be completely masked but she'd know that aftershave anywhere. Clean and earthy at the same time. She'd inhaled it enough times when she'd chatted with him before he left on one date or another.

"Sorry," he muttered, steadying her with his hands at her elbows.

"No, my fault." She pitched her voice lower than normal. Not that she figured Clay would recognize it anyway. She was just Next Door Bridget, unremarkable to him in any way. He probably dropped her from his mind the minute she pulled away from his house. She dabbed at his silk shirt with the tiny bar napkin.

"Don't worry about it." His deep voice cut through the music and hubbub. "It's probably only the first of many tonight."

Okay, Reilly. Do what you came here to do.

"I hope your wife or date won't be upset that your shirt's wet."

"No wife, no date. How about you?"

Yes! He was actually showing some interest!

She shook her head. "Just me. By myself."

Am I making it too obvious? But I just have tonight. I can't afford to waste time.

"The men in this city must be nuts if they weren't standing in line to escort you tonight."

She laughed, wondering if she sounded as slightly hysterical to him as she did to herself, and sipped more wine to calm herself. "I really just came tonight as a favor to a friend."

As they'd been talking he'd maneuvered her away from the bar and out of the line of traffic to a nearby corner.

"There," he said, when they were away from the press of the crowd. "At least we won't get run over. So where's the friend you're doing a favor for? How come he isn't with you?"

"*She* will be here later." *And I'd better be out of the ballroom by then, although there's no way she'll recognize me in this outfit.*

He lifted an eyebrow. "She?"

"Um-hum. And I'm pretty sure she has her own plans for the evening. I wouldn't even have come tonight but I hated to buy the ticket and waste the money."

He plucked her wineglass from her fingers and set it on the nearest table.

"Since we've cleared up that there's no *he* involved, I think we should dance."

"Dance?" God, she sounded like an idiot.

"Yes." His lips, the only part of his face that was visible, curved in a sensuous smile. "You know. Bodies moving to music. Come on."

Before she realized it they were on the dance floor, the orchestra was playing something slow and dreamy and she was finally in Clay Randall's arms. And oh god, it felt so very, very good. His body was so hard, his muscles like stone. His arm around her was a band of steel and he held her close enough that she could feel the hot length of his cock even through all the layers of their clothing. She wanted to rub herself all over him like a cat.

Clay bent his head so his mouth was close to her ear, close enough that she could hear him over the conversation and music. "If you aren't here with a date or your friend you're doing a favor for, won't you be pretty bored?"

Bridget wet her lips. *Now or never. No time to waste. I can do this, right?*

"I came to have an adventure."

He lifted his head and looked down at her. "Yeah? What kind of adventure?"

She tucked her head into his shoulder. "Oh, I don't know. Maybe I'll meet a dashing pirate and run off with him for the night."

His arm around her tensed and the hand that was holding hers tightened. "Really. But you've already met the pirate, right?"

"Um, yes, so it seems." Her heart was pounding so hard with nerves she was sure he could feel it.

"Or are you still looking?" His tone was light. Teasing. But also definitely questioning.

29

And the arm wrapped around her lowered enough so his hand swept lightly over the curve of her ass. Every hormone in her body jumped to life and surged through her system.

"That depends on you." The music came to an end and she let him lead her back to their spot against the wall.

"How so?"

"Well, if I can seduce you then I can stop looking for pirates. Right?"

Even with the mask covering most of his face his eyes were still visible through the slits. When he looked at her she saw surprise in them. "You don't waste much time, do you?"

She lifted one shoulder in what she hoped was a delicate shrug. "I only have tonight so I have to work fast."

"Why? Do you turn into a pumpkin?"

Worse. An ugly toad.

"No. Just an ordinary person."

"Why do I have the feeling there really isn't much ordinary about you?"

"You'd be wrong to think that. But for tonight," she gestured at herself, "for tonight I can be the mysterious seductress who woos the devilish pirate."

"I think I need to get us a drink." His hand rested briefly on the column of her neck. "After all, can't have a good seduction without a proper drink, right?"

"I guess not."

"Wine, right?"

She laughed. "And this time I'll try not to spill it on you."

He bent his head to her again. "If you do I'll just have to make you lick it up."

Visions of that sent a shiver skating over her skin and cream soaking her bright-red thong. Oh, she definitely wanted her mouth on hm. His chest. His nipples. Every inch of his skin. His cock. She shivered again. Tonight she wanted to act out every fantasy she'd written about in her erotic romances.

This is really going to happen.

If I don't screw it up.

Clay waited as patiently as he could to get to the bartender. He wanted to fetch the drinks and get back to his tiny piece of paradise in the corner of the ballroom. Where the hell had she come from, this lady in red? And why had she sought him out? Had bumping into her just been an accident or had she manipulated it? Set her sights on him and planned it?

Oh, yeah, right. How big is your ego, dipshit? With all the men wandering around in this room she deliberately sought you out?

Okay, accident then. He'd have to pay homage to the goddess of fate. If the night turned out the way he hoped, of course.

She felt so delicious in his arms, soft and curvy, not like the lean women he usually dated whose bones clanked with his. So why the hell did he keep going back to them if he found them so distasteful?

Because all men think with their dicks and their dicks have been taught that tall and thin is the badge of honor.

Well. Whoever thought that up is fucking damn stupid.

Because feeling Miss Red Dress in his arms, her soft breasts pushing against the wall of his chest, letting his hand drift to that luscious curve of her ass had him hard enough to drive railroad spikes. Just dancing with her had him mentally stripping that red dress from her body and imagining the creamy skin beneath. He wondered if the curls on her pussy were the same rich shade of gold as those piled on top of her head.

"Sir?"

31

He looked up, realized it was finally his turn at the bar and the bartender was looking at him impatiently.

"Bourbon on the rocks and a glass of white wine."

He stuffed a couple of bills in the tip jar and managed to work his way back to the lady in red without spilling anything.

"Thank you." She took the glass from him with graceful fingers.

Fingers that he suddenly wanted to suck individually, licking them with his tongue.

Jesus! Had she cast a spell on him?

"You haven't told me your name," he pointed out.

"Oh, but isn't that the point of a masquerade? To keep your identity secret?"

He chuckled. "I guess you're right. But I have to call you something besides Hey You."

She lifted the fabric of her dress and let it drop. "How about Red?"

He cupped the tiny portion of her chin not covered by her mask. "Okay. Red sounds good to me."

"But what about you?" she teased. "Should I call you Black Jack? Since you're all in black?"

"How about just Black? Then we'll be like the roulette wheel—Red and Black."

Her laugh was like the sound of silver chimes. "Works for me."

"So what's the next step in your great adventure?"

She lifted one shoulder gracefully. "Maybe another dance?"

He placed his glass on the edge of the table next to them, took hers and set it beside his own. "Then I think this is our song."

He was grateful that it was another slow melody, bluesy in its flavor. A song made for lovers. He was grateful for its tempo, unwilling to expend the energy he hoped to need by gyrating on the dance floor.

He swung her into his arms as if he'd been doing it for years. She fit perfectly against his body, her scent drifting in a tantalizing wave across his nose. His hand against her back drifted down to the swell of her buttocks again, bunching the material and sliding it back and forth. She hummed against his chest, a little sigh of pleasure that made him want to yank the fabric up to her waist and find the naked skin of her ass.

Wait! Stop! This is her adventure. Let her take the lead. Don't jump all over her like a horny teenager.

But with her pressing her body against his, moving in that slow, sexy rhythm with him, what was he supposed to do? He was, after all, a red-blooded male with all the right equipment and reactions.

"Do you live in San Antonio?" he asked, trying to divert his thought processes.

"Yes, I do."

"Too bad we've never met before. I like an adventurous woman." He shifted and turned them in a new direction. "Although I'm gone a lot."

"Oh? Do you travel on business?"

"Yeah, you could say that."

She moved her body against his, rubbing her breasts against him in a barely noticeable movement. He felt her hard nipples even through the satin of her dress and the silk of his shirt. His cock flexed, demanding freedom. Wanting to feel her heat.

"Are you deliberately trying to drive me crazy?" he asked in a strangled tone.

"Why, Black." She moved her hips forward. "Whatever do you mean?"

"Maybe you should tell me a little more about what this adventure of yours is going to entail. Just so I don't get myself in hot water."

Did she tremble or was it his imagination?

"I told you. I mean to seduce a willing pirate and have my way with him. All night long."

"Just for one night?" He turned her in yet another direction, needing to do something, anything except stand practically still with their bodies glued together.

"Oh, but that's the key to an adventure. One night of total erotic bliss with an exciting stranger. Someone with whom you can toss away all inhibitions. If you had to see the person again you might feel…feel…"

"Embarrassed?"

"Maybe."

"But what if you enjoyed it so much you wanted to do it again? With the same person."

"No, that's the key to an adventure like this," she insisted. "No names, one night, exciting memories."

Clay swallowed. "Then why are we wasting it on the dance floor?"

She lifted her head, the little he could see of her eyes suddenly uncertain.

"Unless you've changed your mind, of course." He tried to tamp down the disappointment that surged forward.

"N-no. Not at all." She released a little shuddering sigh. "So are you telling me you're already seduced?"

"Enough that I want this to continue someplace a lot more private."

Again he felt the little shudder and she stopped moving, stepping away from him.

"Wait here for me. I'll be right back." Lifting her skirt in both hands so she didn't trip, she hurried from the ballroom. Clay stared after her then retrieved his drink and downed the rest of it. He hoped she'd hurry, because he was more than ready for whatever she had in mind.

Bridget hurried as fast as she dared, down the escalator and through the busy lobby to the reservations desk. While she waited with barely concealed impatience she looked around, hoping she didn't spot Joni. Of course, who would recognize her the way she was dressed? Joni had never seen her like this and the mask covered all of her face except her pupils, her lips and a tiny bit of her chin.

"May I help you?"

The voice of the clerk dragged her back to her errand.

"Yes. I'd like a room for the night. Please."

The clerk did his thing at his system computer then looked up and smiled. "We don't have too much because of the ball. A lot of people have taken rooms." She laughed. "I guess so they don't have to worry about driving."

"But you still have something available."

"I do. But all I have are suites."

Bridget bit back a sigh. More digging into her secret stash. "How much?"

"We have a special on for the event. Four hundred dollars."

"Are you kidding me?"

"It's normally almost twice that but the owner is on the ball committee so he set special rates."

Oh well. At least it will be worth it. I hope.

"Okay. I'll take it." She handed over her credit card, filled out the registration form and accepted the key card the clerk slid across the counter to her. "One thing, though."

"Yes?"

"If anyone asks who rented this room, please tell them that information is confidential." The last thing she wanted was for Clay to quiz the staff and find out her name.

"Not a problem. I'll pass the message along to the next shift and note the account."

"Thank you." She let out a sigh of relief.

"We hope you enjoy yourself," the clerk told her.

"Oh, I plan to. Yes, indeed."

Back to the escalator, up to the next floor, down the hall to the ballroom. What if he'd changed his mind? What if he was gone? Or worse yet, had hooked up with someone else?

Please, please, please be there.

She shoved her way through the knots of people in the broad hallway, ignoring the snotty remarks until she reached the ballroom again. And there he was. Still leaning against the wall, looking sexier than any man she'd ever met. Bridget let her breath out in a whoosh, settled her nerves and made her way toward him slowly.

His lips, visible below the mask, curved in a warm grin. "I wasn't sure you were coming back."

"I just went to make the arrangements for the next part of our adventure."

"And did you?"

She nodded and shielding her actions with her body slid the key card from her pocket so that just the edge of it showed. "You still feeling seduced?"

Please say yes.

"Not as much as I expect to be if we use that card in your pocket." He put his hand on her elbow, aware that fine tremors were vibrating through her system. "Red? We can call this off right now if you've changed your mind."

She kept walking. "Not me. How about you?"

"Are you crazy? Just show me the way."

She was glad for the secure feeling of his elbow steadying her as they made their way to the elevators. He was a solid presence behind her while they waited, his big body shielding as if sensing her nervousness about the crowd. At last the elevator arrived, they stepped on and she pressed the button for the twentieth floor with a hand that trembled only slightly. Neither of them said a word when the doors opened at their floor. But as they walked down the hallway he took her hand and squeezed it gently.

"I think this will be my adventure too, Red."

"Really?" she asked in a breathy voice.

"Really," he assured her.

When she had the door open he followed her inside. Closing the door with his elbow, he turned her to face him and brought his mouth down on hers.

A stunning jolt of electricity sizzled through her straight to her pussy.

Oh, god. This was going to get far more complicated than she'd bargained for.

Chapter Three

℘

The kiss made Bridget so weak in the knees that she had to cling to Clay's arms to hold herself steady. His lips were firm and warm, pressing against hers lightly at first but then increasing the pressure and using his tongue to trace the closed seam. He lightly licked her upper and lower lip before pushing until she opened for him. He swept inside, his tongue everywhere lighting fires like a dancing flame.

Someone moaned and she was sure the sound came from her. His tongue glided over hers, searching her mouth relentlessly. Licking, caressing, drawing her own tongue into his mouth. Her breath was trapped in her throat and heat consumed her. At the point where she was sure she'd pass out from lack of oxygen—and didn't even care—he lifted his mouth from hers and stared directly into the part of her eyes he could see.

"Jesus!" he breathed. "Your kisses should come with a warning."

"Yours too."

She reached past him to find a switch on the wall beside the door and flipped it on, turning on two small table lamps.

Clay looked around at their surroundings. "A suite?"

"Only the best for my adventure," she told him.

"Then I'd better do my damndest to make it worth your while."

His mouth cruised over her neck, kissing, nipping, licking. He paused at the hollow of her throat, pressing the tip of his tongue against her hammering pulse before trailing kisses along her collarbone. Again he scattered little nips that he soothed with his tongue then moved to the upper swell of her breasts. When he stopped she cried out in protest.

"I think we need to be a little more horizontal for what I want to do."

She was pleased to discover his breathing was just as uneven as her own.

"I think I'm the one who's supposed to be taking the lead here."

His grin was wicked. "Then I say lead on."

Still quaking inside she took his hand and led him into the bedroom, which was as huge as the living room part of the suite. Spotting the king-size bed that seemed to be the focal point, she took another deep breath and urged Clay over so he was sitting on the edge of the bed.

"Showtime," she said in a voice almost a whisper.

I can do this. I can. Just keep it light. Nothing heavy. Don't scare him away.

He sat with his hands on his thighs, his eyes behind the mask burning with intensity.

The dress had a zipper running the length of it in back. Bridget had practiced at home and found she could reach back over her shoulder and pull it down halfway, then reach upward and slide it down the rest of the way. She did it now slowly, tugging the head of the zipper until the material parted and the dress slipped from her shoulders. Pushing downward from her hips she shimmied until the dress pooled at her feet then daintily stepped out of it. She now wore only the outrageously expensive lace-and-satin demi bra and the barely there thong in salacious red. And her wickedly high heels.

She was rewarded by the hiss of Clay's indrawn breath and the tightening of his fingers on his thighs.

"Holy shit, Red," he breathed. "If I say you are every man's wet dream will I offend you?"

She laughed, giddy. "Not at all. Praise a woman lives to hear."

"That's good because it's the damn truth."

She did a slow turn, pivoting on her stilettos, letting him look his fill of her from every angle. Only the anonymity of the mask gave her the courage to do this and she took full advantage if it, cocking her hip at a saucy angle when she finished.

"Surely you aren't going to stop now." His voice held a hint of unsteadiness.

"Not on your life."

She put the tip of one forefinger on her lower lip and bit it gently. Clay sucked in a breath and Bridget watched his fingers dig so deeply into his thighs she wondered if he'd leave grooves. She was so turned-on just from watching his reaction to her that moving to the next step seemed almost natural. Turning away from him, she widened her stance and bent over from the waist, giving him an unobstructed view of her ass, the thong riding in the crevice and the lips of her pussy flaring out on either side of the insubstantial crotch material. Just for good measure she wiggled her hips. She was getting bolder by the minute and enjoying it in a way she'd never imagined

"Jesus, Red." Clay's voice was hoarse with barely controlled lust. "When do I get to touch?"

"First you have to get naked," she told him, turning around. "I want to see your body too."

He rose and began to pull his shirt from the waistband of his pants but Bridget was on him in a flash.

"My job," she said, making her voice low and sultry. "After all, I'm in charge of this seduction. Right?"

"For the moment." He dropped his hands and stood immobile while she finished freeing the shirt then nudged him to bend slightly so she could pull it over his head.

Ohmigod!

Bare of any clothing his shoulders looked even broader, muscles rippling, brown hair scattered across his chest and arrowing down to disappear into his trousers. Licking her lips again, Bridget lifted a hand and ran it over the curls, finding his flat nipples and scraping her fingernails over them lightly. Clay tensed beneath her touch but otherwise made no move or gave any indication of a reaction. It pleased her to know that her touch made him dig for his self-control.

Her hands trembled slightly as she unfastened the drawstring on his pirate pantaloons and undid the fly. The soft fabric fell easily past his hips and hung over the tops of his boots. Hesitating for only a moment Bridget hooked her fingers in the elastic of his boxer briefs and dragged them down too.

Holy shit!

Nothing she'd ever written about prepared her for the thick, swollen, erect cock that sprang free from its cradling nest of wiry hair, the head dark with the blood that had rushed to it, a tiny drop of fluid sitting teasingly on the slit. Below it hung the heavy sac with his testicles, resting against his solid thighs. She couldn't seem to tear her eyes away from the sight.

"Like what you see?" Clay's voice had a provocative tone to it.

"I think you'll do." She tried to match his tone.

"What about the masks?"

She shook her head. "That's part of the mystery. The unknown factor. The masks stay on, so the people behind them will be forever hidden."

"But what if I want to see you? I could just rip it off, you know."

Bridget backed away from him, out of reach. He wouldn't do that, would he?

"If that's what you have in mind then we stop right now. The masks stay on." She waited nervously for his answer.

He held up his hands. "Okay, okay." He grinned. "Enhances the mystery, right?"

"Right."

Moving closer to him again she yanked back the covers and pressed her hand against his chest. "You'll have to sit down so I can get your boots and, um, pants off."

Obligingly he dropped back down to the bed but when she glanced into his eyes she saw laughter and a hint of mischief. For a moment she felt as if she were playing with a real pirate.

Kneeling down she tugged each boot off individually before sliding the pantaloons and boxer briefs down legs with muscles that were as hard as rocks, and pushing everything to the side. Then, with a confidence born of the security of the mask, she wrapped her fingers around his shaft and brought it to her mouth, glad that she'd opted for the three-quarter mask that left her lips totally accessible.

Clay's breath hitched as she closed her lips over it and ran her tongue around the head, tasting the salty sweetness of his fluid.

"Jesus," he hissed and cupped her head with his large palms.

Bridget hummed in satisfaction and continued to lick and suck and savor. Her other hand stole between his thighs and cupped his balls, manipulating them with her fingers. His grip on her head tightened and he tried to thrust himself deeper inside her. But her experience with this was limited and she hadn't figured out how to accommodate anyone's full length let alone Clay's enormous size.

She pulled back and wiped her lips with her fingers. "My show," she reminded him.

"Can I just say that you're killing me?" he asked in a strangled voice.

"Oh, I don't think so." She licked the head once more before rising. "Not yet, anyway. I'm just getting started."

"Oh, lord," he muttered. "When is it my turn?"

"When I say so."

She pushed him back onto the bed and nudged him to move his body until he lay with his head on the pillows. Clambering up to straddle him, still wearing the sexy lingerie and fuck-me shoes and balancing herself with her hands on his shoulders, she pressed her mouth to his and thrust her tongue inside. Lordy, but he tasted good. She caught the scent of her own musk as she worked her tongue into every corner of his mouth, dancing with his tongue, licking every inner surface.

When she'd drunk her fill she moved down the line of his neck to his chest, finding his nipples and nipping each in turn. His big hands came up to stroke her back, fingers tracing the length of her spine. She was sure where her cunt pressed against him there was a patch of her cream. Could he feel the tiny flutters inside her? Were they vibrating into his body?

Shifting position she moved her mouth to his stomach, tracing the indentation of his navel and following the line of hair down to his groin. She kissed his hipbones, his hard flat abs, the inside of his upper thighs, encouraged by his groans and sounds of pleasure. Her fingers followed the trail of her mouth, brushing against the hot flesh, loving the soft feel of him beneath his taut skin.

He was all male, that was for sure, and she explored him as she might a dish of candy, touching, tasting, rolling the flavor around in her mouth.

His big hands grabbed her shoulders and dragged her up his body. "Darlin', if you don't get serious pretty quick this show's gonna be over before it starts."

"But I'm seducing you," she protested, planting a wet kiss on his chest.

"Believe me when I tell you I'm seduced. Even beyond seduced. So could we please get down to business?"

She laughed. "I thought I was."

If she got any more down to business Clay figured it would be all over but the shouting. And he hadn't had any fun himself yet. Although he'd enjoyed the hell out of her seductive mouth and hands. In desperation he pulled her farther up his body, grabbed the ties at the sides of her thong and yanked them loose. Next to go was the bra, her breasts now free and tempting. He tugged her forward so he could take one nipple into his mouth, the sensation sending jolts of lightning straight to his already bursting cock.

He wanted to lick her pussy too, and lunge his fingers deep inside her, but he was too close to the edge.

And then a devastating thought struck him. He opened his mouth to let her nipple plop free and tightened his hands on her arms.

"I don't suppose you set out on this seduction prepared at all, did you?" he asked, desperately trying to remember if he had one lone condom stashed in his wallet.

She bent forward and gave his chest another slow lick. "Like the Boy Scouts I am always prepared."

Gracefully she hopped off the bed, tossing the now loosened thong and bra to the side, and picked up her dress from the floor. Reaching into what appeared to be a very deep pocket she pulled out a string of condoms. Clay's eyes widened.

"You just stuck them in your dress like that? What if they'd fallen out?"

"I didn't want to carry a purse so I found a costume with several deep pockets."

He stared at the string in her hand. "Planning on making a long night of it?"

She climbed back onto the bed and straddled him again. "Just as long as you can hold out, Black."

He started to say he was a SEAL and they had legendary endurance. But this wasn't the time to exchange personal information. This was the time to launch the mission. Plucking the condoms from her hand he separated one foil packet from the rest, tore it open and handed her the latex sheath.

"Care to do the honors?"

"Absolutely."

She sounded confident but he could see her hands trembling again. He wondered just how often Red indulged in one of these seductions. Exactly how experienced she was. Part of the pleasure her mouth had given him was the sudden realization that she was sort of learning as she went along. For whatever reason she'd chosen him tonight he was eternally grateful. But she was unknowingly playing havoc with his emotions too. From the connection of that first kiss something more than physical attraction had been at work here, Clay didn't know whether to embrace it or run like hell.

He was jerked backed to awareness by the feel of her slender fingers rolling the latex down the length of his rock-hard cock, smoothing it into place.

"I think we're ready." There was just the tiniest catch in her voice.

"Almost," he told her, sliding a hand down his stomach to find her pussy.

Her breathing hitched as he rubbed the hot flesh between her thighs, finding it slick with her juices, her clit already swollen. When he caught it between two fingers she jerked then rocked herself back and forth on his hand. He manipulated his hand to ease two fingers up into her tight, grasping sheath, pressing his thumb on her clit at the same time.

Oh, yeah, she was definitely ready. Time to take control.

In one smooth move he rolled her to her back, tucking her beneath him and nudging her legs wide. She was so tempting, spread out the way she was, her nipples wet from his mouth, her skin flushed with desire. He wished like hell he could see her face, but there was no mistaking the heat in her eyes. That was blatantly visible through the slits in the mask.

Bedroom eyes, he thought. Hot and seductive. Eyes a man could get lost in. Damn he wished she'd take off the mask.

Positioning his body, he wrapped the fingers of one hand around his cock and nudged her opening with the head. Her small hands came up to clutch his shoulders and she spread her legs even wider. Clay took his time sliding into her, enjoying the bite of her nails into the skin of his arms as he stretched and filled her. When he was fully inside her, his balls touching the lower curve of her ass, he closed his eyes, enjoying the moment.

Clay had been with a lot of women, probably more than he'd like to admit, but not once did he ever experience what he was feeling now with Red. It wasn't just the physical contact, although that was off the charts. He felt again the same connection that had hit him when he'd kissed her earlier. Intense. Emotional. Reaching deep inside him.

Better put that thought away, macho man. This is a one-time fantasy. You'll never see her again.

The thought saddened him and he deliberately blanked it from his mind.

Bending his head he pulled one nipple into his mouth again, sucking hard and grazing it with his teeth until she cried out, arching up to him. When the plump bud was swollen in his mouth he turned to the other one, all the while his cock telling him to get to it. To move. To fuck her the way he wanted to.

And finally he did, moving slowly at first, gliding in and out of the wet sheath, the head of his dick bumping up against the mouth of her womb. Then faster. Faster yet, until he was slamming into her again and again and her cries of pleasure echoed in the room. Her cunt gripped him, pulling at him, hips thrusting until…

Yes! God, yes!

The orgasm shook him so hard he forgot everything except this woman and her body and the intense spasms rocketing them both over a cliff into a black velvet oblivion. He pumped and pumped and pumped, wishing there was no latex barrier between them, until the last drop of semen had been wrung from his cock.

When he collapsed he rolled to the side, taking her with him, still connected to her body, his arm wrapped around her holding her close. His heart was banging against his ribs and his breath sounded like a ripsaw in the air as he fought to get himself under control.

Jesus! If he was given to abstract feelings he'd have said the whole experience was spiritual. Because it sure had gone way past just the physical. Emptying himself into this woman was a bonding more than an exercise.

He smoothed his hands over her damp skin, following the line of her back and the sweet curve of her ass. Oh, yeah. Her ass. Before the night was over he'd have her there too. She was like a drug in his system. If he was only getting this one shot he wanted it all. Every bit. Memories that he could pull out at night in the jungles of Africa or the unforgiving Hindu Kush mountains.

"You okay?" he asked when he was sure he could speak.

"More than okay." Her voice was soft and when she spoke her breath was like a soft breeze against his chest. "I think the seduction worked."

He laughed unsteadily. "More than." His hand was still wandering over her body. "Now it's my turn to take care of you."

She tilted her head back. "What do you mean?"

"I mean, under other circumstances I'd pick you up and carry you into the shower with me. You have no idea how sexy showering together can be." He paused. "You ever done it before? Showered with someone? Had great shower sex?"

"Um, sure. Of course I have."

But he didn't believe her. He heard the thread of uncertainty in her voice. What kind of life did she lead? How

47

had she reached this point, where sexual exploration was so uppermost in her mind that she'd set out to seduce someone, yet came to it so obviously lacking in experience? He'd give a month's pay to know her background.

But that wasn't what tonight was about. And her combination of wickedness and innocence was an incredible turn-on.

"Well," he went on, "since you insist we keep our masks on we can't exactly dunk ourselves. So as the very happy recipient of your charms I'm going to give you a sponge bath."

She pushed away from him and sat up. "A what?"

"A sponge bath." He cupped her chin and tilted her masked face up to him. "You'll love it. I promise. And it will give you time to rest before the next act."

"The...next act?"

He brushed his mouth against hers. "Surely you didn't think we were finished. Did you?"

"Um, no, I guess not."

Bridget stared at him. She couldn't imagine what was going on in his mind but she was eternally glad he hadn't told her it was time to leave. She didn't want her fantasy to be over so quickly. If she only had one night with Clay Randall she was going to wring everything from it she could.

Because she had just realized an all-important fact—she was definitely in love with Clay Randall. Not that it would ever come to anything. She'd probably be carrying her heart around in pieces for a long time.

But it's worth it. Oh, it's so worth it.

She lay back on the pillows, inhaling the air still redolent with the combined scents of their musk, the ripeness of sex. Her limbs felt like limp noodles, her body so filled with lassitude that she couldn't have moved if she had to. Not even in her wildest imagination had she expected an orgasm as intense as the one she'd just experienced. Anything else in her pitiful sex life not only paled by comparison but disappeared into nothingness. Now she knew what authors meant when they wrote about exploding rockets and falling through space.

When Clay strode back to the bed from the bathroom she couldn't help but notice that his cock was still semierect. This whole night was turning out even better than she'd expected.

"Lie back and relax."

He sat down on the bed next to her, moving her over just enough to give him room. In a moment he was stroking a warm cloth over her, beginning at her neck and working his way down to her breasts, her tummy, the sensitive flesh of her pussy and down her legs. His touch was light, almost feathery, whispering over her skin, arousing her as much as it soothed.

She moaned, a little whimper of pleasure, as he brought the cloth back to her cunt and nudged her thighs apart with his hand. The slightly rough texture of the cloth brushed her clit and her pussy lips sensuously. The walls of her cunt began to quiver, already responding to the stimulation. Her legs moved restlessly and her hips arched slightly.

"Feel good, darlin'?"

Good was too tame a word for what she was feeling.

"Mmm," was about all she could manage.

He leaned closer to her. "I'm going to make you feel even better now that I've got you cooled off a little."

Cooled off? Was he crazy? Her temperature was about to zoom off the charts.

He dropped the washcloth into the little dish on the nightstand, moved back onto the bed and knelt between her thighs, slipping his hands beneath her ass.

"I've been dying to taste you ever since you slipped out of that red dress and I got a full view of that luscious body. And now I'm going to do it."

He lifted her to his mouth and took a long, slow lick the length of her slit. Bridget quivered beneath his touch, every nerve in her cunt firing, her cream lubricating her.

"Yum." He had his lips against her clit, his voice vibrating against that hot little button. "Just as tasty as I thought."

He did it again. And again, leisurely swipes with his tongue capturing her liquid. Nuzzling his face against her, inhaling her scent. Pulling her clit into his mouth and sucking on it. Swirling his tongue around it.

The flutters intensified, turning into tiny spasms, spreading through her body.

"Black!" she cried, thankful she had enough sanity left not to call out his real name.

"It's okay, Red." He placed an open-mouthed kiss right on her clit. "Go with it."

And then he moved one hand to slide two fingers inside her, his mouth still busy with her button of swollen flesh, and just like that she came again. He fucked her with his fingers, adding a third one, his lips and tongue never leaving her pussy. She shuddered, heels digging into the mattress, hands fisted in the sheet. Spasm after spasm rolled through her and still he never let up, until the final tremor subsided and she collapsed, completely spent, every muscle limp and lax.

Then he eased her down and smoothed his hands over her sides and her breasts, his mouth finally taking hers. She could taste herself on his tongue, an intoxicating flavor that slithered through her. She sighed, wishing she could take off the mask and kiss him without its restraints.

But she had bigger problems than that. The last thing she'd expected was this powerful connection to the man she'd only thought to have a one-night stand with. A night to treasure that would probably never be repeated. It was more than just lust. More than just passion. Without realizing it she'd just ripped her heart out of her body and handed it over to this man.

"This seduction thing seems to be working pretty good," he teased, bringing her back to the moment.

"Yes," she breathed. "Better than good."

Too much better than good.

He gave her another brief kiss—a mere brush of the lips— then stood up. "We missed the goodies at the ball. If you plan to keep on seducing me I think we need something to give us some energy. Room service or the minibar?"

Not room service. If Clay happened to get nosy when the waiter gave her the slip to sign the game would be over.

"I think the minibar will be just fine."

Chapter Four

ॐ

Clay found a silver tray on the credenza next to the minibar and plundered the snacks the hotel provided. Cheese crackers, cookies and pretzels weren't his idea of romantic fare but it was better than nothing. He'd actually been relieved when Red decided against room service. That would have meant both of them pulling on the complimentary robes hanging in the bathroom and he wanted her naked every possible minute. If all he had with her was this one night he wasn't about to spend any of it without her naked.

As he poured wine into the goblet on top of the bar and added ice cubes to his bourbon he mulled the situation over in his mind. It bugged him that she wouldn't take off her mask. Or let him remove his. Who was she? Was it possible she was someone's wife, out for a wild night to get what she couldn't get at home?

But the moment the thought popped into his head he dismissed it. He'd learned to be a pretty good judge of people during his years in the SEALs. Often that ability meant the difference between life and death. No, Red wasn't anyone's wife. Or very experienced at what she was doing. Although the secrecy the mask provided seemed to give her unfamiliar courage.

One thing was for sure. He'd never enjoyed a woman as much as he was enjoying this one. Nor felt such an instant emotional connection. He wanted more than sex with her. A lot more. How to approach it, though, was the problem. Come hell or high water, somehow he'd find out who she was, because he had no intention of letting this end when morning rolled around.

When he carried the tray back into the bedroom Red was still stretched out on the sheet, one arm thrown over her forehead, the other hand resting on her slightly — and delightfully — rounded little tummy. He stopped for a moment, thinking he could stare at her like this for the rest of his life.

The rest of his life?

Shit, Randall. You've got it bad and after only a few hours.

"I think you actually have to bring the tray over here for me to reach any of that," she joked.

"What? Oh, sorry."

He placed the tray on the nightstand, waited while she hitched herself up with the pillows behind her then handed her the wine goblet. Taking the tumbler with his own drink he touched it to her glass.

"To seduction."

Below the edge of the three-quarter mask her lips curved in a smile.

"To seduction."

He sat on the edge of the bed, nudging her over to make room for himself. "So, is this playing up to your expectations so far?"

I cannot believe I asked that dumbass question. She'll think I want her to stroke my ego.

Well, I do. And something else along with it.

"Why, Black, are you worried you might fall short of my expectations?"

"Not a bit." He leaned forward and ran his tongue over her lips. "Just checking. The night isn't close to being over."

"Good." She licked her lip where his tongue had been, the gesture sending urgent messages to his cock. "That's good."

He lifted a pretzel from the bowl he'd dumped them into and held it to her mouth, waiting while she took a bite of it before bringing it to his own lips. Again that little tongue glided over her full bottom lip, catching the crumbs from the

53

pretzel. God, she was just the sexiest little thing he'd ever met in his life. Clay was sure by the time she ate the whole damn thing he'd be harder than concrete. He needed to distract himself.

"Is it against the rules for you to tell me about yourself?" he asked, picking up another pretzel.

"But then the mystery would be gone, right?" She bit down on the pretzel.

"Maybe we could stay away from things that are too personal. For instance, what's your favorite movie?" He popped the rest of the pretzel in his mouth and chased it with some bourbon.

"It's an old one and you'll laugh when I tell you."

"Why? Because it's a typical chick flick?"

She shook her head. "Not at all. *Delta Force* with Chuck Norris."

Clay laughed. "That's probably the last answer I'd expect."

"See? I'm still a woman of mystery. Now you. Your favorite."

"Also an oldie. *The Hunt for Red October.*"

"Hmm. So we both like military thrillers. Okay. Favorite kind of music."

She took a sip of her wine. "Easy. Anything country."

"No kidding? Me too. Although I tend to like the older stuff better."

He picked up a chocolate cookie and put it to her lips. She bit down on it, the action more sensual than he would have imagined. She swallowed the bite but little chocolate crumbs stuck to her lower lip. Clay couldn't help himself. He leaned forward and captured them with his tongue, the softness of her lips as intoxicating as the rich taste of the chocolate. Clay was sure he'd never enjoyed minibar snacks this much before.

"Favorite food," he continued.

"Pizza," she answered at once.

"Steak and fries," he came back.

She giggled. "Why did I know you were going to say that?"

He cocked an eyebrow. "Too cliché? Typical macho fare?"

"Uh-huh."

He smiled. "What can I say? I play to type. Okay, favorite color?"

"Red."

"Mine too," he grinned. "Especially after tonight."

"Really?" Her glance flicked to the rumpled pile of his pirate clothes. "I would have thought black."

"Black is only who I am for the night. All this talking must be making you hungry."

"I'm not sure that's what revved up my appetite."

He fed her another bite then waited while she chased it with a swallow of wine. Everything she did, from drinking her wine to chewing the cookie to all things sexual, she did with incredible grace. Yes, he could definitely get off on watching her for hours.

"So, are we through with Twenty Questions yet?"

Her hand, resting on his thigh, was moving casually back and forth, closer and closer to his cock, which definitely wanted to come out and play again.

"I guess talking is highly overrated," he growled, unable to stand it a moment longer.

He placed both of their glasses on the tray and stretched out on the bed beside her, shifting her so she was spooned against him. One hand cradled a breast, the fingers idly pinching and tugging at the nipple, while the other drifted down to the softness of her pubic curls and the damp heat of her cunt. She was still delightfully wet, the lips warm to the touch. His fingertip just grazed the tip of her clit, drawing a quick intake of breath from her.

"Feel good?" he breathed in her ear.

"Oh, yes."

He lifted her top leg and moved it so it rested on his thigh, giving him greater access to her. Slowly, gently, he stroked her clit, squeezing her nipple in a matching rhythm. Red moved her hips in a slow, liquid tempo, riding the movements of his hand. What he really wanted to do was play with her until she was nearly to the point of madness, pull her to her hands and knees and fuck that sweet ass that made his mouth water.

But he hadn't come prepared for that, hardly expecting that the woman of his dreams would seduce him into an impromptu one-night stand. And he was sure she hadn't. In fact, he was pretty damn sure her ass was virgin. He wanted to be her first and so he didn't want to do anything to hurt her. Damn! He was going to have to find a way to see her again. Somehow. Some way.

The more she rocked her hips against his touch the harder his cock became and the more his balls ached. He wanted to shower kisses on her cheeks but the damn mask was in the way so instead he bent his head slightly to kiss the graceful column of her neck. Erotic little sounds were whispering from her mouth, soft cries that threatened his control.

He increased the tempo of both hands, tormenting the nipple as he alternately worked her clit and thrust three fingers in the grasping heat of her pussy. She was breathing hard now, the little moans increasing in intensity. The harder she rode him the hotter he got until he reached a point where he had to be inside her. Right now.

If he couldn't take her ass tonight he'd at least have the next best thing. Grabbing one of the condoms from the nightstand he ripped the foil with his teeth and sheathed himself with one hand. Rolling her onto her tummy he lifted her so she was on her hands and knees and pulled two pillows beneath her to brace her body.

Kneeling between her legs he placed his palms on the cheeks of her ass and unable to help himself spread them wide to see the winking rosebud of her anus. Impulsively he rimmed it with his tongue, eliciting a shudder from her and a louder moan.

"I'd love to take you here," he rumbled, "but I'm afraid to hurt you." He kissed each cheek. "But one of these days, Red, your ass will be mine."

One of these days? He didn't even know her name.

Before she could say anything he placed the head of his shaft at the opening of her cunt and drove in with one swift stroke.

Oh, Jesus!

He closed his eyes, letting her wet heat grip him and the feeling of pleasure sweep through his body. And then he began to ride her, plunging in and out, making himself keep to a steady, even pace. But as she bucked back against him, matching his rhythm, his pace increased until he was pumping into her harder and faster. Balancing himself with one hand on her hip he slid the other one around until he found her clit.

He rubbed the hot little bundle of nerves and flesh, faster and faster, carrying them both over the edge into a climax that shook him to his very core. Nothing existed except for him and this woman and the racking spasms shattering them both.

"Red?" he murmured.

"Mm-hmm?" She nestled against him, feeling so good next to his body.

"You now we have something going here besides just good sex, right?"

She tensed. "W-what do you mean?"

"I think you know exactly what I mean. This is more than just sex."

"But damn good sex, right?"

"Don't try to distract me. I'd like to see you again. More than just tonight."

She was still taut, her body strung like a bow. What was with her?

"I...I can't do that, Black."

He kissed her blonde curls. "Why not? You're not married, are you?"

"N-no. Nothing like that."

"Then what? I think we've got a good thing going here. I don't want to lose it."

She was silent for so long he wondered if she'd fallen asleep. Then she said, "How about if we talk about it in the morning?"

"Okay. But just so you know, I'm not letting you leave before we do."

After what seemed like a long time but was probably only minutes he withdrew from her and headed to the bathroom to dispose of the condom. When he climbed back into bed he could sense from the relaxed state of her body that she was seconds from sleep. Pulling her against him and wrapping his arms around her, his last thought before his eyes slammed shut was that she'd find her again if it was the last thing he did.

* * * * *

Bridget opened her eyes and looked around, disoriented at first in her surroundings. A hotel room, and a pretty fancy one. Something was covering her face and when she reached a hand up she realized it was a satin mask. Mask! The masquerade ball! The second thing she realized was a warm, very male body was in bed next to her, curled around her with a hand cupping her breast.

Clay Randall! Ohmigod! She'd actually done it.

No wonder her body felt sore in so many places. Make that delightfully sore as the memories of the night before came crashing back on her.

Glancing at the little bedside clock with its red LED numerals she discovered it was five thirty in the morning. Time to get the hell out of here before Clay woke up and made leaving difficult. Or worse yet, pulled off her mask. Besides, he'd been very insistent he wanted to talk to her in the morning about seeing her again, and that was just not possible.

As gingerly as possible she slid from his embrace and wriggled her way out of bed, groping around for her dress and shoes. She had no idea where her bra and thong were. She'd just have to go commando. Her keys were in one of the deep pockets in her dress along with her little change purse and her credit card. Once she was dressed she'd be good to go.

Clay shifted on the bed and mumbled something, his arm reaching out for her. She froze, holding her breath but in seconds he was back asleep, snoring softly. Tiptoeing into the adjoining living room she pulled on the dress and managed to get herself zipped into it. She eased the door open then closed it softly behind her, slipped on her shoes and headed for the elevator. She had no idea what condition her hair was in and she knew she was bound to get weird looks with the mask on her face but she wasn't about to take it off. Not yet.

In the lobby she ignored the stares of people milling around, checked out and accepted a copy of her bill then asked the parking valet to get a cab for her. She finally breathed easily when the cab pulled away from the hotel out into traffic and she was heading home.

Last night was definitely one for the memory books. Clay Randall was every bit as magnificent and sexy as she'd imagined. The ball had provided her with the one opportunity to have this night with him. She'd be replaying it in her mind over and over again, reliving every single moment in vivid detail. It had been more than she'd ever expected it to be, worth the price of the ticket and the suite and even more than that.

But that would be the end of it. She couldn't go around wearing the mask forever and once Clay got a look at her eyes she'd be lucky if he even socialized with her over their garbage cans.

Her problem, however, was that, just as he'd said, the night ended up being about far more than sex. Clay had touched her feelings, brought up emotions she hadn't expected to come into play. Now she wanted more, and not just more sex. She wanted everything. With him. The whole nine yards.

Except she knew she couldn't have it. It was just a fragile dream.

She was so lost in reverie she didn't even realize the cab had stopped moving.

"Hey. Hey, lady."

She looked up to see the driver leaning over the back of the front seat.

"Yes?"

"We're here." He pointed out the window. "This is the address you gave me."

"Of course." She pulled out her change purse, paid the driver and eased herself out through the door. "Oh, and here." She handed him a twenty-dollar bill. "Please. If someone tries to find out where you took me can you ask the dispatcher not to give out my address?"

"Sure thing." He frowned at her. "You gonna be okay going inside by yourself?"

"Yes. I'll be fine. And thanks again."

She gathered up her skirt and hurried up to the porch, unlocking the door and practically falling inside. Just in case Clay managed to wake up right after she left and headed home she wanted to be tucked away in her house before he could see her. Leaning against the closed front door, she paused a moment to catch her breath. Then she ripped off the mask and tossed it onto the little wall table.

I'll bet that thing made a mess of my hair and face.

In her bedroom she got herself out of the dress and hurried into the bathroom, staring at herself in the mirror.

Oh, yes. A mess. Her golden curls the stylist had carefully arranged on top of her head were falling this way and that, drooping now across her forehead without the mask to hold them up. And the mask itself, after being worn for so many hours, had left lines on her forehead and cheeks and reddened her skin.

It had more than been worth the damage but now it was time to turn back into plain old Bridget with the ugly eyelids. As she looked at herself in the mirror it seemed to her that the heavy fold of skin had grown even bigger but that had to be her imagination. Didn't it?

Sighing, she turned on the shower and when the water was hot enough stepped into it and let the spray beat down on her. She hated to wash Clay's scent from her body but last night was over. Finished. She needed to get rid of everything but her memories.

Bridget spent a long time in the shower, lathering her body twice with scented shower gel and thoroughly shampooing her hair. Then she took even more time drying off, blow-drying her hair until it hung in its usually straight curtain to her shoulders. She rubbed lanolin-rich cream into her face, soothing the places where the mask had cut into it and finally, when she'd done all the repair to her body she could, she pulled on a t-shirt and a pair of yoga pants and went into the kitchen to make tea and toast. Skipping dinner and spending the night in hot sexual activity should have given her a bigger appetite but she could feel the adrenaline that had kept her going all night washing out of her system. And with it her appetite. She knew she'd be crashing any minute now. That was okay. She could fall asleep and dream about Clay and the erotic things they'd done together. Later she'd make herself a better meal.

She brewed another cup of tea and was sipping the hot liquid when she heard the sound of a car in the next driveway. Clay! She set the tea down on the counter and hurried into the living room. The blinds on the picture window were closed but she peeked between two of them, just in time to see Clay's car pull into his garage. She glanced at the funky wall clock hanging by the door. A little after seven.

Had he slept an hour after she left then left the hotel? Or had he spent part of that time trying to find out who had rented the suite, or checking with the head valet to see if she'd taken a cab or driven herself? Had he actually gone looking for her or had he just written it off as one night of hot sex and goodbye?

And why do I even care? Nothing will ever come of it.

A car moved slowly down the street, stopping at each house. The newspaper carrier. Her own paper landed on her porch with a *thunk!* Making sure that Clay was nowhere in sight she opened the door, scurried out to get the paper and ran back inside, slamming and locking the door.

And why would I care if he saw me? I take my newspaper in every morning.

She was just spooked, that was all.

Sighing, she tossed the paper on a small table and headed to her bedroom. The adrenaline crash was about to overtake her completely and she needed a bed.

* * * * *

Clay took off the pirate garb and tossed it onto a chair in his bedroom. In his bathroom he turned on the shower, letting it get as hot as he could stand it then stepped in under the punishing spray. His body ached from head to toe and he had no idea why. This wasn't the first sexual marathon he'd been involved in so why was it this time his muscles were protesting? Was it because he'd worked harder, been more intense this time? Because for the first time in ages it had really meant something?

He soaped his body, wishing Red was in the shower with him. He'd love to see the drops sliding down that lush body, beading on her breasts and nipples, leaving droplets on the dark-blonde hair covering her mound. He closed his eyes and leaned against one wall of the shower, remember every dip and swell of her body, the roundness of her breasts, the swollen buds of her nipples.

In a flash he recalled the feel of her sweet, sweet pussy, so tight, clenching around his cock, milking it. The taste of it, sweet and tart, rich on his tongue and lips. He licked his mouth now as if he could still taste her. He wanted to suck that sweet little pussy, thrust his tongue into its hot walls. Scrape it against her sweet spot and feel her convulse in his hands. Hear those wonderful little whimpers of pleasure.

God, fucking her had just been so sweet. More soul-shattering than anything he'd ever done with any other woman. Burying himself inside her was like coming home.

Washing carefully, he paused when his fingers reached his cock and his balls. For an instant he recalled the feeling of Red's soft fingers around his shaft, her hand cupping his balls. Her touch was so exquisite it made him hard just thinking about it.

The images crowded his mind again and he stroked himself without even realizing he was doing it. He gripped himself with one hand, his other cupping his balls, as he remembered and stroked, pretending it was her hand on his cock. Breathing hard, he spread the drop of fluid that gathered at the slit over the engorged head then slid his fingers up and down, up and down, up and down.

Before he realized it he was rhythmically squeezing his balls and his cock was about to burst. One last stroke and his semen spilled over his fingers, washed away by the beating spray of the shower.

Spent, he struggled to catch his breath, but even after jacking himself off like a horny teenager all he could think about was Red.

Where the hell had she come from? How and why had she chosen him for her night of seduction? Despite her audacity and brashness he had a deep-down feeling that she was playing a part. He just couldn't see Red in that role on a regular basis. She seemed too...too... He searched for a word. Nice. Yeah, nice. Maybe.

She'd certainly been a wild woman in bed. Uninhibited and imaginative and willing to not only follow his lead in anything but take it herself. She gave herself unselfishly, something he wasn't used to lately with the women he took to bed. They either wanted their performance graded or they wanted it all for themselves. It was all about what he could do for them.

Clay wondered if there was a way to find out who had purchased tickets to the masquerade ball and track her down that way. But in the next instant he realized how futile and foolish that would be. Oh, there'd be a record of all the names. Everyone received a charitable deduction receipt. But the list would be endless. Anyway, what could he say? *I want to find a woman with whom I had a spectacular night of sex? And she didn't give me her name?*

Yeah, right. Way to look like an idiot.

He rinsed himself off thoroughly then turned off the shower and pulled a towel from the rack. Dry, he found a pair of sweats in his drawer that he put on and wandered into the kitchen for something to drink, something to quench his sudden raging thirst.

He'd been ten kinds of pissed to wake up and find her gone, his woman in red. He'd meant what he said about wanting to see her again. Which was probably why she'd ducked out the way she did.

What was her big secret, anyway? He'd believed her when she said she wasn't married. And he was pretty sure she didn't have some guy in her life. So what the fuck was the problem?

He vaguely remembered her slipping from the bed but he wasn't sure if it was a dream at the time and he'd been too spent and exhausted to force himself awake. But then he finally did wake and the bed was empty. He'd roared around the suite naked, calling her name. When he couldn't find her he'd sat back down on the bed, dragging his fingers through his hair and over his unshaven face. And then on the floor, peeping out from the edge of the bed where they'd landed, he saw that wicked thong and matching bra.

He didn't even remember how long he'd sat on the bed, holding the fragile garments, inhaling her scent like some crazed addict. Reliving the night. Craving just one more touch of her soft skin, one more tight clasp of her hot, wet pussy. Until he'd finally dressed in his now rumpled pirate costume and tried to ignore the stares of people as he attempted to browbeat the desk clerk into giving him her information.

No luck there. Or at the valet stand or with any of the cabbies.

Finally, frustrated, he'd retrieved his car and driven home.

Now he stood on his small back porch drinking orange juice straight from the carton and wondering if there was any way to find her at all. He couldn't get her eyes out of his mind. Bedroom eyes. Seductive. Fiery with passion. If only he could have seen more than the vivid blue that the slits in the mask allowed. Every time he looked those eyes pulled him in.

Swallowing the last gulp of juice he headed back inside and tossed the empty carton in the trash. He still had three weeks of leave left before his next mission. Somehow he'd find a way to learn who she was. Maybe his captain's wife could help him.

But first some much-needed sleep, or he wouldn't be doing anything.

Chapter Five

ഐ

Bridget opened one eye and glanced at the clock on her nightstand. One o'clock.

Holy shit!

She'd slept half the day away. But then she'd really needed it. She certainly hadn't gotten much the night before. Her muscles protested when she stretched, another reminder of the previous night's activities. But a pleasant reminder. Oh, yeah. Much more than pleasant.

Closing her eyes she recalled the feel of Clay's masculine hands on her body, his hot mouth coaxing responses from her body. His thick cock filling her and stretching her as he rode her to one explosive climax after another. One hand slipped beneath the waistband of the yoga pants she was still wearing and found her pussy already damp as memories blasted at her.

Taking a deep breath she stroked herself slowly, pretending it was Clay's hand in her pants. On her flesh. She slid her fingers along the inner lips the way he had, moving them up and down, capturing her clit between the knuckles.

Oh, Clay!

She stroked herself, slowly at first, then faster, rubbing her clit in a swift, circular motion. More, more, more. Her other hand moved under her t-shirt to find a nipple already hard and needy. As her hand moved more rapidly on her clit she pinched and squeezed her nipple. Her mind called up Clay's face, not as it had been when it was mostly hidden by his pirate's mask but as she remembered its familiar planes and angles from all the times she'd seen him.

Her hand moved faster and then she was there. Right there! She jackknifed on the bed, shoving three fingers into her cunt and riding them as she pinched her nipple. Hard.

She pulled her hand from her yoga pants, spent and trembling, and loosened her grip on her nipple. Panting, she lay in the afterglow, wishing with all her might that it had been Clay's hands on her body. Clay bringing her to orgasm.

But of course it wasn't. He wasn't about to be lying next to her again, any more than she was going to realize her dream of being a writer full-time and introducing herself in public. For some people dreams never got to be a reality.

She dragged herself out of bed and grabbed her laptop from her desk. She picked up the newspaper on her way into the kitchen and scanned the headlines while she waited for her coffee to brew. Then she took everything to the small table in the breakfast nook.

"Email first," she mumbled, opening the computer and booting it up.

Her family was scattered everywhere and email was the glue binding them together. Okay, first her brother stationed in Iraq. She emailed him every day, knowing whenever he could access email he hungered for the messages from his family. Then her sister, living in California with her husband, who managed actors and actresses. And did a damn good job of it, as far as she could tell.

Next came the weekly newsletter from her mother, from Vermont where Bridget's father was on the faculty of a small but exclusive liberal arts college. God, she missed them. All of them. Somehow when they'd all been together her problems weren't quite so bad. Maybe it was just the fact that her family was so used to seeing her the way she was that no one commented.

And when she had a bad day there was always someone to prop her up.

But career choices had scattered them. She was happy for all of them but at times, like right now, she longed for the comfort of their presence. Especially for her sister Moira's wisdom.

She skipped through some inconsequential emails, finally opening one from her editor that only made her situation all the more intolerable. Her publisher was hosting a first-time convention for its authors and readers, arranging opportunities to interact with all the readers who would be there and to be interviewed by industry publications. Her editor explained what a great opportunity it would be for her, especially with the big book fair on Sunday.

The worst of the email was the information that this first one would be held in the city where Bridget lived. The publisher's public relations people wanted to hype the "local woman makes good" angle with the media.

Bridget thought she might throw up. No way could she go to something like this looking the way she did. Readers would wonder how anyone with her deformity could write such emotional books, think she was a fraud, and she'd lose her audience.

Damn.

She'd have to figure out an appropriate response, when her brain was functioning better. Meanwhile she fixed another cup of coffee, put her laptop aside and opened the newspaper, turning immediately to the lifestyle section. She always checked to see if any of her favorite authors were in town for a signing, living vicariously through their success. Instead what caught her eye was an article headlined *Durban Trust Funds Another Success Story in Reconstructive Surgery.*

Bridget smoothed out the paper and sipped her coffee as she read the story of a philanthropic trust that helped people who needed plastic surgery. People with real problems and unrealized dreams.

The Durban Trust, she read, *was established by famed Hollywood star Evelyn Durban, who left funds in her will to*

68

continue the Trust. She fulfilled her dream of stardom by her own cosmetic surgeries and wanted to pass on the ability to realize their own dream to other people. Since her death the Trust is administered by her sister Georgina, a star of some magnitude in her own right. She is assisted by a team of lawyers and medical advisors. All the applicants are vetted by Georgina's son as well as a psychologist before being recommended to local surgeons and psychological counselors.

But there are certain conditions attached. The applicant must have a dream that he or she wants to fulfill, and must write to the Trust explaining why the surgery is important and what their dream is that is at the moment unattainable. Following the surgery the applicant is required to keep the Trust updated, finally recounting if their dream is realized.

Bridget read on, studying the snippets of stories of people who had been helped through the Durban Trust, her pulse escalating just the tiniest bit as a kernel of hope took root deep inside her. Was it an accident of fate that she read this story today of all days?

She scanned the article again. At the bottom were both the snail mail and email address of the Trust and a footnote stated that all letters be directed to Georgina Hawthorne.

Bridget sipped at her now cooling coffee, her mind scattering in a million directions. Could she bare herself to strangers? Tell them about her anger and hurt and share her dreams with them? How long would the process take?

She stared at the article for a long time, not actually seeing the print, running possibilities over and over in her mind. This would be a major step for her but maybe, just maybe, she could make that big change in her life that up until now had seemed so unattainable.

Nibbling her lower lip, she pushed the newspaper aside, pulled her laptop over in front of her and opened up a new document.

"Dear Miss Hawthorne," she began.

* * * * *

Clay slept until well into the afternoon, took another shower and dressed in jeans and a t-shirt. While he drank a cup of coffee he mulled over his predicament. If he was really serious about hunting down the mysterious Red—which he was—then he had to look at all of his options.

He could go online, look up the Fiesta executive committee and find out who the overall chair of the masquerade ball was. He could scan all the committee names to see if by chance he recognized anyone. Or he could suck it up, call his captain and throw himself on the man's mercy. That might be the most painful but was probably the most efficient.

So at four o'clock that afternoon, freshly shaved, his t-shirt replaced by a button-down one and every bit of him spit polished, he rang the bell at Captain John McCord's house, hoping he wasn't about to make a total ass of himself.

"Well, Clay! Hi!" Annie McCord grinned up at him and held the door wide for him to enter. "I told John the other day we don't see nearly enough of you. Living in the same city we need to have you and the others around here over more often when you get a break in your missions."

"And I told her I get to see enough of your ugly faces as it is." The man himself had come up to stand behind his wife, one hand on her waist, the other outstretched. "Glad you stopped by."

Annie closed the front door. "John, why don't you guys go out on the patio? I'll bring out a couple of beers."

McCord chuckled. "Got her trained right."

Annie swatted at him playfully. "Oh, you. You'll be lucky if I don't put hemlock in your drink."

But the affection between them was a living thing, so strong that Clay was struck with the sharp blade of envy. After all the playing around he'd done, all the reluctance to commit to anything permanent because of his career as a SEAL, he realized two things. He wanted what the McCords had and he wanted it with Red. A woman he'd only known for a few hours but who had imprinted herself on his soul.

He followed the captain out through the kitchen to the patio, settled himself in one of the chairs at the umbrella table and thanked Annie for the cold beer she handed him. He took a swallow, trying to think just how to begin.

"I'm glad to see you, Clay," McCord said. "And Annie's right. I need to make sure the team members in the area know that you're all free to drop in any time we don't have plans." He studied Clay with slate-gray eyes. "But I have a distinct feeling that this isn't just a social call."

Clay adjusted himself in the chair, trying to find a comfortable position and figuring out that in this case there really wasn't one.

"See, it's like this," he began. "I'm trying to find a woman."

McCord burst out laughing. "That's probably the last thing I expected to hear from you. As I understand, your problem isn't finding them. It's beating them off."

Clay's cheeks heated. "This is a little different." He took another swallow of beer. "And I might need Annie's help with it."

McCord's eyes widened a fraction. "My wife? You must be in pretty damn bad shape if you need Annie to find a woman for you."

"Well it's...uh...it's a particular woman."

McCord watched him for a moment in silence. "Clay, in all the years I've known you there are plenty of times when you've been a man of few words but never one who's at a loss for words. Maybe you'd better start at the beginning and tell me what the hell this is all about."

Clay chose his words carefully. "It's about the ball last night," he began. In stilted sentences, omitting most of the details, he explained about meeting Red, spending the night

71

with her, never seeing her face or getting her name and now being desperate to find her.

"Desperate?" McCord grinned.

"I know, I know." Clay raked his fingers through his hair. "Sounds stupid, right? To feel this way after less than twelve hours with someone?"

"I've got two things to say to you. She must be one hell of a woman, and one hour after I met Annie I knew she was it for me. So what do you need from my wife?"

"She was on the ticket committee. I'm hoping they keep some sort of master list of everyone who buys tickets."

"And you'll…what? Contact every unattached woman on the list to see if she's the mysterious Red?"

Clay shrugged. "Sounds stupid, I know."

"I just don't want to get a call that you've been arrested as a stalker." He laughed again. "But let's see what Annie has to say."

"We do keep a master list," she told them when John pulled her outside and into their conversation. "But I don't think we can make that available for public use."

"Of course." Clay fiddled with his bottle. "I should have been smart enough to figure that out."

"And we've got a lot of people selling tickets," she went on. "This Red could have bought hers from anyone. Especially if it was one of the lowest price tickets. She wouldn't have been given a reserved seat or been invited to the private cocktail party before the ball."

"So what you're saying is there's really no way to find out who she is."

"I'm not sure. Let me give it some thought. There's an executive committee meeting on Monday and then the ticket committee Wednesday night. I can ask some questions. See if it rings a bell with anyone."

"I'd really appreciate it." He stood up and held out his hand to McCord. "Thanks for letting me barge in like this. My apologies to you too, Mrs. McCord."

"Annie," she reminded him. "I'm just hoping I can help you." She grinned. "I must say it's interesting to see the big player Clay Randall get his shorts in such a twist over a woman."

"You know what they say," he groaned. "Payback is hell."

"We'll do what we can to see if we can make that payback any easier," McCord said. "Just so you don't hold out any hope for miracles."

Clay had given up on miracles a long time ago. But on the way home it occurred to him he might pick the brain of his neighbor. He and Bridget Reilly had lived next door to each other for two years and really didn't have more than a nodding relationship. But she seemed smart enough, even if she did wear those strange tinted glasses all the time. Maybe she could give him a woman's point of view on this. Something that could point him in the right direction.

* * * * *

Bridget spent most of Saturday and Sunday pacing her small house and avoiding Joni's telephone calls. She also made herself stay inside her house at all for fear she'd run into Clay. Her dreams every night had been filled with erotic images of him, memories of their night together. She needed to put a lot of space between them until she could get a good grip on her feelings and lock her heart away. Maybe if she had the surgery… The letter she'd written sat in her computer, ready to be emailed. All she needed was to hit the final keystrokes and she'd be good to go.

What was she waiting for? The worst they could say was no, right?

But if they did, the chance to have the surgery now would be gone—and she'd be back to saving money for who knew how long to pay for it herself. In the meantime Clay Randall would be off on more missions, hanging out with a variety of arm candy in between and probably find someone else to plan the rest of his life with.

By Monday morning she was a wreck. Should she do this? Shouldn't she? Finally, before she could change her mind again, she pulled up the email to the Trust and hit Send. Now the waiting began.

At work she did her best to avoid Joni and her prying questions, even bypassing their usual quick coffee and a muffin at the Starbucks in the lobby. But at ten when she went to the break room there her friend was, eyes flashing.

"What's the matter with you? You didn't take any of my calls over the weekend and you skipped our usual Starbucks. What on earth is going on? You bought that ticket at the last minute—out of the blue, I might add—and won't tell me a thing about it. Was the masquerade ball a disaster?"

"No. No, it was fine." She busied herself at the coffee machine. "I just had a lot to do this weekend."

Joni looked at her, concern evident on her face. "Did something bad happen to you, Bridget? It did, didn't it? I was worried about that very thing. You don't get out enough to have good experience with the assholes that show up for these things."

Bridget sighed. "It was nothing like that. Honestly. I went and had a good time. End of story."

"I looked for you there and didn't even see you," Joni said accusingly.

"I told you I was there. But there were so many people. We just probably missed each other."

Joni sighed. "Okay. I guess you aren't going to spill whatever's on your mind." She put her hand on Bridget's arm.

"I just want you to know that whatever's going on, I'm your friend and I'm here for you."

Impulsively Bridget hugged her. "I know. And thank you. When I get my brain straightened out I'll let you know. Can you just give me a little space right now?"

"Of course. Want to grab a bite to eat after work?"

"No date?" Bridget teased.

"On a Monday? Are you kidding?"

"Just kidding. And thanks, but no. I've got some stuff to do at home."

Joni studied her. "You *always* have something to do at home. Do you have some secret project I don't know about?"

Yes, and you aren't going to know about it if I can help it.

"No. Just…stuff. Listen, I have to get back to my desk. But I'll talk to you later, okay?"

But she was buried all afternoon at her desk and didn't even get to leave until after six. Deciding to treat herself she stopped to pick up Chinese takeout. Now if she could just pull into her garage and get into her house…

But no such luck. When she turned into her driveway Clay was outside trimming the shrubs around his porch.

Okay. Get out of the car. Take the packages. Wave nicely and hurry into the house.

No luck there either. When she climbed out of the car Clay was standing in her open garage doorway, looking delightfully male and sweaty. Her heart thumped and butterflies began doing the tango in her stomach. How in hell was she going to handle seeing him without giving herself away?

"Hey," he said.

"Hey yourself." She reached in and pulled out her purse and the sack of takeout. "I'd hang around and chat with you but I want to eat this food while it's hot."

He sniffed the air. "Is that Chinese I smell? Food of the gods, right?"

"Some might say. Is there something I can do for you, Clay?"

He scratched his head then shoved his hands in the pockets of his cutoffs. Bridget could hardly tear her eyes away from his long muscular legs, his broad chest and the impressive bulge at his fly. Was her mouth actually watering because she knew what was hidden behind that denim? She needed to get away from him before she embarrassed herself. Or blurted everything out.

"Yeah. Um, I wondered if I could talk to you for a few minutes. About something."

She held up the paper sack. "Food. Hot. Waiting to be eaten."

His mouth curved in that sexy-as-hell grin. "That looks like it might feed two. I could bring the beer."

"Clay," she began.

"Come on," he coaxed. "For a neighbor. I don't ask anything of you very often. Like almost never."

Which unfortunately was true.

"Besides," he went on, "you won the bet."

She frowned. "The bet?"

"You know. Dinner if I met a woman and she seduced me."

Every muscle in her body tensed. She had totally forgotten about the idiotic wager, the one she'd thought to herself was so cute at the time. "You mean it really happened?"

He nodded. "Idiotic as it might seem. So since this was your bet you get to listen to me whine."

"I thought you said the seduction worked."

"It did." He shifted his weight. "But now I have another problem."

Please don't ask me to help you find this woman.

But he didn't seem to be taking the hint.

"All right," she sighed. "Bring the beer and meet me on the back porch. I've got a nice little table out there. I'll take care of the food and plates."

He lifted his eyebrows. "Outside?"

"I'm, um, inside all day, and it's nice out. I'd like some fresh air." And between the fading light and the tinted glasses he won't be able to see these ugly eyelids.

"Okay. Fine. See you out back."

He jogged back to his house while Bridget carried everything inside.

I can do this. I can do this. I can do this.

She kept repeating it like a mantra while she stripped off her work clothes and tugged on a tank top and shorts. In quick order she had plates, silverware and the sack of Chinese food. Bumping the door open with her hip she brought it all out to the back porch just as Clay came around the fence into her yard. He held up both hands, each of which held two bottles.

"I'm optimistic," he grinned as he took the stairs to the porch with one long stride. He set the bottles on the round table between the containers of food.

"If this is too cold I can heat it up," Bridget said, fussing with the silverware.

"I'm sure it will be fine." He sat down in one of the chairs. "Relax. We're just having some conversation, okay?"

"Sure. Okay." She sat in the other chair, being careful not to look at him directly. The more oblique the angle to her eyes the better off she'd be.

He popped the top on two beers and handed her one, taking a long swallow and waiting for her to help herself to the food.

"You first," she said. "Please."

She watched the play of muscles in his arms as he served himself, remembering how those arms felt around her body.

Cool it, Bridget. Just keep it together. Hear him out and send him on his way. What on earth does he want, anyway?

She forced herself to eat while he made idle chitchat. She wasn't even sure what he said, to tell the truth. But when the food was gone and the dishes piled to the side, he opened the other two bottles and leaned back in his chair.

Okay, here it comes.

"There's really no good way to jump into this," he said, "so I'll just spit it out. I've met a woman."

Bridget didn't know whether to laugh or cry. On the one hand she had a dreadful feeling that she knew what was coming. On the other, should she be insulted that he thought her so sexless he could discuss another woman with her? Sitting out here with him was hard enough, feeling the sexual charge snapping in the air, her own body responding as her nipples peaked and the walls of her pussy contracted.

She took a slow drink of her beer. "A woman?" She hoped she sounded casual enough. "Surely that's nothing new for you."

He gave a short laugh. "Why is it everyone I talk to seems to think I have women falling out of my pockets?"

Bridget almost giggled at the image. "You mean you don't?"

Clay heaved a sigh. "Okay, okay. So I'm a bit of a player. My job has a high stress level and I relax between missions. But this is different."

"Oh? In what way."

She listened while he told her about the mysterious Red who had seduced him at the masquerade ball and how she'd reached into his heart in just a few hours.

"This hit me like a ton of bricks," he told her. "I never thought I'd fall for someone like this."

Bridget wasn't sure she could keep it together. She wanted to yell at him, *Me! It's me! I'm right here.*

But then he'd make her take off her tinted glasses and that would be the end of that.

"And you're telling me this because?"

"I want to find her, Bridget." He took a long pull of his beer. "I mean, I really want to find her. He leaned across the table. "This was more than just some fu—hot night of sex. We made a connection. I know we did. Why wouldn't she tell me her name? How am I supposed to find her?"

Bridget looked away, not wanting his face to get too close to hers. "Maybe she had some personal issues," she suggested.

"Issues?" he was bewildered. "What kind of issues?"

"I don't know. Personal problems, maybe." She stood up and gathered up the empty plates and containers. "Look, Clay, I'd love to help you but I really have no idea what to tell you. If I think of anything I'll let you know. But my guess is, if she wants to find you she will."

As soon as she's ready.

"You think so?"

She forced a smile. "Sure. If she got the same vibes you did, she'll work out whatever her problem is and hunt you down. I can almost guarantee it."

He rose from the chair and picked up the empty bottles. "I probably shouldn't have bothered you with this, but it's not like I have a lot of females I can talk you. At least, not one—" He stopped, as if realizing he was about to put his size twelve foot right in his mouth. "I mean... That is... What I meant to say..."

"It's all right, Clay." She hoped her smile looked real. "I know exactly what you mean and I'm fine. I'm flattered that you felt you could talk to me about this."

"Really?" His eyebrows rose. "Because I'm pretty sure any of the other women I know—"

"I'm not one of the other women you know and everything's fine. But I really need to get inside."

"Bridget, listen…"

She dug up a bright smile from somewhere and flashed it at him. "Thanks for sharing dinner with me. And bringing the beer. Good luck with your search."

She was inside with the door closed before she could fall apart.

Dumping the dishes and silverware in the sink she dropped down into one of the breakfast room chairs, closed her eyes and leaned her head on her elbows. This was worse than she could imagine. When Clay Randall was unattainable it was bad enough. But after one very hot night with him she realized she was hopelessly in love with him. And he was in love with a woman who didn't really exist.

What the hell was she going to do?

Chapter Six

ॐ

Bridget sat in front of her computer, staring at the screen. A project at work had kept her long after her usual quitting time. Then she'd had errands to run so it was well after eight o'clock by the time she got home and close to nine by the time she wolfed down a tuna sandwich and made it into her home office to write. But email first, as always. So she'd clicked on her email program and there it was.

The letter.

The letter.

Dear Miss Reilly,

The Durban Trust has reviewed your case and I am delighted to be able to provisionally offer you the treatment requested. This offer is subject to a successful series of interviews and examinations, beginning with our psychiatrist and followed by a medical examination. We enclose a list of the doctors approved by the Trust in your area. He or she will do his or her examinations before agreeing to undertake the procedure.

But prior to that the chair of the Trust, Ms. Georgina Hawthorne, would like to have her own interview with you. Since distance is a consideration we would like to set up a video chat between the two of you. Please reply as soon as possible, so we may set up a schedule.

They'd answered her. They'd really answered her. Not only that, but she had a provisional agreement that they would provide the funds for the procedure.

Ohmigod!

She read it through for the umpteenth time, still trying to process what she was seeing. Yes, she was really one step closer to her dreams. Clay. And fully embracing her career as an author.

Taking a deep breath to steady herself she hit Reply and wrote:

Thank you so much for your reply and for the provisional offer. I am available any evenings and weekends for the video chat with Miss Hawthorne, and I have a camera in my computer. Just let me know what's convenient for her.

Thank you very much.

She hit Send. It seemed like such a puny reply for such a wonderful gift but she didn't know what else to say without gushing. She watched until she got the Message Sent indication then picked up her glass and headed toward the kitchen for more water, wishing she had some wine to celebrate with. Some wine and maybe some*one*. Like Clay Randall. Maybe after the surgery. But in the interim ice water alone would have to do.

She had made it as far as the refrigerator when the lights flickered twice then went out and the house was suddenly completely dark. Bridget stopped with her hand on the refrigerator, trying to adjust to the blackness, feeling the fear swamp her. She knew it was irrational but nothing she tried had ever helped. Now that she lived alone she slept many nights with the light on and she always had nightlights glowing. Of course with no electricity they didn't do her any good.

Forcing a calmness she didn't feel she moved sideways four steps and reached out for the handle of the drawer where she kept two flashlights, just in case. Opening it she fumbled inside until her hand closed over the smooth length of one of the torches. Okay, good. She pushed the button to turn it on.

Nothing.

Don't panic. Don't panic. Don't panic.

But as always she felt the dark closing in on her and choking her.

She fished around until she found the other flashlight, bigger and sturdier, and pressed the switch on it. Again nothing. Frantically she pushed it back and forth but still nothing happened. How was that possible? The last time she'd checked the batteries everything had been working just fine. When had that been? Shaking she scrabbled in the drawer for spare batteries, nearly jumping out of her skin when someone knocked on the back door.

"Bridget? Hey, it's me. Clay. You in there?"

Clay!

She didn't care what had brought him over only that he was here. Guiding herself with the tiny sliver of light that sliced in through the closed blinds her made her way to the door, unlocked it and opened it.

"Bridget?"

She fell against him, almost sobbing with relief, wrapping her arms around his waist.

"Oh, god, I'm so glad you're here." She plastered herself to him like a barnacle on a ship.

"Hey, hey, hey." His muscular arms cradled her and his hand stroked her back. "The power's out on the whole block so I just thought I'd check on you. What's going on here?"

"N-nothing." Her voice was muffled against his chest. "It's just so...dark."

"Sure is." His hand continued its soothing motion up and down her spine. "That a problem for you?"

"No." But she couldn't seem to unpeel herself from him. Over thirty years old and still terrified of the dark. "I'm okay."

He chuckled. "Liar. Now I'm glad I came by. I've at least got a working flashlight."

He flicked it on and Bridget pressed her face harder against his chest. "Turn it off. Please."

"Huh? I thought—"

"No. Now that you're here I'm better. Maybe we could just...sit down?"

"No problem."

As if she weighed nothing he lifted her in his arms, kicked the door shut and made his way into her living room.

"How can you even see where you're going?" she asked into his t-shirt.

"I'm a SEAL," he teased. "Don't you know we have to see in the dark?"

How he managed to find the couch she didn't know but in the next moment he was sitting on one end of it with her cradled in his lap.

In his lap! I'm sitting in Clay's lap!

"I'm glad one of us can." Her anxiety level was decreasing but she still clung to the safety of his body.

"Don't you have any flashlights of your own in the house? You must not have been a Girl Scout."

"I have them. But it seems the batteries are dead." A feeling of stupidity was slowly replacing anxiety. "I'm usually better about making sure everything works. Anyway, now that you're here I'm not so frightened."

"But then I wouldn't have any excuse to hold you on my lap, would I?"

And that quickly the air between them became electrically charged. She felt the thickness of his cock pressing into her buttocks through the denim of his cutoffs, the rough texture of his hard-as-stone legs against the bare skin of her own.

"Um, Clay?" She knew she should move but it was the last thing she wanted.

"Feeling better?" His voice had taken on a husky note and his hand had slipped from her back down to the curve of her ass.

"Yes," she whispered, trying to decide if she should press harder against him or get up and run like hell.

"Bridget?" His mouth was close to her ear and one hand cupped her chin.

"Uh-huh." Her breath was trapped in her throat.

"This may be a big mistake but I'm gonna do it anyway."

The moment his mouth touched hers fire exploded in the pit of her stomach and fanned out to every part of her body. She knew her crotch was suddenly damp with her juices and she worried that Clay could feel it through her thin yoga pants. Her breasts tingled, just begging for his mouth.

His tongue traced the seam of her lips before urging them open and slipping inside. He licked gently everywhere, his tongue gliding over hers. His fingers threaded through her hair, cupping her head and holding it in place so he could slant the kiss this way and that. At first it was gentle. Coaxing. Testing. But as she found herself sinking into it an urgency crept in and the contact became hot and fierce.

It's pitch-black in here. Only a tiny sliver of moonlight. He can't see my eyes. Or my body, and compare it to his mysterious woman. I can be totally anonymous again.

And that quickly she let herself fall into it, sliding her hands through the silk of his hair and pressing herself against him.

"Jesus, Bridget." He tore his mouth from hers, his breath coming in uneven rasps. "What the hell are we doing here?"

"You tell me," she whispered, and wriggled her ass against his thickening cock.

"Do that one more time and you'll be in big trouble."

In answer she moved again.

"Don't say I didn't warn you," he ground out and slid his hand beneath her t-shirt.

Bridget suddenly remembered she wasn't wearing a bra. She always took it off when she got home and changed into comfy clothes for the evening. Now Clay's large callused palm was sliding up her rib cage and cupping her breasts, the contact of skin against skin electrifying.

"Sweet," he breathed and pinched her nipple.

She jerked in response and a tiny moan whispered over her lips as she arched into his touch.

He pinched her nipple again and tugged at it lightly. His tongue was back in her mouth again, firing her senses. She moaned again as his hand moved down over her tummy beneath the waistband of her yoga pants and into the nest of curls. He nipped the end of her tongue as his long fingers slid against the lips of her pussy and found her opening, circling with a slow movement.

Automatically she moved her thighs to give him better access and one finger slid easily inside her. Bridget ran her hands over his shoulder, down his arms and beneath the fabric of his shirt to find the dusting of hair on his chest and his flat nipples.

He groaned and added a second finger to the first. She clenched around him and rocked back and forth in tiny movements. With each shift of her buttocks she rubbed the thick ridge of his cock.

"Okay," he gasped, tearing his mouth from hers. "Enough fooling around, I just hope to hell one of us knows what we're doing." He pulled his hand from his body and cupped her cheeks. "Bridget. Listen to me. I have to go home and get a condom. They aren't usually part of this outfit. When I come back if you've changed your mind it's okay."

Her throat was so dry she could hardly speak. "I-I won't change my mind."

He kissed the tip of her nose. "If you do, I'm just telling you it's all right." He set her on the couch and stood up. "I'll leave the door open so it won't be quite so dark in here."

Then he was out the door with his long-legged stride.

Bridget nibbled her bottom lip, wondering if she was making the biggest mistake of her life. After she had her surgery—*if* she passed all the qualifications—and she told Clay she was really Red, would he be mad as her for the whole seduction episode? Madder yet that she had sex with him as Bridget without telling him? If so, maybe she should grab on to the unexpected opportunity and run with it.

Deliberately she made her mind a blank she removed her t-shirt and yoga pants along with her thong and lay back down on the couch, her heart pounding like that of a racehorse. Her breath caught in her throat when she heard Clay's feet on the back porch followed by the closing of the door. Then he was standing beside her and he was shucking his clothes.

His fully erect and swollen cock brushed her cheek and she closed her fingers around it, stroking the familiar velvet-over-steel that she remembered from their night together. Once. Twice. Then her hand slipped down to cup his balls and run her fingernails lightly over the sac that held them.

Clay brushed her hand away and she heard the crinkle of the foil wrapper, sensed him sheathing himself in the latex. He knelt between her thighs on the couch but instead of entering her he bent his head to kiss her again, his cock rubbing against the mound of her pussy.

She rubbed her hands over the hot skin of his back, feeling the play of muscles beneath it, her tongue meeting his in a delicious duel.

His broke the kiss and trailed his mouth across her cheek and down the column of her neck, pausing to place a kiss behind one ear and at the hollow of her throat where her pulse was beating wildly. Then downward until his lips closed over one nipple, sucking on it deeply before turning his attention to the other. Over her stomach, his tongue drawing circles around her navel and finally to her pussy, where he licked the length of her slit.

Bridget was on fire, the need in her so strong it engulfed her. She pressed her feet into the couch cushion, thrusting herself to his incredible mouth as he licked and stroked and tasted. His tongue swirled around the nub of her clit, sending fire spearing through her.

"Oh, oh, oh," she murmured as his very educated tongue drew incredible responses from her. "Please. *Oh*, please."

He lifted his head. "Please? Please, what?"

She could hardly get her breath. "Please. Inside me. Now."

The head of his cock nudged her opening and then he slid in smoothly, filling her completely. He paused a moment, letting her adjust to him although the feeling was so familiar it brought tears to her eyes.

Yes, yes, yes!

This was what she'd hungered for every night since the masquerade ball. What she'd dreamed about.

And then he moved, slowly at first then faster. Bridget wound her legs around his waist and lifted herself to him so she took him deeper and his balls slapped against her with each thrust. She clamped her inner muscles around him, riding him, nothing existing in the pitch dark except her, this man and the incredible soaring feeling rising inside her.

He moved one hand between them to find her clit, rubbed it, rubbed it, and then they were plummeting into space together, bodies shuddering as spasms rocked them. A long time seemed to pass before the heavy tremors began to subside. Clay collapsed on her then eased himself out, his breathing still choppy.

"I don't want to crush this sweet, sweet body," he rumbled, his voice still ragged.

Bridget struggled to get her own breathing under control. "I'm okay. Honest."

She was vaguely aware of him standing, doing something—disposing somehow of the condom—then sitting beside her on the couch. Pulling her into his arms.

"Bridget," he began.

"It's okay," she said, her voice muffled as he pulled her to his chest. "Just please don't say you're sorry."

"No. It's not okay. And I'd be lying if I said I'm sorry, but I feel like a real shithead."

"Don't," she protested. "Please do not say you're sorry. Do *not* do that. I wanted this as much as you did." *Maybe more.* "It...just happened."

He brushed her hair back from her face and she wondered in panic if somehow he could see her features in the blackness.

"I worry that I took advantage of you in a vulnerable situation." He sighed. "And then there's..." His voice trailed off.

"Your mystery woman," she finished for him, her heart twisting.

"Yes. There's her."

Silence stretched between them until she couldn't stand it anymore. She lifted her hand, searching until she found his face. She smoothed her fingers against the stubbled skin.

"Let's just say you helped me when I needed it and let it go at that." She pushed herself up and gave a slightly hysterical giggle. "I think I'm relaxed enough now and you need to go."

"I feel like a bastard walking out on you like this."

"You aren't walking out. I'm giving you permission to leave. Really. Go. Please."

She heard his sigh. "Let me take you into your bedroom and do this right. Please?"

In her bedroom? Was he kidding? Does his male ego just demand that he give a better performance? Not on his life.

Secretly she'd hoped that her body would be familiar to him. That he'd somehow recognize Red. That the feel of her around him would trigger the memories.

Apparently not. And maybe she'd made a mistake falling for him in the first place and going through with the elaborate charade. Now she wanted to scream at him *Just get out* but instead she scrabbled around for her clothes and began pulling them on. "How about this? You were a whole lot better than a drink or a tranquilizer, and the memory will be more pleasant. We're good, Clay. Really."

"This will sound stupid but are we still friends?"

Friends. The word suddenly took on a whole new meaning.

"Of course. And I might even find a way to help you locate your mystery woman."

She heard the rustling of fabric as he dressed then felt his lips on her forehead.

"Don't forget I owe you dinner."

"I'll be sure to collect." *Not in this lifetime.*

"If you're sure you're okay?"

"Fine. I'm fine." *Go. Now.*

Actually she was an emotional wreck and about to explode but she wanted him out before that happened. The darkness was no longer the only thing threatening her sanity.

"I'll check on you later." His lips found her forehead in the darkness.

"Actually, I'm going to grope my way to bed now so I'm good. Thanks. Really."

She kept her head averted as he opened the back door, afraid a sliver of moonlight might cast itself on her.

"Bye, Bridget."

She heard the soft snick of the door closing and stretched out on the couch, her arm over her forehead. The lights chose that moment to come on, flooding the house with light.

Thank god Clay has already left.

But as if he might return any minute she hurried into her office to find her glasses. Back in the kitchen she finally got her

90

glass of ice water and sat at the breakfast table sipping it. Holy god, what had she done? She could only chalk it up to the intense need to be with Clay again and the overwhelming panic of the blackout.

What would he think? His head was so tied up with his mystery woman, by tomorrow she wouldn't even be a blip on his radar. How would he react when he found out the truth of the situation? Be happy? Hate her?

She chugged the rest of the water and stuck the glass in the dishwasher. She still had a good hour of time to write tonight. Maybe she could lose herself in the pages of her book instead of the mess that her life was becoming.

* * * * *

Well, that was certainly a fucking mess.

Clay slammed his back door. The power was back on so he stuck the flashlight in a kitchen drawer. Maybe he should stick his head in with it. What a bonehead thing he'd just done. Probably ruined a good friendship at the same time.

Bridget was…Bridget. The really nice next-door neighbor who he chatted with over the fence or the garbage cans. Who he'd just recently poured his heart out to about a woman he'd fallen in love with. That he was desperate to find. And tonight, when she'd been frightened out of her wits, what had he done? Fucked her like some bimbo he'd picked up and brought home.

Shithead.

He pulled a cold bottle of beer from the fridge, popped the top and took a long swallow. It seemed as if lately he'd been doing a number of really stupid things. Like crawling into bed with a strange woman, fucking her brains out while they still had their masks on, falling in love in less than a twelve-hour time slot and letting her leave without getting her name or any idea of how to find her.

To make matters worse he'd dumped all over his captain and the captain's wife as well as Bridget. But having sex with her just now was the frosting on the cake of stupidity. What kind of person tells a woman he's in love with someone else, someone he can't even find, then fucks her in the dark like he did. She probably thought she was a poor substitute for his mystery woman. So what kind of asshole did that make him? The kind of asshole he detested?

As if that wasn't bad enough, the whole time he'd been with her, short as it was, he had the weird feeling that he'd done this same thing with her before. There was a familiarity about her body, about the way her tight pussy clenched around his cock. About her breasts, as stupid as that sounded. Maybe it was her laughter or the gentle cadence of her voice.

But he knew that was unreasonable. He and Bridget had never been intimate before tonight.

Intimate.

Now there was a word to describe what he and Red had experienced. More than fucking. More than sex. Better than just making love. They'd been *intimate*. It sounded hokey to say it but it felt as if she'd touched his very soul and unlocked something that had been isolated for a long time.

What was it about her that had turned him on so unexpectedly? A sudden thought left him thunderstruck and he stopped where he was, every brain cell frozen. Was it possible... No. Now he was really letting his mind run wild. No way could Bridget and Red be the same person. He was just superimposing memories on the real thing, because he wanted to find her so badly.

So now he was in deep shit twice. He had no idea how to find Red, a woman he found himself feeling unfaithful to, and he may have ruined his relationship with Bridget.

Way to go, dickhead.

Chapter Seven

ॐ

Bridget settled herself at her desk, having checked her blouse, her hair and her makeup at least ten times. It was just shy of eleven o'clock Saturday morning and she was about to have her video chat with Georgina Hawthorne. She was so nervous she hadn't even been able to eat any breakfast.

What if they decide I'm not a good candidate?

Stop it. They contacted me, didn't they? I'll just have to make my case.

The video chat was all set up. At eleven o'clock exactly her computer dinged to let her know she was getting an incoming call. She clicked on the icon to open the program and there, in front of her, was one of the most elegant women she'd ever seen. She could have been anywhere from fifty to seventy, slender in a pretty shirtwaist dress with her hair perfectly coiffed and her makeup flawless.

Bridget felt like a gnome by comparison.

"Good morning, Bridget." The woman's voice had a musical quality to it. "It's so very nice to meet you."

"G-good morning, Miss Hawthorne."

"I was very much impressed by your letter," the woman continued. "You expressed yourself very well."

"Thank you. I tried to write from the heart." Did that sound stupid? She wasn't exactly sure how you spoke to a living legend, much less the woman who held your future in her hands.

"And you did." She lifted a sheet of paper, obviously a printout of the email. "I see you're a writer."

"Yes." She nodded. "Romance novels."

93

Georgina smiled. "Romance is such a wonderful world to lose yourself in. I checked your website. It's very well done."

And a place where anonymity is queen.

"Thank you."

"And the blurbs and excerpts of your novels sound fascinating. I can see why your publisher wants you to create a presence for yourself at their conference." Her smile was sympathetic. And I understand your reluctance. In my generation people were judged solely on appearance and it was a truly artificial world. One that destroyed many."

"As I said in the email, this is something I'd really like to do. That is, if…" She let her voiced trail off.

"If you have the surgery." Georgina looked down at the email again. "And there's a man in the picture." Her lips curved in a smile. "I think the way you went about arranging an evening with him is extremely inventive and took a lot of guts. That's what I look for, Bridget. Guts. And wouldn't it be nice to be able to be with him without the masks?"

"Yes, it would."

"Tell me a little more about yourself."

So Bridget told her about her family, about how they were all following their own dreams. About her fantasy of becoming a writer and her desire for Clay. How desire had turned into love so quickly and unexpectedly and she wanted the opportunity to find out if it was real.

Georgina stared at her through the video camera for what seemed like the longest moments in Bridget's life.

"Could I ask you to remove your tinted glasses for me, please?"

With a hand that trembled slightly she removed them, leaving her feeling naked and exposed.

Georgina studied her for what seemed an interminable amount of time. Then she nodded.

"I'm sorry that you've been dealing with this in your life, although you have a lovely face, my dear. Elegant bone structure. But I do believe that having the surgery will be a gift you won't misuse."

"Oh! Oh, thank you, Miss Hawthorne."

"Georgina," the woman reminded her. "And you are truly welcome. Someone will be in touch with you about the psychological evaluation. Once that's completed we'll forward a list of recommended surgeons in your area. Let us know which one you select and we'll take care of everything else. Bye, now."

Then she was gone and Bridget was staring at a blank screen.

It's really going to happen!

It was a long time before she was steady enough to get up from the chair and leave the room. She wanted to sing. To shout. To tell someone about her great good fortune. She was sure she'd pass the psych eval. And then...

Yes. And then.

Needing to do something with her sudden abundance of restless energy, she decided to do her grocery shopping. In a few weeks she'd be cruising the mall, shopping for new clothes to go with her new look.

As she backed out of her garage she happened to spot Clay just come out of his garage, dressed in fatigues. She had avoided him since the night of the blackout, but in the security of her car she could at least wave and say hello.

She rolled down her window. "Off to play war?" she teased.

"Off to the real war." His face was impassive. "The team has a new mission assignment. I'm leaving here any minute."

"Oh. Sorry. I didn't mean to sound so flippant." She wet her lower lip. "How long will you be gone?"

He shrugged. "Probably a month." Then he grinned. "Don't let anyone steal the house while I'm gone."

"I'll guard it with my life."

He walked over to the car and she was glad she had her heavy sunglasses on. "I haven't seen you since the night of the blackout. You hiding from me?"

"Not at all." *Liar.* "Just busy. Find your mystery woman yet?"

"No. Not even a hint of her. And lord knows I've tried every possible contact I could dig up." He scratched his head. "You know, it's the funniest thing. The other night I almost..." He paused.

Bridget's pulse quick-timed. Had her body been familiar to him? Had it triggered a memory?

"Never mind. Just my brain playing tricks on me." He slapped his hand against her car door. "Drive carefully. I'll see you in a month."

And maybe the new me, she thought as she nodded and backed out into the street. If things worked out right she might have a special surprise for Clay when he was back from wherever he was going.

* * * * *

"Only for you would I get up at five o'clock in the morning," Joni teased, tucking the hospital sheet around Bridget a little more snugly.

"I really appreciate this, you know."

"Of course I know, sweetie. I'm happy to do it. More than happy."

Georgina Hawthorne had written to let her know that she'd passed the psych eval with flying colors and forwarded a list of recommended surgeons to her. She'd decided making an appointment with each of them was the best way to make a decision, and she felt the most comfortable with Harlen Richards.

Telling Joni about the procedure had been at once frightening and exhilarating. But Dr. Richards had been adamant that she couldn't be alone, at least for the first couple of days. She'd be groggy from the anesthetic plus she needed ice on and off her eyes every twenty minutes for at least twenty-four hours.

She managed to have the surgery scheduled for a Friday and Joni had eagerly taken two personal days at work. She spent Thursday night with her and drove her to the hospital. She'd be staying at Bridget's through the weekend and bringing her for her post-op appointment on Monday morning. Since arrival she'd signed enough paper to build a house, had everything checked again but her teeth and had her "before" picture taken.

"I should be mad at you for keeping your books a secret," Joni said. "And for not telling me all about the masquerade ball." She brushed a stray hair back from Bridget's cheek. "But after listening to you last night I understand it and forgive you."

She'd been told not to eat or drink anything after midnight so they'd opened a bottle of wine with dinner and Bridget had spilled everything. The ball, her feelings for Clay, how she'd started writing the books and the small success she was having. And her publisher's request that she attend the conference.

"I should have told you before, but it just hurt so much to talk about it. Especially since I never expected to be able to do anything about it. Until now."

"Until now," Joni agreed.

"Good morning." Dr. Richards swept into the room in his scrubs, smiling at her. "All set?"

"More than I've ever been," she assured him.

He motioned to another man beside him clad in the same kind of scrubs. "This is Dr. Heisler. He'll be giving you some happy juice and keeping you comfortable through the procedure."

He went on to explain again what they'd be doing and while he talked Heisler inserted the IV line and hung a bag of fluid on the pole at her head. It seemed only seconds had passed before her eyelids drooped and she drifted off to sleep.

When she woke up someone was holding her hand and there was something heavy and cold on her face. She tried to lift her other hand to touch it but the same someone grabbed it.

"Uh-uh." Joni's voice. "Ice. You have to leave it on for a while. The nurse will be by in a bit to check on you."

"How…how did I do? Was the surgery successful?"

"One of the best I've ever done." Dr. Richard's voice right next to her. "Men will swoon when they see your eyes," he teased.

"I'll just be happy if they don't run screaming in horror."

The doctor took her free hand in his. "Bridget, I can promise you, no one is ever going to make comments about your eyes again, except to tell you how beautiful they are."

She closed her eyes and drifted off again.

She was in and out of sleep all day, only obliquely aware of the ice being lifted from her eyes then sometime later replaced. Of Joni sitting beside her, talking to her when she was awake.

"Have you been in that chair all day?" she asked when she felt more alert.

"Mostly. I'll be glad to leave, though. The hospital coffee will rot your stomach."

"Leave?" She had a moment of panic. "Where are you going?"

"To take you home. Think you can sit up enough to drink something? They won't let you leave unless you can swallow and pee. In one end and out the other. So get busy. Dr. Richards will be making evening rounds shortly. You've done so well if you get a handle on this he'll be signing you out."

"How do I look? I've had ice on my face almost all day."

They just took the most recent ice pack off. Let me crank you up and you can see."

Joni handed her a mirror and what she saw shocked her on many levels. The heavy epicanthic fold was gone, replace by redness and a line of stitches. And of course some swelling. But she could actually see her eyes! It was astonishing.

"Keep the ice on schedule for twenty-four hours and you won't even have any bruising." Neither of them had noticed Dr. Richards come in. He leaned closer, examining his handiwork. "Good job if I do say so myself. Okay. Let's do what we need to and get you out of here."

Bridget was eternally grateful for Joni, who was religious about the ice packs and made sure she slept with the special goggles they gave her. And fed her. And amused her. And encouraged her.

The post-op appointment showed better than good progress and each day as the week passed the surgical site improved. The swelling continued to go down, she had no bruising and she couldn't stop looking at herself in the mirror. On Friday afternoon Dr. Richards gave her a huge smile and told her he'd see her in two weeks.

"You're my star patient," he said, and gave her copies of the "before" and "after" pictures. Then he said something strange. "Keep these to remind yourself that it's really the person inside who counts."

She celebrated by emailing her publisher to let her know that the conference was a go and by pulling up the conference site and registering. She felt as if she'd climbed a mountain. Her first day back at work she got up early to carefully apply her makeup, especially eye shadow and eye liner. This was the first time she could really use it properly. When she looked in the mirror it startled her to realize she didn't look like she was squinting. That her entire iris was visible. And sparkling!

What a change!

She wondered how long it would take before someone noticed she didn't have her tinted glasses on. It wasn't until she went for fresh coffee in the break room and ran into three coworkers that someone actually commented. But by the end of the day she was basking in the compliments, even if no one realized what they were for. Everyone assumed she'd gotten contacts and that was why she'd ditched the specs. She didn't care. She felt good about herself for the first time in longer than she cared to remember.

Telling her family had been a bigger hurdle. Her mother and sister were upset she hadn't consulted other doctors and even more so that she hadn't asked either of them to come and stay with her. But they'd been amazed at what they saw during video chats and now she only had one hurdle left to leap.

Clay Randall.

"Be careful how you do this," the therapist working with her cautioned. "You have high expectations and I don't want you to be upset by anything."

"By what?" she frowned. "Are you thinking Clay won't find me attractive after the surgery? Won't be glad that he can find his mystery lady?"

"I'm thinking he might not be too happy."

"I don't understand. And I won't let you spoil this for me."

By the time Clay was back home nearly all the swelling was gone and she was ready to put her plan into motion. At midnight on Friday night she snuck out to his mailbox and left a note in an envelope for him.

Your mystery woman has been located. She will arrive at your house promptly at seven Saturday night looking for her pirate. Wine and snacks would be appreciated.

Saturday after running the errands she needed, including a trip to the costume shop, she sat in an agony of indecision. Should she have mentioned the snacks? Was that too unromantic? Should she have just asked for wine? Would he be shocked when he opened the door and there she was, in ball gown and mask?

Too late now. Everything was in motion. If she backed out she'd never forgive herself. She'd missed Clay desperately every day he'd been gone, distracted only by her surgery and recovery. Soon the waiting would be over. She just hoped and prayed that the connection they'd made the night of the ball was still there.

She took a long time getting ready, spreading lotion over every square inch of her skin, spraying perfume on all her pulse points. Carefully applying her eye makeup. Getting herself into the ball gown and mask. Promptly at seven she rang his doorbell.

"Red!" His eyes lit up when he saw her.

He looked so good, in dark slacks and a plaid shirt with the sleeves rolled up.

"Can I come in?" she asked.

"Oh. Of course." He opened the door wider to let her cross the threshold. "I didn't know we were dressing formally tonight."

"Only me," she said. "And only for a little while."

"I hope that means what I think it does." His voiced was edged with lust and something deeper. He waved at the coffee table in front of the couch. A cooler filled with ice and two bottles of wine sat on a tray with two goblets. "As requested." He winked. "Snacks later, when we need to replenish our energy."

"Thank you."

He poured two glasses of wine and handed her one, touching his glass to hers. "To us."

She nodded. "To us."

101

"I don't know who found you or how," he said, "but I owe them big-time. I nearly went crazy when you left without giving me your name or a phone number. Do you know I've dreamed about you nearly every night since then? Wanted you? Missed you?"

"But it was just one night," she reminded him. "A night of seduction."

His face sobered. "No. Maybe that's the way it began but it was much more than that. Right? Don't try to deny it."

Her heart was beating erratically as nervous shivers jittered over her skin. Now they were starting to get to the meat of things.

"And if I agree?"

"Then you'd better have a damn good reason for running out the way you did." He wasn't smiling now. "Tell me what it is."

Instead she set her glass down and slid down the zipper on her gown, letting it pool around her feet and stepping out of it. His eyes widened.

"You're getting naked when we haven't even finished our discussion?"

She tried another smile. "I thought maybe I could distract you."

"Not this time. Tonight I want to see the face of the woman I'm making love to. With." His voiced lowered. "The woman I think stole my heart."

Bridget unclasped her demi bra and let it drop, then shimmied out of her thong. She stood before him in just her ridiculous high heels and the mask.

"How's this?"

His eyes traveled over her slowly, taking in every naked inch, fire dancing in his eyes.

"Good. But not good enough."

"Oh? What else would you like?"

"I'd like the mask off too."

Bridget took in a slow, deep breath.

"Are you sure that's what you want?" she persisted.

"Absolutely. I'm not going to let you walk out of my life again and me not knowing who you are. I want to know right now. Because I truly believe we stated something special and I want to know who it's with."

"Okay, then."

With shaking hands she reached back to unfasten the lacings that kept the mask in place. Slowly she pulled it away from her face and tossed it to the floor with her gown. Here it was, the moment of truth.

Clay's eyes widened and he nearly dropped his wine. "Bridget?"

She trembled with uncertainty. "In the flesh. So to speak."

"What the hell is going on? *You're* Red?"

"Is it so hard to accept?" She reached down for the dress and held it up like a shield, needing something so she didn't feel quite so exposed.

"But why? I had no idea you even felt that way about me." He swallowed half of his wine. "You never even let me get close to you. Never. Where are your glasses? I thought you had trouble with your eyes?"

"I do." She bit her lower lip, wishing she hadn't thought this was such a good idea. "Did."

"Bridget, what the fuck is going on here?" Then his face hardened. "Did you pull that whole stunt at the ball to win that stupid bet?"

She was stunned. "What? No. Of course not. I just...wanted to be with you and there was no way you'd ever..."

"Ever what? It might have helped if you'd given me a signal here and there. Was it just the sex? Was it, Bridget?"

She shook her head, tightening her hands into fists at her sides. "Of course not."

But he wasn't hearing her. "Thought you'd have a good roll in the hay with the military stud next door? Was that it?"

"No." Tears were burning her eyes. "Nothing like that."

"Then what?" His eyes widened as if a thought had just stabbed his brain. "Wait a minute. Why didn't you say anything the night I… We… When…"

"Yes," she said in a low voice. "The night."

"Yeah. Wouldn't that have been a good time to mention it?"

She lowered her gaze. "I had my reasons."

"I hope they're damn good ones, because right now I'm feeling like the fool of the century. And it isn't a good feeling, I promise you."

This wasn't going at all the way she'd planned. "Maybe I should just show you the pictures."

His eyebrows flew up to his hairline. "Pictures? What pictures?"

"Not the kind you think." She stepped into her dress, shoving her arms into the sleeves just enough to hold it up, gathered up everything else and fled out the back door.

She'd left her own door unlocked, knowing she wouldn't be far away. In her bedroom she tossed the dress, the lingerie, the mask and the shoes in a corner, trying hard to stave off the threatening tears. Finding a big t-shirt and a pair of shorts, she dug the pictures from Dr. Richards out of her top drawer and hurried back to Clay's, her heart threatening to pound its way out of her chest all the while.

He was still standing in the living room, right where she'd left him, like a mountain of stone, his face looking as if it was set in concrete.

"Here." She shoved the pictures at him. "This is why."

He took the pictures from her and glanced at them then looked again, harder. "What's this?"

"That's me. Before," she pointed, "and after."

He looked at the pictures for so long Bridget was almost afraid to move. She was shaking so badly she had to clutch her hands together.

"Say something. Anything. Please."

At last he lifted his gaze and looked at her. "So you had a problem with your eyelids. And now you've had surgery. Right?"

She nodded.

"You didn't think you could tell me the real reason you wore those glasses? Or let me know your were interested in me without that whole charade?"

"Oh, right. You would have jumped at the chance. Just like all the other men who took a look at me and made crude jokes. Just like the people who stared at me as if I were a freak." Anger was fast replacing the anxiety. "I've seen the women you date, Clay. And I was very aware of how I looked. You would have taken one look at me and run in the other direction. You told me I had bedroom eyes. Well, you wouldn't have taken them in your bedroom if you'd seen me as I was."

He tossed the pictures onto the coffee table. "You obviously have a very shallow opinion of me, Bridget. I go into war zones where I see things so much worse than this they'd turn your stomach. I want what's inside a woman, not what's outside." He paused, staring at her hard. "Did you ever wonder why I never saw these women more than once or twice? Or why I never settled down?"

"I-I thought it was because you're a SEAL. You go away so much you didn't want to have to leave someone behind."

"Do you know how many SEALs are married? My captain's about to celebrate his tenth anniversary." Clay came to stand in front of her, glaring down at her. "I've been looking for a woman like Annie McCord. Someone strong and independent, who loved me unconditionally for who I am, not what I am. Who would make a home for me to always come back to. Who understood what I do. In the short time we spent together I had the feeling you might be that person."

"Please." It seemed to be the only word she could force out of her mouth.

He turned away from her. "But if you think so little of me that you can't be honest with me then you aren't that person. If you wanted the surgery we could have discussed it together. I would have been here for you, even just as a friend. But if you think all I'm looking for is a pretty face you're very much mistaken. Go home, Bridget. We're done here."

She picked up the photos and walked out, proud of herself that she made it all the way inside her house before falling apart. Then she huddled on her sofa as night fell, sobbing until she was sure she had no more tears left. Her eyes felt swollen, her throat was raw and her chest hurt. Or maybe it was her heart. Never in all her planning had she ever thought Clay would not understand. That he'd be so angry with her.

What right did he have? Until that night they'd never had more than the most casual contact. Okay, so that night had been intense. And yes, it had touched feelings in each of them she hadn't expected. She was sure he hadn't, either.

The therapist's words echoed in her head. "You might not be happy with what you get."

So now what did she do? How could she live next door to him after this disaster?

She had no idea how long she sat curled up on the couch, rocking back and forth. Once she thought about calling Joni but she wasn't yet ready to share her humiliation with anyone, even her closest friend. First she had to figure out how to handle it herself.

Finally she managed to find her way to her bedroom and crawl into bed with her clothes on. She hoped tomorrow would be a better day. It couldn't be much worse.

Chapter Eight

෨

Clay stood in his kitchen watching the sun begin its slow descent in the sky, washing away the vivid shades of gold and red. Red. That made him think of Bridget. Red. With her golden hair.

Shit.

Well, he'd fucked this up royally, that was for sure. He hoped he didn't get floor burns on his ass from sliding around with both feet in his mouth. He couldn't remember the last time he'd been as much of a total jerk to a woman. Of course, he'd never been shocked by his feelings like this, either. He was fucking in love with her, for shit's sake.

In love!

Him. Clay Randall, the big bad SEAL who didn't do love or anything even close to it. He'd always fooled himself that the reason was the hazards of his chosen career. He didn't want some woman sitting home waiting for him wringing her hands in despair. Of course he'd completely ignored the fact that his captain as well as three other members of his team were deliriously happily married to women who had their shit together, provided a wonderful sanctuary between missions and supported each other when their men were away.

Maybe he was just a selfish bastard who didn't want to give away a piece of himself to another person. But meeting Red had changed that. And when his one-night seduction and his friend from next door had blended into one he should have felt like he'd won the fucking jackpot. Instead he'd felt insulted she hadn't trusted him and yelled at her like some grade A idiot.

Good going, jerk-off.

Leaving the wine where it was, he tossed some ice cubes in a glass and poured himself a stiff shot of bourbon, tossing back half of it in one shot. Standing at the breakfast room window he stared out into the fading twilight, replaying everything in his head.

Why hadn't he figured it out the night of the blackout? Was he so desensitized that one body was the same as the other? What the fuck did that say about the kind of person he was? He'd been so busy chasing a ghost he hadn't realized she was right under his nose.

He should have been smart enough to understand what kind of courage it took for her to do what she did, everything from the seduction the night of the ball to having the surgery to exposing herself to him tonight. And he couldn't begin to imagine what her life had been like all these years. He knew exactly how cruel people could be, how devastating and brutal their remarks.

She'd come to him and practically laid her heart at his feet, exposing herself physically and emotionally, hoping that he'd just be so excited at finding her that nothing else would be important. And what had he done? Taken his bruised ego out on her.

His mother and sister would be so proud of him. *Not.*

He couldn't just let it lie there like an elephant between them. The plain truth was he was in love with her. He wanted her. In his life. In his bed. In his heart. So now what did he do? Groveling came to mind, and plenty of it. But he figured if he just went over there and tried to push his way in he wouldn't get past the closed door.

No. He needed a plan. And a good one. If, indeed, there was one.

* * * * *

"Looking very, very good." Dr. Richards snapped off the light on the complex examining machine and rolled backward in his chair. "Among my best work, if I do say so myself."

"I'm glad you're pleased." Bridget forced a smile. This was good news. She should be very happy about it. Instead she sat there with her heart like a lump of concrete weighing her body down.

Dr. Richards studied her. "I sense something a little less than overwhelming happiness here. Is there something I should be aware of?"

"No. Not at all. I'm fine. Just a little tired."

He pushed the machine aside and took one of her hands. "One of the things patients who have any kind of plastic surgery often are faced with is a lack of fulfillment of their expectations. Is that what we're dealing with here?"

"No." She shrugged. "I don't know. Maybe."

"Have you met with the therapist again? This is one of the reasons the Durban Trust insists it be one of the conditions of the surgery."

"I'm seeing him again tomorrow night."

"Good. I'm sure he'll be able to help you through whatever the situation is."

I doubt it.

"Okay, then," Richards said. "One month from now we'll take another look." He smiled at her. "Good luck, Bridget. You deserve it."

If only the Good Luck Fairy thought so too.

She was really trying to see things from Clay's point of view. At least after she'd finally finished sobbing enough tears for a tsunami and gulping down half a bottle of wine. Maybe she *had* misjudged him, but he hadn't walked in her shoes all these years. Been the brunt of cruel humor and tasteless jokes. Hidden at home rather than socializing because being out with people was too humiliating. In fact, she was still very fragile in that area.

But apparently he had looked at the whole thing differently than she did. She'd expected him to take a look at her very naked body when she ripped the mask away and pull her into his arms.

So much for that.

She was still lost in her very private pity party, still trying to see things from Clay's perspective, when she pulled into her driveway and had to slam on the brakes. On the driveway, in the center of the closed garage door, stood an enormous red vase filled with a thick arrangement of red roses. A red ribbon was tied around it, the ends trailing onto the concrete.

What the hell?

She jammed the gearshift into Park and got out of the car to pick it up. A rectangular white envelope was sticking up between the blooms and she plucked it out.

For the woman who stole my heart. C.

Bridget read the card at least six times, her heart doing a jitterbug, and finally picked up the vase, put it in her car and drove into the garage. Inside the house she set it in the center of the breakfast table where she'd be sure to see it every morning and night, then just stood back and admired it.

Okay. He'd sent flowers. Great flowers. But did he send them to Red or Bridget? He hadn't indicated either. Should she call him and thank him? Go over to his house? No, she wasn't ready to face him again. Her feelings, her emotions, were still too raw. And anyone could send flowers. It was an easy fix.

Still, shoving her sunglasses back on, she stepped out onto her back porch and looked over at Clay's house to see if he was outside. No, nothing stirring. She sighed. Okay, so he was just easing his conscience.

Then why didn't he call?

Yes, Bridget, and say what? "I'm sorry I was such an idiot."

111

Somehow she had a feeling apologizing didn't come easily to Clay Randall.

Okay, enough dwelling on that. The conference her publisher was sponsoring was in two weeks and she had a lot to do to get ready for it. For one thing she had to get with her publisher to decide which ebooks to feature so they could print covers for her to sign. Promotional items to check on. And definitely an appointment at the salon the day before so she looked her very best.

Stripping off her work clothes she changed into old shorts and a faded tank top and stuck a frozen dinner in the microwave.

Ah, the glamorous life of an author!

She was better the next day, especially after her session with the therapist.

"Focus on the good things happening to you and not on things you can't change," he told her over and over. "Life is different for you now in many ways."

She hadn't been in the house for ten minutes before her doorbell rang. Looking out through the blinds she saw a kid in his teens on her porch carrying a huge straw basket and the delivery van from a gourmet food store in her driveway.

What the hell?

She opened the door cautiously, leaving the safety chain on. A girl couldn't be too careful.

"Bridget Reilly?" he asked.

"Yes."

"I have a delivery for you."

She frowned. "I didn't order anything."

He looked at the tag on the handle and shrugged. "All I know is I'm supposed to deliver this to you. Can you please open the door wider?"

Sighing she released the chain and reached out to take the basket.

"You gotta sign." He slid a small clipboard from beneath the handle and held it out to her along with a pen from his pocket. "Thanks," he said after she scribbled her name, and loped down the steps to the van.

Bridget closed the door and carried the basket into her kitchen. Whatever was in it was completely covered with opaque red cellophane. When she pulled it away she saw dozens of chocolate hearts of all sizes. On top of the candy was a note.

You have all the pieces of my heart in your hands. C.

She couldn't help the smile that curved her lips. Well, she'd have to give him marks for inventiveness. Just like the previous night, she walked out onto her back porch and looked over at his house, but nothing was stirring. There wasn't even a light on.

Sighing she turned back inside. Maybe she could work all this into her current work in progress.

Each night for the remainder of the work week she came home to find a new gift. One night it was a big red teddy bear wearing a t-shirt that said, *I'm an idiot.* Well, yes he was. And where had he gotten a tiny shirt like that? Another night it was wine. But the one that made her laugh the most was the gift on Friday, a stuffed donkey with a note that said, *I am such an ass. C.*

She sat in the living room cradling the toy and munching on one of the chocolate hearts. Clay had still been suspiciously absent all week which was not only weird but also driving her crazy. Was the man deliberately avoiding seeing her? The gifts were wearing her down little by little, especially the cute little donkey. But if they never spoke to each other they'd never resolve anything.

His house remained ominously dark that night. Finally she forced herself to sit down at her computer. She had only one week before the conference and she needed to make sure she had everything together. Then she'd get back to her work in progress. And tomorrow she was going shopping for some new clothes for what she thought of as her coming-out party.

And I won't be wearing anything red.

But in the morning when she opened the garage door there was another basket sitting in the driveway. All it contained was a wine bottle and a note. Curious, she picked it up, saw the bottle was empty and frowned.

"You have to read the note," a deep male voice said from behind her.

Startled, she nearly dropped the basket, looked over her shoulder and saw Clay standing less than two feet away.

"What—"

"Read the note," he repeated.

Looping the handle of the basket over her arm she slid the note from its envelope and opened it.

If you'd like to exchange the empty bottle for a full one, provided by a man groveling on his knees, show up next door promptly at seven tonight. Dress entirely optional. C.

She stared at the note for a long moment then turned to ask Clay about it, but he'd left as silently as he'd appeared. Every nerve in her body suddenly snapped to life and the pulse deep in her cunt beat hard enough to send out messages in the jungle. Anticipation raced through her like a wildfire.

Setting the basket in the garage she backed out onto the street, her mind whirling, hope blossoming like a new flower.

* * * * *

Bridget wet her lips nervously, smoothed her hands over the skirt of her brand-new sundress and rang the doorbell at Clay's house. She barely had time to take another breath before the door was pulled open and there he was. For a long moment she could only look at him, drinking in the sight of his lean, muscular body, the masculine face, the deep brown eyes.

"H-hi. It's um, seven o'clock."

Clay reached out a hand, tugging her into the house and into his arms. One hand cupped her chin, tilting her face up so he could take her mouth in a hungry, predatory kiss. His tongue swept inside, licking every surface while one hand stroked her back and the curve of her ass. She was pressed so tightly against him she could feel the hard ridge of his cock pushing against her.

Just at the moment when she was sure she'd run out of breath Clay lifted his head and stared into her eyes. Her *new* eyes.

"I don't know where to begin to tell you how sorry I am. How much I regret every single word." He grinned. "You're free to kick my ass if you want."

She studied his face, trying to read him. "It took a lot of courage for me to come here that night and do what I did," she reminded him.

"I know. And I reacted like an idiot." He stroked her cheek. "I can't begin to know what you've gone through all these years. But I want to get this out before anything else. I think I fell in love with you before we ever had sex. Made love. Whatever we call it. All those times we spent talking, even when you hid behind those dark glasses. It's the person I want, Bridget. Please understand that."

"As long as you understand how important is for me, finally not to be afraid to let people see what I really look like."

"Think I could see what you really look like now?" he drawled, one corner of his mouth kicked up in a grin.

"You mean all of me?" she asked, teasing him.

"Wait." He took a half step back. "I promised you wine and groveling. The whole nine yards. First things first."

She shook her head, suddenly so eager to feel his naked body against hers she wanted to rip off her dress.

"Maybe the wine could wait. Even the groveling." She tugged his shirt from the waist of his jeans and with fingers that trembled only slightly opened the button and pulled down the zipper.

"Someone's anxious," he noted, mischief sparking in his eyes. "I think I see Red making an appearance."

"Is that who you want?" She searched his face, trying to read his expression. "I've been a nervous wreck all week. Even with all those great presents I wasn't sure how you really felt. And if you wanted Red or Bridget."

"I want both." He captured one of her hands and pressed it against his cock. "Does this answer your question?"

"Yes," she breathed.

"Then I think we need to move to someplace more comfortable."

He fastened the button on his jeans, swept her up in his arms and carried her down a short hallway to his bedroom. Her breath caught as she noted the candles placed everywhere waiting to be lit and caught the scent of jasmine in the air.

"I'd never have figured you for such a romantic," she said.

"I think there are a lot of things about me you don't know. But tonight I'm going to show you as many as I can."

He undressed her slowly, kissing each area of her body as he exposed it. She hadn't worn a bra with the sundress so when it pooled around her feet she stood in front of him wearing only a thong and sandals. The look in his eyes could never have been faked. It was more than lust. It was a deep-down hunger for a lot more than sex.

He kissed her cheeks, her jawline, the sensitive spot behind one ear, the hollow of her throat. Then he kissed her eyelids, so tenderly she felt tears gathering.

"The real you isn't what covers your eyes but what they tell me."

"And what do they tell you?" she asked in a breathless voice.

"That you're the only woman I've ever met who could fit into my life."

Before she could respond he cupped her breasts in his palms and put his mouth first to one nipple then the other, pulling, sucking, tugging until they were hard and pebbled and aching. Bridget tried to unfasten the button on his jeans again but he pushed her fingers away.

"Not yet."

Dropping to his knees he looked up at her. "This is only partially groveling," he teased then licked the seam where hip and thigh met, letting his tongue dance lightly over her skin. She was trembling, clutching at his shoulders to keep herself upright as his tongue licked and lapped and teased. Very slowly he pulled the insubstantial fabric of the thong down her legs, pausing only to let her step out of them before parting the lips of her pussy and running his tongue the length of her slit.

"Oh, oh, oh," she whimpered, so close to the edge already that she could feel the little spasms gathering force deep inside her.

Clay lifted her to the bed and placed her carefully on the edge, bending her legs so she was completely open to him. He stared down as her while he yanked off his shirt, undid his jeans and pushed them down along with his boxers. His eyes were like hot coals burning into her as he wrapped his fingers around his shaft and stroked it slowly from root to tip.

Bridget ran her tongue over her lips, hungering for the taste and feel of him.

He knelt down again and went to work on her cunt with his mouth, licking the wet flesh of her lips, swirling over the hard nub of her clit and thrusting his tongue inside her.

"So sweet," he murmured. His mouth pressed against her.

"I—I want to taste you too," she protested, barely able to form words.

117

"You will, darlin'. Plenty of time for that." He worked her with tongue and fingers until she thought she would lose her mind with need. Over and over again he brought her just to the edge, only to back off, soothe her with little kisses then start all over again.

She dug her heels into the edge of the mattress, lifting her body to him.

"Please," she sobbed. "Oh, please."

He slid two fingers inside her again, curving them to hit her sweet spot. At the same time he nipped gently on her clit.

"Clay," she wailed.

His laugh was deep. "Oh, yeah. I think we're ready."

He moved her up on the bed and turned her over, pulling her to her hands and knees. One big hand slid over each cheek of her ass.

"Ever been taken here, Red?"

She shook her head, too embarrassed to answer him and too aroused to form a coherent thought.

"Good. Because after this you'll belong to me completely. Forever."

Hot kisses covered the globes of her buttocks and his hand slipped easily along the crevice between them. His hand left her for a moment, she heard the sound of a drawer opening and closing then something cool touched her anus. She jerked, startled at the touch.

"Just some lube," he told her in a soothing voice. "The last thing I want is to hurt you."

One finger spread the gel around the tight ring before slowly easing its way in. His other hand reached around her hip and between her thighs to find her clit, stroking and rubbing it until all she could concentrate on was the sensation spreading from it. He kept it up in a steady rhythm so she was shocked to realize that he now had not one but three fingers in her ass, stretching her and massing her tender tissues.

"Hang on, darlin'. I think you're ready."

So was he if the rough edge of his voice was any indication. Bridget was at a point where she didn't care about anything except finally reaching the edge of that cliff and falling over it.

She heard the crinkle of foil and a slight tearing sound then she felt the head of his cock pressing against her opening.

"Deep breaths, Red," he told her as he drove into her with a slow but steady thrust. "Breathe in, out, in, out."

And all the while his fingers still played with her clit, driving her until every bit of him was inside her. Filling her so full that he was everywhere. That she didn't know where she ended and he began. Then he was moving, slowly at first then faster, rocking against her, one hand one her hip, the other still rubbing her clit.

The orgasm crashed through her so unexpectedly that it shook her entire body, threatening to splinter her with its cataclysmic force. She heard Clay shout her name, felt his cock throb and flex inside the latex sheath as he pumped into her again and again. When she finally collapsed forward Clay was right with her, wrapping his arms around her and kissing her shoulders and back even as he fought to steady his breathing.

Bridget was limp, totally spent. When Clay eased himself from her ass and stepped back from the bed she had a sudden sense of loss. But then he was back, lying down next to her, turning her to face him.

"I love you, Bridget 'Red' Reilly," he told her in his warm-as-molasses drawl. "I think I fell in love with you long before I realized it. If you hadn't decided to show up at the ball as Red, I hate to think how long I would have stumbled around not knowing we were right for each other."

She placed her hand against his cheek. "I love you too."

He ran a fingertip along the crease of each eyelid. "Your doctor did a damn fine job here. No doubt about it. But I want you to know that I love what's inside. What's outside isn't all that important." He grinned. "Except for the bedroom eyes, of course."

* * * * *

Clay had insisted on attending the first day of the conference with her.

"I want to bask in your glory," he teased.

She laughed. "My glory at the moment wouldn't fit on the head of a pin."

But he stood near her proudly when she was introduced at the opening meeting and when readers ran up to her to get her autograph.

"What's your next book about?" one woman asked.

She smiled up at Clay. "About a woman who discovers what the real meaning of love is."

But the most important thing she'd written was in her computer, an email just waiting to be sent.

Dear Miss Hawthorne,

I can't begin to thank you and the Durban Trust enough for providing the surgery that has made such an impact on my life. I am appearing at the conference my publisher is sponsoring, the one I discussed with you. But the most important thing is that I am marrying the man of my dreams. But it seems my eyes wouldn't have made a difference to him because he really loves me for who I am. The surgery just gave me the confidence to take that person out in public.

Thank you from the bottom of my heart.

Bridget Reilly (soon to be Randall)

STRANGERS NO MORE
Lynne Connolly

ഔ

Chapter One

✁

Neville's decision didn't surprise Whitney one bit. She kept her expression bland, but inside she decided to tough this one out, to take a stand. To make him *say* it.

"Why not?"

Neville blinked, surprise showing for a bare instant in his heavenly blue eyes, eyes that had fooled many an interviewee into thinking he was a pushover. "What do you mean, why not?"

Whitney sighed and shook back the curtain of dark hair framing her face. She'd have to go at this the hard way and tell him straight out. He wanted to humiliate her, make her admit it. Open questions were Neville's stock in trade on his top-rated interview show, but she knew him better. She'd force him into saying something. Then she'd sue his ass. "Why won't you give me the job? I'm qualified for it, much more than some of the bimbos I've seen coming in for interviews over the last few days. I've worked at NewsInc for five years now, so I know my way around and what the company expects. I can do it."

He sighed and glanced away. "Some of those *bimbos* are highly qualified," he said. "Beauty and brains in one package is hard to resist."

At least he admitted it. He wanted a beauty to cover the foreign correspondent's job, or someone did. Neville helmed and edited the wildly successful show that had attracted the sharks to NewsInc. A mixture of current affairs and chitchat, it was unlike anything else on TV, as it combined real news reporting with lighter fare. Whitney wanted the heavier job, the news side.

She held her ground. She was probably being unfair to some of the women she'd seen trooping into Neville's office over the last week, but she'd take the chance. Neville was being unfair to her. "Not as well qualified as I am. Would they stand in the center of a battle zone with a mic and camera propped up against a stone, shouting to be heard above the barrage? Not if it spoiled their perfect hairstyles, they wouldn't." She'd done the job for the smaller company she'd worked for before NewsInc, but now Nev and the new owners wanted to expand the show and they needed new personnel. She could do it and she was tired of working in the back office, doing radio and research.

He clamped his mouth shut and she suddenly had a vision of editors in years gone by, clenching their lantern jaws on their cigars while the presses rolled. What made Neville different from other talk-show hosts was that he remained a newsman, never let the glamour take over. And the new situation had chafed him more than somewhat, she knew because she'd spotted the occasional twitch or frown. She was a journalist, after all, expected to notice these small signals.

Because of their respect for his abilities and the way he'd flashed through the broadcasting universe like a shooting star, everyone who worked here had let him get away with too much. Not this time. "You said you wanted more than a pretty face, someone with experience and nerve, someone who'd go out in the field and send reports back from the front line."

These days the news got out almost as fast as it hit Twitter. And it needed professional journalists like her to deliver it. "It's no good sending someone into the field who doesn't know both the company and the background to the news. You know that, Nev." None better. Nev had earned his battle scars, though none of them were visible on his smooth, handsome outer shell. He'd been in the Near and Far East, Iraq, Afghanistan and other trouble spots, he'd been there and ducked the bombs. He didn't look quite so smooth and glossy out there either. She preferred the journalist Nev to the anchor

Neville. Today he wore an Italian tailored suit and a button-down white dress shirt—the open neck the only sign of casualness about him. His dark-blond hair was smoothed back, maybe even gelled, and his face closely shaved. She'd rather see the grubby journalist in the crumpled jeans and T-shirts. But that was just her.

"These girls have some impressive credentials."

Girls? Shit, she had no chance here, not if her boss thought of the applicants as "girls". Not that it would stop her trying. She owed it to herself, to the rest of the women fighting to make a serious name in modern journalism. No, fuck that. She wanted this job, period. She wasn't doing it for anyone else, she was doing it for her. "So there's no problem, right? I have the experience and the knowledge. I even have the qualifications." *What more does he want?*

Neville shifted in his chair, the worn leather not giving out even a squeak, he'd done it so often. He'd brought the chair from home, something that had some kind of relevance to him but she had no idea what. He glanced away, down to her application, which currently lay on his cluttered desk. "It's more than that."

And then she knew. He wasn't telling her the entire truth. It wasn't Nev, it was Mattson—the big guy, the disgustingly wealthy man who'd just added NewsInc to his portfolio of media interests. He was notorious for effecting change, putting in his own people when a natural vacancy occurred. Or he'd just order those below him to do it. Old Man Mattson had told Neville to employ the pretty ones.

Nev sighed and rubbed his jaw, his discomfort palpable. "I'd hire you if I could. You're good at what you do. But I want someone who's comfortable in China."

Fuck, oh fuck. She didn't have much experience in that part of the world. If he lucked on a bimbo who'd visited China, who knew it better than she did, she wouldn't stand a chance.

"Do you speak any Chinese languages?"

"Some." Not well enough. "But I can get up to speed fast." Even if it killed her. But she didn't know her way around China, had few contacts there.

"I interviewed a few interesting candidates today." He was looking more comfortable now, an easy smile slowly spreading over his face. "One of them is fluent in Mandarin and she lived in China for a couple of years."

She'd lost.

* * * * *

Although she tried not to show her disappointment, Whitney dropped her notebook next to her laptop with a harder thump than usual. It was enough. Jay would notice.

Jay glanced up, took one look at her face and crossed the room. He sat on the side of her desk, perching his deliciously tight ass on the lucky piece of wood. "Do I need to ask?" He flicked away the long part of his hair, the bit at the front. She envied him the glossy dark curtain, but when she'd asked him what he did to get it that way, he'd told her that he just washed it in the shower. Some people were born lucky.

"No. The bastard wants a babe." She didn't say which bastard—Neville fucking Harrison or Bastard John Mattson. It didn't really matter from where she was sitting.

Jay raised a brow. "And he didn't want you?"

Right at that moment, she could hate him. "Don't, Jay. I know the difference between them and me." She'd lived with it all her life.

He gave her a slow up-and-down look that heated her instantly. But she had no chance with Jay. His career took first place. As a colleague, he couldn't be beat, and she knew she was no oil painting. Some women thought they looked plain, ugly even. She knew it. A charity case, someone who had a great body but a plain face, lots of intelligence but no beauty. Usually she could live with it, but sometimes it sucked to be her.

She'd had boyfriends, but Jay, with his movie-star looks, square jaw, dark, melting eyes and lean, muscular physique, was way out of her league. Jay Preston O'Neill attracted the best. Several of the women coming in for interviews today had given him the eye, and some had dropped business cards on his desk on the way past. They'd have recognized him from his broadcasts, but it wasn't his reports they wanted him for. Not that Jay was promiscuous. He hadn't had a steady girlfriend for a while, but considering his job that wasn't surprising.

He'd appeared in public with some notable women, but she'd been in this business long enough to know that might mean nothing. Maybe both of them needed a career boost, a note in the media, so they'd go on a few dates. He was a high-profile journalist and reporter, and he wrote wildly successful thrillers. And the camera loved him.

She was working on a biography of Rock Hudson in her spare time, and researching his life made her even more aware of the way the media could be manipulated if money and popularity were involved. And what a tightrope these people walked. Jay had every opportunity to exploit that, instead of letting them exploit him.

Not that there was a chance of that kind of fame happening with her.

Jay leaned forward, so close that his breath heated her cheek. "You have too much of a hang-up about your appearance. You look just fine."

She blew a raspberry. "Jay, you're my best friend, but don't kid me. I know I'm not completely repellent but I've also heard that I'm best naked, with a paper bag over my head." He drew back, his brows drawn together in an angry frown, but she held up her hand. "Don't, please. It's not my imagination, you know it and I know it. My looks are best described as distinctive. I can live with that. And frankly, most of the time I don't care. I don't have to look at it. Do you know my last date had the nerve to tell me he could do some work for me cut price. Serves me right for dating a cosmetic surgeon. What was I thinking?"

That he'd see past the superficiality he dealt with on a daily basis. Some hope that had been. He'd spent their entire date describing how he could make her look like Angelina Jolie. No thank you. She wanted to look like herself. Only a little bit improved, that was all. She quelled the wistful thought firmly. No chance. She was what she was.

"Why not get the work done?" he asked gently, so softly only she heard. "You're a great journalist, one of the best I've ever worked with. You can stand in front of a crowd of baying revolutionaries and not one will touch you because they trust you to tell their story. You can put a complex political situation into two crisp sentences. So if something is holding you back, why not do it?"

There was a whisper of air against her cheek as he brushed the merest kiss against it, and she wondered if he'd had to brace himself to do it. After all, that was where the worst of her moles were.

She gave a forced laugh. "I can't afford it." But it was more than that. She was afraid. Of going under the knife, of something going wrong. Of not being herself anymore.

He grunted. "I'll front you. I know you're good for the loan."

Whitney wouldn't do that. It went against what standards she had left after working for nearly ten years in this business. "No thanks. In any case, that's giving in to the people who think everyone in front of the camera has to be beautiful."

"No it's not. You know that."

She gave him a venomous glare. She hated that he knew it, hated that he knew she hated the way she looked. But stubborn principle kept her from taking that last step. That and the lack of the money to get it done properly — and the fear.

Her mind in turmoil, she pressed her lips together, afraid that anything she said wouldn't come out right. Jay raised his brows and grinned, as if he knew it. "Think it over," he suggested.

He got to his feet and strolled across the room to his own desk, with only the slightest limp. The reason for his deskbound activities over the last couple of months was a broken leg, sustained while leaping from a moving vehicle. It was either that or get shot, he'd told her, and she believed him. Jay was a great reporter, but under fire he did what the commanding officer told him and didn't get in the way. No bravado for the camera's sake. That was one of the reasons the military tolerated him, because he followed orders when necessary. But he didn't always tell the story they wanted him to. Like her, he told it like he saw it.

Moving from radio to visual media had been a snap for Jay. Not for her.

She couldn't even say that it was because he was a man. Jay was indecently good-looking and the camera loved him. He could have fronted any program he chose, made a fortune narrating the endless reality shows that littered TV screens these days. As it was, he definitely upped the ratings of the station they worked for.

During his recovery, they'd had him present the prime-time evening news program alongside Bethany James, a popular favorite and a beautiful woman. Neville had been only too glad to step aside for a while and concentrate on managing the company. But however hard she tried, Whitney couldn't hate Bethany. The woman was pretty, vacant, without a vicious bone in her body. Not one.

Her fate was to be surrounded by beautiful people she couldn't hate. And sophisticated women and men who played games around her—nasty, possessive games in which they gave no quarter. The world's trouble zones had nothing in intrigue on NewsInc, Corp.

She stroked the length of her nose, a habit she tried to avoid, but this time, the cause of her failure to get the job needed acknowledgement. Long, full, flared at the end and the bane of her existence. But also the thing that had made her what she was. Character building, her mother called it.

She'd call her tonight.

* * * * *

"Mom, I didn't get the job."

Her mother's voice came down the line, firm and cheerful. "Oh dear, that's a shame."

Whitney choked down her tears. She wouldn't let her mother know how much the failure had affected her. "They said they wanted someone who spoke Mandarin."

"And you don't."

"Not fluently," she admitted. She found the side of her chair and gripped it hard to stop emotion creeping into her voice. "But it wasn't that, really. It's my looks. It's my nose and these moles."

"Oh no, Whitney, I'm sure it wasn't —"

She couldn't bear to hear it again, her mother's eternal optimism. She should have been called Pollyanna, not Ellen. Her mother had guided Whitney through some sticky situations, given her courage, but this time it wouldn't do.

This time she had to face facts. "Mom, no. I can get by in Mandarin, and NewsInc already has a fluent speaker on the payroll. But this was for a position in front of the camera. A promotion. I've been providing copy and reporting off-camera so far. This was a chance to claim the credit for my work. To make a name for myself. But I'm not pretty, Mom, and they want pretty."

As her mother began to protest, she continued, "No, Mom, no excuses, not this time. Thanks to you and Dad, it hasn't made a difference to the way I feel about myself, but now it does." She hated to say it, not least because her nose came from her mother's side of the family. But where her mother was tall and stately, Whitney barely topped five foot four, and she was slightly built. The nose that made Ellen Carmichael appear distinguished, like a latter-day Virginia Woolf, made her smaller daughter look, frankly, odd.

Silence followed. Then her mother took a breath like a gasp. "How about journalism in print? You know, newspapers, articles and the like?"

"I already blog, Mom. But it doesn't pay the rent. It just gets my name out there. I could apply to one of the majors, but they're laying off and using freelancers. I can't afford to do that. And no, I'm not coming home. I won't go backward." She glanced around her apartment. Small but choice, in a good enough part of town and with its own parking space—worth more than gold dust in L.A. "I could move to the East Coast. They're not as obsessed with looks there. But the studio is here. I'd have to start again." And that would take time, money and the kind of soul-destroying assignments she'd already worked her way through here in her unofficial apprenticeship. Or maybe they just put the ugly ones through that. Anyhow, not something she'd do except as a last choice.

"Whatever you want to do, sweetheart, we're behind you. You know we'll help you any way we can."

She wouldn't ask them for money. Ever. As the child of two academics, she'd never gone hungry, but they'd never had money to spare either. Besides, she didn't need it. She had rainy day money, enough to tide her over from one job to another. Not enough to cope with giving up altogether. "Well, I still have this job. I'm owed a ton of vacation, so I might take some and think things over."

"That's a good idea. Come over for a break. Timmy misses you."

"I miss him." Her parents always had at least one cat and Timmy, an affectionate tabby, was a robust ten. They didn't allow pets in this building or she'd probably have one of her own. Cats didn't care about appearances.

131

No. She stopped herself as she had so many times before. Feeling sorry for herself was something she never allowed. When she thought of the things she'd seen and heard in her career, she knew how incredibly lucky she was. A job she loved, food on the table and some great friends, together with a supportive family. No way. What were a few moles and a big nose compared to that? She'd despise herself if she gave in.

No, she wouldn't allow herself that either. Nothing but honesty would do. In a different world, in a different situation, she'd have the work done. Face her fear, as she'd done before in other situations, and go through with it.

After half an hour with a tub of cookie-dough ice cream, Whitney had made up her mind. She'd look for another job, discreetly because the world of journalism was small and getting smaller. In the meantime, she'd look for a few paid columns and cut down on the free stuff. Slowly start to make a difference to her life. Then, when she felt more secure, she'd jump ship and leave NewsInc.

Maybe she'd take to novel writing like Jay. He'd started the stories to amuse the military personnel he spent so much time with in war zones. The glamorized accounts of their activities had amused them, then they'd urged him to send the stuff out. He had, and he'd hit the bookstores at the right time, when they were gagging for something grittier than the polished fare that was then glutting the market. And Jay Preston had been born. Using his middle name had distanced him from his news persona, and now he had two careers. The journalism he loved and the novels he enjoyed writing. The military still loved his stories, but Whitney knew for herself how realistic they were and how cleverly Jay balanced the glamour and the reality.

She cut off her thoughts with a slice of her hand, wincing when she hit her kitchen table harder than she'd expected. Thinking about Jay wouldn't help. Her best friend was mouthwateringly sexy and he went through girlfriends like a knife through butter. She frowned. Not so many recently, actually. Perhaps his injury turned them off, or perhaps that broken bone had done more damage than he admitted. Anyway, she hadn't been able to tease him quite so much recently. Fewer pictures in the gossip columns.

All these wandering thoughts were doing her no good at all now that she'd decided on her new course, but she was still too wired for sleep. She needed a distraction.

Smiling, she reached for her laptop and switched it on.

Chapter Two

Later that night, Whitney slid her keycard into the slot of a hotel room door in downtown L.A., the kind of hotel that hosted conventions and business meetings. Anonymous and huge. The green light flashed and she pushed the door open.

Someone dragged her into the room and slammed her against a wall. The door clicked shut, blocking out the only light available. The room was in pitch darkness, the windows covered, the lights out. She hit the wall with a soft thud, her face against the paper.

Her attacker grabbed her around the waist, his free hand dragging her head back by her hair, and then his mouth crashed down on hers, taking her with a hot desperation that flung her into the whirlwind. Now she couldn't think. Now she could only feel. His hips pressed against hers at an awkward angle but he twisted them against her and she felt the insistent bulge of his erection.

The moment his lips came into contact with hers, she knew him. Knew that pressure, the way his mouth felt against hers, the way he flicked her lips with his tongue in an unspoken request—demand—that she open for him.

When she didn't obey immediately, he nipped her bottom lip and when she opened her mouth to protest, he surged in, soothing the bite with his tongue in a gentle caress before resuming his fierce attack on her. She tasted him, peppermint and a touch of something else, something fruity. He'd had a glass of wine recently. He never met her drunk, but he sometimes tasted of wine and sometimes brandy. She loved it. It added a tinge of danger, the threat that he might get carried away and ignore her needs. But he never did.

134

"Never" being three times. They said that three times and one was hooked. Three cigarettes, three shots of heroin, three "Stranger Danger" encounters. The man with no name gave her what she needed, what she craved. He fed her addiction and she fed his.

He took her mouth with an intensity she could respond to only with the kind of helpless acceptance she never demonstrated in her real life. The life outside this door. Whimpering, she followed him when he withdrew, begging for more. With a grunt, he turned her around so her back pressed against the hotel wallpaper. Her backbone rolled against the hard surface but she welcomed the discomfort. He wasn't going to stop. He seemed as desperate as she was. That had connected them from the first time, and he was no less desperate now. He wanted her.

Here, in the dark. No excuses, no explanations needed here.

He connected with her again, tilting his head to bring his mouth down on hers in a deeper, harder fusion. He swept his tongue around her mouth in total mastery. She opened for him and lifted her chin to meet his demands. He was much taller than she but then most people were. He must be over six feet, with the kind of abs a girl could get lost exploring. *What a way to lose direction.*

She grasped his shoulders, felt the rough edge of a T-shirt under her palms and groaned into his mouth. She loved the mounds and dips of his body. Fuck, this guy was ripped. Whoever he was.

He pressed against her, his pecs to her shoulders, and bent to kiss her. Sliding his hands around her waist, he lifted her with a convulsive motion, making her gasp for breath. The thick cotton of his pants rasped against her jeans, the only sound in this hushed room. Lifting his head, he spoke in Greek. He had a deep, gravelly voice and he rarely spoke much. Just to give her instructions. Her Greek was better than her Mandarin, but hardly fluent. In this situation, it didn't have to be. "Skirt," he said now. "Not trousers."

It took her a minute to process the words, and she had to concentrate. Maybe it was time to buy that teach-yourself-Greek DVD. By the time she'd taken a step, he was on her, dragging down her zipper before he shoved her jeans down her legs. He thrust his hand between her thighs but the pants weren't far enough down her legs for her to open them properly. Bending, he dragged off her sneakers and tossed them aside. They landed in dull thumps. Then he was back, tugging at her jeans again. He got one leg completely off but the other leg tangled around her ankles. She kicked, but it didn't help.

With a rough word of frustration, a word she guessed must be a Greek curse, he stood once more, lifting her and setting her on a nearby table, dumping her as if she were a doll on the polished surface. She could only hope it would hold her weight because he didn't give her a chance to protest. She gripped his shoulders as he pressed his nose against her crotch through her panties and inhaled noisily. His soft groan told her he liked it, that he wanted her.

He stood and her hands dropped to his chest, slid down the thin fabric over his lean but powerful muscles. Not bulky with gym-pressed goodness but strong as if he used them for his work. Maybe he was a builder or a construction worker, or maybe he worked at sea. Maybe a soldier.

She wanted him hot, exploring her near-naked body, taking her, forcing her to do what she wanted. Because he knew she wanted it too. He must know, from her response and the perfect way he took her.

He pushed his hand between her legs, forcing them open, and slid a finger under the elastic of her panties. She'd worn red silk for him. Stupid, unless she told him the color, but the texture was great and *she* knew she was wearing red. She needed that jolt of courage before she came here, or wherever he told her to be. Always a hotel, a good hotel. She found the keycard waiting for her at the desk when she asked for Nikos Sandaloros. Not his name, she was sure. She'd Googled it and found nothing relevant. She never called him Nikos. Only "Stranger".

She called him that now, gasping the name into his mouth when he kissed her once more. His fingers moved along her crease, touching her clit, teasing it and then, as she pressed against him, desperate for relief, down to her entrance. When he pushed a finger inside her, she sucked him in, her hot walls closing around him. She tightened her muscles in a way she'd learned at yoga class and he groaned. Deep, rumbling, demanding. Two fingers now and he twisted them so they hit her G-spot, sending a jolt of sensation through her. Now it was her turn to groan. "Ah shit, ah fuck, please, more, please!" Christ, she was easy. But only here, in this anonymous room with Stranger.

She'd known when she first signed on to the site "Stranger Danger" that it could be truly dangerous. But she'd been desperate enough to do it. That first time, she'd come armed with mace and kept her finger on the speed dial number for 9-1-1 that she'd programmed into her phone. But the mace had never left her purse, and she'd dropped the phone on the floor, desperate to get more of this ripped, gorgeous man who made her feel beautiful when he took her.

He slapped a packet into her hand. He always did that — gave her control over applying protection, or made her aware that he was using it. It gave her assurance. She did it now, reaching for his cock with shaking fingers. He'd slipped his pants down far enough, his boxers too she noticed when she missed and touched the soft cotton instead. She slid her hand up his thigh, gasping at the hairy, masculine strength under her palm but grabbing his cock with determination.

She'd ripped the package open before she reached for him and now she put the thin circle over the tip. His cock was already greased with his own lubrication, sliding under her fingers. She'd caress him next time, if there was a next time.

She'd contacted him late tonight and they might not have time for a second round.

Helplessly, she groped for the right words in Greek but settled for English. "You feel so good, so hot. So *long*." Because his cock was the longest she'd ever encountered, and it had a curve when erect, standing proudly to attention. *Her* attention. Thick enough, especially at the base, that sometimes he stuffed it into her and she felt so full she thought she might burst. But tonight she'd soaked her panties in the car as she drove over here, anticipating what would happen here, in this room. The room she would probably never see.

She didn't linger over sheathing him this time. She wanted to give him another sheath. A living one.

Thrusting her pussy toward him, she leaned back, knowing he would hold her safe and prevent her from falling. He would put her where he wanted her and she'd go. For him. She hadn't known this kind of hot, wild sex before. Now she wondered why she'd waited so long to try it, because this made her crazy hot. Sex with someone she didn't know, in the dark. Perfect.

He thrust hard and deep, only dragging his fingers out at the last minute, replacing them almost immediately with his cock. He slid his hand under her bottom, supporting her through the panties she'd almost forgotten about.

Then she did forget them as he reached her G-spot and kept sliding, kept moving in harder and deeper. His mouth landed on hers again, his tongue thrust in with his cock, then he finished the kiss and touched her cheek, her jaw, with his lips, fastening on the place where her throat and shoulder joined. She cried out, sobbed, "Stranger!"

He grunted and dragged her closer over the polished surface of the table to push hard and deep. Lifting her legs, she wound them around his waist, using her calf muscles to drag him closer.

The only sounds in the room were the dim rumbles of the traffic outside and the thud as the table took the impact when she pushed up, into him, her hands around his neck.

He fingered her through the silk of her panties, rimming her anus, stroking it, as gentle with that as he forcefully pounded into her pussy, rousing the nerves in that sensitive place, adding to the tingles coursing through her. She cried out, a single, sharp "Ah!" and he took that as encouragement, working her more, pushing slightly so a pinch of silk and the tip of his finger entered that small opening. "Mine. Say it."

She understood that well enough. He'd made her promise it before. He must be very possessive. God help her, she loved that too. "Yes," she gasped, although she didn't know how he'd find out if she decided to go elsewhere. "Yours." But why would she want anyone else? He provided everything she needed and more. She craved his touch, dreamed about it, wanted it so badly she thought she'd go mad sometimes. And she didn't know if the situation or the man was the greatest appeal.

Right now she didn't give a damn as long as he kept doing what he was doing.

Her gave her no quarter but rammed into her, withdrew and then slammed in again, a resounding slap of flesh providing a counterpoint to her needy cries. He set up a rhythm she fell into—slam, retreat, then he'd circle her anus before ramming into her again. She waited for the next onslaught, catching her bottom lip between her teeth until he prevented her from doing it with a kiss every bit as savage as his fucking. No more tasting but a long, lavish taking of her.

She loved it. And she loved that he knew it.

Her climax rose, then the pause before she plunged into the abyss—the eye of the storm, the moment when everything seemed to stop, even her heart. She gasped, then screamed as she tipped over the top and plunged down, taking him with her. He broke away from her mouth and roared his pleasure in a voice deeper than his speaking voice. But Whitney wasn't in

139

any state to note it for more than a fleeting moment. He shattered her and she went willingly. Into his keeping.

Chapter Three

What the fuck is this? Two weeks later, Whitney arrived at work to find a large white envelope covering her desk. She shifted it, booted up her computer and then opened it. She couldn't put it off any longer. Terrified it contained her marching orders, her fear and her anger rising, she scanned the cover letter.

Dear Ms. Carmichael,

We received your letter and have reviewed your case, and we are delighted to be able to offer you the treatment requested. This offer is subject to a successful series of interviews and examinations with our psychiatrist and our medical expert. We enclose a list of the doctors approved by the Trust in your area. He or she will almost certainly appoint someone to assess your mental health, and do his or her examinations before agreeing to undertake the procedure or procedures.

Furthermore, the chair of the Trust, Ms. Georgina Hawthorne, would like to see you. This is not a condition of the offer and you may choose to decline, but she has expressed an interest in meeting you. Please reply as soon as possible so we may schedule appointments.

Whitney couldn't decide which astounded her more—the offer or the meeting with Georgina Hawthorne. The woman was a legend. She and her sister, Evelyn Durban, had been shining stars of Hollywood in the 1950s and 1960s. But while one sister had had new breasts, a new nose and several other procedures—some of them experimental—the other remained *au naturel.* One did glamour films and musicals, the other did drama and comedies. And for a scant few years, they ruled Hollywood.

She'd kill to do Georgina Hawthorne's biography. Nobody had yet been authorized by the great lady herself. She had a colorful past, had known everybody who was anybody back in the day, and had one great, legendary love, who was unfortunately married for most of their liaison.

Whitney had to take this opportunity. The dichotomy between private and public personas had always fascinated her. That was why she started looking into the life of Rock Hudson, whose sexual preferences were kept secret for most of his life so successfully that he'd become a matinee idol. Evelyn Durban had her secrets, as did her sister. They'd had entrée everywhere. The prospect of meeting Georgina Hawthorne, maybe persuading her to do an interview, made Whitney's mouth water.

Her mind raced. Georgina Hawthorne rarely gave interviews. If she could persuade Ms. Hawthorne to go public, give her something on the record, that would be a start. Maybe a biography, maybe a series of extended interviews. Even one interview would put her on the map.

But the cosmetic surgery? Her brain came to a screeching halt and backed up. She hadn't applied; she would have remembered something like that. But coming hard on the heels of that latest rejection, she was tempted. Fuck, was she tempted.

She read over the letter again, then flicked through the documents clipped to it. Information about something called the Durban Trust. She vaguely remembered it being mentioned when Evelyn Durban had died, four years or so ago, but apart from giving a moment of quiet thought to the passing of a woman who had done things her way, she hadn't paid much attention to the story. She had been wholly focused on her foreign correspondent's radio job then. She checked the date. Someone had applied for her two weeks ago, just after her disappointment in not getting the on-air job.

Now it had landed on her doorstep. Or rather, her desk.

"What's this?"

She wasn't fast enough to prevent Jay seeing the letterhead. "Wow, the Durban Trust? What do they want?" He snagged the letter before she could snatch it back.

She shrugged. "Do you know anyone who might have applied to the Trust for me?"

"Without asking you?" He turned the letter over and she leaned back, resigned to sharing. No point hiding it from him now. He gave a low whistle and lowered his voice. "An interview with Georgina Hawthorne? Fuck, you've got to take it."

"But I'd have to agree to the rest of it," she paused, "the surgery."

"What's wrong with that?" He bit his lip. "Sorry. But after not getting that job..." He shrugged and left the rest of the sentence hanging. He didn't need to say anything else.

Usually she preferred honesty but in this instance it cut too deeply. Even Jay thought of her as a friend, not a potential lover. Well, she had Stranger, and he had her. That gave her the courage to go on.

Lifting her chin, she typed the name of the Trust into her computer.

She swallowed. More than reputable. Some people had come out and detailed their experiences with the Trust. She found them on non-affiliated websites, and she found reports about Evelyn Durban and the Trust that she'd established in her will all over the place.

She could employ a lawyer to go through all the legal stuff and act as her advocate—she could find a good one on file right here at work. But the more she stared at the screen and checked the facts, the more she leaned toward getting the work done.

Jay stayed with her, reading the facts. "Do it," he murmured into her ear. "But for you, not for anyone else."

He was right. She deserved this. Her only problem would be her mother. How would she feel? Whitney would have to talk to her tonight, not leave it for her to discover for herself. Her mom had worked so hard trying to get Whitney to accept herself for what she was and to love herself despite her looks that it would surely disappoint her to learn that her daughter was giving in to current thinking and getting the work done.

But inside, the growing excitement refused to die. This was right. She felt it in her bones, in her heart. People sometimes had a stroke of luck, and this had to be hers. She could persuade them to do minimal work, maybe leave the nose. But no, that would be—she paused and laughed.

"What's so funny?" Jay had an enchanting smile. It took away the lines at the side of his mouth, the ones that gave him that grave look he'd worn since he returned home.

"Cutting off my nose to spite my face!" she explained before exploding with laughter. The strain of the last couple of weeks, the pain of losing the job to someone from the outside, it all came to a head and she couldn't stop laughing.

But this time Jay didn't smile. He stared at her. "I wouldn't have you any different," he said. "You're perfect as you are. Don't do it for you, do it for the job."

"Bullshit." So used to rebuffing attempts to be kind, she could almost believe him from the way he stared at her. "You are so full of it, Jay Preston O'Neill."

His expression froze. She couldn't read him at all. "Not this time." He straightened and returned to his desk, his limp giving him a halting rhythm.

An hour later, she'd arranged for her leave to start the next week. She had only one more thing to do.

* * * * *

Could a relationship be based on weekly fuck sessions? Was his growing obsession with Whitney and her needs something he should control? Jay had no idea. But he could do nothing but let it take him where it would. If she hadn't contacted him about this meeting, he would have done it. He'd miss her when she left, more than he cared to think about.

He arrived first, as usual. He closed the curtains, careful to ensure the blackout drapes met, securing them with the piece of tape provided for that purpose. That was one reason why they met in four-star hotels, places that guaranteed blackout curtains. He'd have preferred five-star, but that might have clued her in to the fact that he had money. And she kept putting cash into that stupid PayPal account she'd opened to pay her half, money he had no intention of touching. He could afford it, she couldn't. Simple as that.

He checked the bathroom and the toiletries, then switched off the light. Going back into the bedroom, he turned down the covers on the queen-size bed. Glanced around. Moved the coffeemaker from its precarious position at the front of the small table to the floor near the window. Unlikely he'd want to take her there, whereas the table looked interesting, and they wouldn't need the coffee. Then he memorized the room and the position of the furniture as best he could. Bumping into solid wood in the dark tended to be a passion killer.

This could be the last time. Her leave started next week. She had the interview with Georgina Hawthorne, then she'd go into the clinic and the rounds of pre-procedure consultations. The procedure itself, rhinoplasty and mole removal, would take up to a month, including recovery period, according to the research he'd done on the internet. She'd told only him about it, no one else, not even Nev as far as he knew. According to the other people at NewsInc, she was taking a break. He wondered if she'd worked out how to handle her return to work transformed.

He sighed. Should he come out to her tonight? Tell her how he felt, what he wanted?

His obsession with her had started with admiration. He'd heard her on the radio reporting from Afghanistan, cool and in charge of her broadcast. So he'd admired her before he saw her, before he met her. They'd met in an airport, and only her voice had alerted him to her identity, because he hadn't been able to find her picture anywhere.

He realized why when he saw her. Not ugly, as she kept saying, but distinctive, much as the aristocratic actress Edith Sitwell had been. But where Sitwell had turned her distinctive looks into distinctive style, Whitney moved away from them and tried to disguise them. In these days of perfect features, she was out of fashion. An oddity. Ugly. Or so she thought. But she had a body to die for and a mind as sharp as a whip.

It was that nose. It cast unfortunate shadows under strong studio lighting. But if she'd been some kind of celebrity, they'd have moved heaven and earth, and lights, to have her. They should have done it. He'd listened to her broadcasts when he was in 'Stan, had recorded them, used them to ease the tension of nights under fire. She had come to mean so much to him then. As if a nose would make any difference to that.

And to find that her body held some kind of addiction for him meant he was in serious trouble.

He checked his watch. Fifteen minutes before the time she said she'd be here. So far she'd been on time or a few minutes early. Once she'd surprised him by arriving half an hour early, obviously intent on setting the scene. He'd barely had time to duck out through the fortunately unlocked connecting door before she'd come in. Because he usually booked the room next to them as well, in case he needed a quick exit or they made too much noise. Not that he'd dream of telling her that.

When he'd seen the entry on the website Stranger Danger he'd thought his heart would stop. She had no idea of the dangers waiting for her, or perhaps she did and didn't care. Mace wouldn't have stopped some of the fuckers out there for long and that was all she'd brought to that first appointment. He'd arranged the meeting and gone with every intention of scaring her, taken a knife, handcuffs, just to show her the kind of thing that could have happened to her, but wouldn't because it was him and not some faceless, nameless person who could have mutilated and killed her. She'd arranged the perfect scenario for murder but she hadn't realized it. His blood turned cold even now when he thought about it. But it hadn't turned out that way. He got hard just thinking how it had been.

He'd arrived first, hours early in fact. When she entered he was on her right away, fastening the handcuffs behind her back before she could deploy her mace. Then he put his mouth on hers to stifle her scream, or so he told himself. That first touch of their lips had changed everything. He moaned when he remembered the shot of pure arousal that had rocketed through his body at their first kiss. Their first-ever kiss and one that ensured he was her slave for as long as she wanted him.

He'd undone the cuffs so he could feel her hands on his body and then improvised. Against the table with the weapons, against the posts of the four-poster bed. He'd have taken her into the shower, but the danger of sliding on the tiles worried him.

Jay gave a wry smile. Well, that memory had primed him nicely.

He stripped and laid his clothes over the hard chair nearest the door in case he needed to make a fast exit. He put condoms next to the bed, on the table and had one ready in his hand. He wanted to fuck her without but she didn't know him, so why should she trust him? But he knew she was on the pill, and he was clean. He'd bet she was too.

Not tonight. She had enough to cope with.

The cardkey scraped in the slot, an almost soundless swipe, but he heard it and snapped off the remaining light. He blinked, squeezing his eyes tight shut and then opening them wide to accustom himself to the dark, and tried to control his wayward breathing.

Shit, this scene excited him. Was that part of the thrill? He'd bet it was, and knowing who was about to walk through that door made it more exciting, not less. To feel those gorgeous breasts in his hands, to slide his arms around her waist and pull her hard against him...

The door opened. He stood behind it in the dark, where she wouldn't see him. He stayed there, breathing quietly. He could remain hidden, a skill hard-learned on his first assignment to a battle zone.

She closed the door quietly and pushed back the hood on the top she wore. Standing silently, she called out, "Hello?"

In their preliminary emails he'd warned her, "If you arrive up to half an hour before the appointed time, don't turn on the light." He'd scanned the room tonight before he entered, using the heatseeker he used to carry in his battle kit. Now it was safely stowed away in the capacious pockets of his jacket.

She took another step. "Are you there?"

Would she turn on the light? Almost, he wished she would. Then this part of their relationship would end and they'd move on. But she might shut him out, might not let him in, and he wanted to be there for her during the next month. She'd need a friend. No, he couldn't expose his identity yet, he decided. He'd remain her friend and leave his needs until after she'd recovered from her surgery. Almost relieved to find a real reason rather than an excuse not to reveal his identity, he moved forward.

Jay took a step toward her, going by a sixth sense that could locate her anywhere. Dim shapes showed in the near pitch-black, just enough to help him navigate.

She stood still. "You're here, I can tell. What is it? What do you want?"

"You," he said in Greek, only just remembering to grunt the word. He didn't touch her. "Strip."

He heard her ragged breath and waited. She fumbled at first, dropping the hooded jacket on the floor and making hard work of the buttons on her top, but he didn't help her. She must know where he was because of the direction of his voice, but she didn't move toward him. She obeyed him.

The top, then her bra. His mouth watered. Her scent freed, a mixture of light cologne and her, the heady scent wreathing around his senses, turning him into raw need.

She bent to remove her sneakers and it was all he could do not to step forward and finish it for her, grasp her backside with both hands and grind his aching cock against her. *No.* He'd wait. Torture them both.

She stood up again briefly to undo her skirt, then slid it slowly down her legs before stepping out of it.

He hoped she'd taken her panties off with her skirt because he couldn't wait any longer. He grasped his cock and stroked it once, up, spreading his essence over the head, teasing himself before he took the stride that separated them and dragged her against him.

They both groaned. "How long did you plan to make me wait?" she demanded.

"Longer."

She spoke in English with the occasional Greek word, and he'd heard enough to know her Greek was rudimentary. He'd chosen the language deliberately to put her at a disadvantage, suspecting she'd like the added obstacle. He'd never worked in Greece for NewsInc, never had to use that language in her presence. And now he kept it to the odd gruff word. He'd never kissed her before their first encounter in the dark, never let her see more of his body than a colleague should, although he'd been tempted. The one time he'd tried, taken her in his arms, she'd pushed away and backed off.

Awkward, always looking for mountains to climb. If he carried this charade on much longer, she'd improve her Greek beyond reason and then she wouldn't be concentrating on what he said rather than how he said it. He'd bet she was already studying.

Now they spoke in the language they both understood and were fluent in—fucking, lovemaking, screwing—he wasn't sure what he'd call it anymore. Only that it invaded his dreams, flooded his mind at unexpected moments during the day. She was close to becoming an obsession. Or these sessions were. Guess he'd find out which in a month or two.

He reached around and handed her the condom. She fumbled, dropped it, bent to pick it up, making his cock butt against her backside, press against her anus. No, not that. He wanted her cunt, that lush, beautiful pussy. Her hand shaking, she pressed the small package back into his hand. "I can't. You do it."

He groaned. Probably best because the way he was feeling right now, he might just come from her touch on his prick. Lucky he always brought plenty of supplies. Tonight he had a few toys, but he doubted they'd get around to using them right now. Or—wait. They were close enough to the table. First things first. He tore open the package and rolled the rubber over his aching cock. Jesus, even that was enough to make him quiver as if he were some kind of animal. And that was what they were doing—fucking like animals, reducing the act to its most basic form. But in relatively luxurious surroundings.

Animals wouldn't care. Neither did he. The only thing that mattered to him now was his woman and getting inside her.

He lost it. With a long drawn-out groan, he found her wet opening and tested it, pushing a couple of fingers inside and rotating them. She sighed into the darkness. He yanked his fingers out and replaced them with his cock, just the head, bathing it in her sweet honey. Her pussy threatened to scald him, the thin latex no barrier between him and the heat at her core. *Hold back.* He tensed his muscles, thought of anything, the salad sandwich he'd had at lunchtime, the cool soda he'd

150

downed afterward. While he was looking at Whitney, imagining what was to come later.

No, no, no!

Another thought, of his beautiful Whitney under the surgeon's knife, just a flash of the horrific vision and he found the control he needed. *Oh God, no.* He couldn't bear it. Now he had to switch his mind away but for a different reason. If he thought about that too much his cock would subside and he'd end up sobbing.

Jesus, he'd faced bombs and knives more easily.

Forcing himself back to the present, Jay realized he needed to heat things up a bit and he reached out, grabbing the first object he came into contact with. Perfect. A small, versatile vibrator, a little silver item with one curved end and one flat end. He reached around so he could use his other hand to twist the item and turn it on.

"Wha—" Startled, she jerked when he touched her stomach with the vibrator then glided it down, slowly. By the time it had reached her clit, she'd got with the program and she leaned into him, straightening up a little. He gripped her around her waist with one arm, determined not to let her get away, and slid the rounded end over her clit and down toward where their bodies joined.

"Oh no, don't stop. Do that again!"

He leaned into her, growled against her neck but didn't say anything. He teased her, teased himself, felt the throb of his cock as it responded to the gentle whirr. Then he slid it back against the ripe bud that yearned for his touch. She jerked again, forcing him deeper inside.

Holding her as still as he could, he began to work her, sliding in and out, setting up a rhythm she could respond to. "Move," he murmured against her neck, and then hummed before nipping her jaw. When she turned her head toward him, he kissed her for the first time that night, taking her with his tongue and his cock, working the wicked little vibrator

151

against her clit, pressing it right into the knot of flesh, now swollen and soaking. His bad leg trembled, threatening to give out. He moved his weight to his other leg and kept at it. Shit, he could do this one-legged. He could do it any way that worked.

She didn't last long. When she cried out, her pussy clenched around him, taking him in convulsive throbs and driving him up to his own, devastating orgasm. He felt hot semen tense his balls, move and spurt from his cock deep into her welcoming body. Sucking at her mouth, clamping her body to his, he shattered.

The vibrator fell from his nerveless fingers, clattering to the floor. It continued to purr, as did she and then it stopped. She didn't. He brought his fingers, wet with her essence, up to their mouths. They licked, hungry to taste their combined juices, sucked at each other, laughed. He'd never tasted anything half so good. Nectar. Addictive.

When he withdrew he nearly slid out of the condom, but he rescued it using the hand that had clasped around her waist, and then grabbed a tissue from the desk, disposing of the package in the wastebasket. He'd flush it later. Now he wanted the aftermath. He wanted to hold her.

It might be the last time. Together they staggered to the bed and slumped into it, half laughing, half moaning with the impact of their fucking. He tugged the covers around them, more for the sensation of security, of having her to himself, than for warmth. He'd ensured the room would be warm enough for their fun and games before he'd switched out the light.

Chapter Four

ഇ

When they'd first met, he'd loosened the bulbs in the lights where he could, but now they trusted each other not to do that. Trust. Precious, fragile and to be treasured. He'd do his best not to break it, which made this situation even harder, because he had already. He could only pray that she'd understand when the time came to tell her. But not yet. Not until he'd helped her through the ordeal to come. If she wanted him.

She rested against him, stroking his chest with the flat of her hand. His leg still throbbed but it was so worth it. He had to be careful not to limp in these encounters or she'd know him for sure. But it hurt like a bitch sometimes. It'd be weeks before it was as strong as ever, despite the hours he spent in the gym. It kept him awake at night. That and the nightmares. As the leg healed, the nightmares got worse. He'd been more irritable than usual, probably a result of his lack of sleep. He should grab some sleeping pills or something.

But he was physically mended. He could have gone back but he didn't want to. Not while she needed him. Nev had never accused him of malingering but had been concerned about battle fatigue, something Nev, for all his fancy suits and designer hair, could still understand. Jay disagreed, thought Nev was crazy for even suggesting it. He'd seen men suffering from PTSD and he didn't think he was nearly that bad.

She didn't go to sleep, as he'd expected, but sighed and stretched her hand over his chest, down his belly. She paused. "What's this?"

Oh fuck, she'd found his worst scar. He had a few but this was his deepest, and if she thought hard enough, she'd remember that Jay O'Neill had sustained a knife wound in the bazaar at Marrakesh when he was investigating a drug cartel. He'd been lucky that someone on his team knew more than basic first aid.

Now he had a brainwave. "Appendix," he said. The first word he'd said to her in English—he made it heavily accented and labored, pronouncing each syllable separately. He still had his appendix, but the scar was in approximately the right place.

She moved closer and kissed his chest then, when he bent down, his mouth. This time their kiss was lingering, tender. He needed to take her mind off exploring his body. He'd been lucky—that knife wound and the broken leg were the only significant injuries he'd sustained. Apart from the concussion, and maybe that huge bruise that had felt almost as bad as a broken arm at the time. In the heat of the moment, what felt like nothing often turned out to be something a lot more serious. He shuddered.

"What?"

Back to Greek again, he murmured, "Nothing." To quiet her, and because he wanted the solace of her mouth, he kissed her again. He smiled at her. Not that she'd be able to see it but she might feel it. She did when she lifted her hand to cup his cheek and he turned his head to press a kiss against her palm before moving away again quickly. He was getting paranoid, trying to keep the Stranger persona intact. Trying not to limp, avoiding her touch in the places where he was scarred or she might recognize, and keeping his voice down to that gravelly tone instead of his usual more mellifluous tones. That throaty growl would give him a sore throat if he did it too much, then he'd be gruff at work, then she'd know. If she found him out, she might tell him to fuck off and die, and he couldn't risk that. Not yet. Not ever, hopefully.

The thought concerned him. Whitney had come to mean more to him than he ever intended. He'd just wanted to avoid her meeting someone in this stupid club who could really hurt her. And if truth be told, he'd always yearned to know what lay under the clothes. Now he knew and it only made him want more.

He'd meant to keep tonight's encounter hot, giving no quarter. So what was he doing pressing gentle kisses over her face and body, caressing her, sliding his hands down her sides to enjoy the smooth curves of her compact body? He should give her another hard fucking and then leave. Let her keep the little vibrator as a souvenir.

But he enjoyed this. Holding her this way gave him clues as to what she liked, how she liked it, where she liked him to touch her. He could fine-tune his approach.

He'd reached the smooth planes of her belly and that sweet little innie of a bellybutton. He kissed around it before dipping his tongue in briefly and moving on. He scented her arousal now, a heady musky odor he wanted to bottle and use as cologne. Shit, that'd go down well with the men he worked with.

"Why are you laughing?"

He couldn't tell her how beautiful she was in English. So he settled for a gruff Greek "*Eisai omorfi*" before continuing on his journey. Every kiss nearer the seat of her pleasure tortured him, but it was such sweet torture. He loved her little moans, some cut off. He guessed she was biting her knuckles to stifle them when she lifted her hand. He parted the fine hair over her pussy and wished he could see it but it was all a dark cleft, no details. So he closed his eyes. Sight was no good to him here.

Instead, he tasted her. She had a unique flavor, totally her, with a heady aroma that drove him wild. He breathed in through his nose, took a deep, savoring gust of air and held it while he swooped down on her pussy and sucked the hard point of her clit in, releasing it just as fast. He didn't need the vibrator, but now he wished he'd kept it because he only had his fingers to tease her opening.

155

It seemed to be enough. He shoved a finger inside without warning, only one, and he knew she was wet enough for it not to hurt. He kept his finger stiff, rigid as it went in and she arched, her body tense against his. He didn't need to see to know she'd pressed her shoulders against the bed and let her head go back, stretching her throat. Her cry didn't sound muffled this time and her fist hit the sheets near her thigh. She couldn't move too far now — he'd put his hands on her hips, curving them around to graze the top of her buttocks, moving them just enough for his short, blunt nails to make contact and create a sharp contrast to his tongue and mouth.

Opening his mouth wide, he sucked her in, nuzzling her clit with his upper lip, licking her cleft just above her opening. Could a taste be consigned to memory? Because he'd know her from taste, smell and touch, from every fucking sense he possessed.

Her moaning changed to sharp cries and pleas. Apart from enjoying her reaction, he ignored her pleas and concentrated on his self-imposed task. He'd do this his way. And she tasted fucking amazing. He could live on her essence. Greedily he lapped, wanting more and knowing what he had to do to get it. Make her come.

He tugged on her clit, gently pulling on it so he could caress the sides and base with his tongue, just flicking it along the length, gauging by the increased wetness that he was hitting the mark. And she twisted under the gentle but firm imprisonment of his hand on her hip, steadying her, reminding her not to move too much or he couldn't continue.

She stilled for a fraction of a second but he knew this was it. He thrust another finger inside, curled both fingers and effortlessly found her G-spot. It took one touch, one graze before she exploded.

She screamed and the walls of her vagina gripped his fingers, released, did it again, the original strong movements eventually dying out via little flutters, barely there. But he felt them, every one. He lapped up the juice that soaked his hand, determined the bed would get none of it. He'd worked for it, he'd take it for his own.

And when he was sure she'd ridden out her orgasm, he surged up her body and into her. He'd applied the condom halfway through kissing down her body, sure he wouldn't lose his painful hard-on any time soon. He'd been right.

Now he knew the precise place where her G-spot lay, he could angle his body so his cock grazed it with each stroke. He could almost visualize it, and the sensations he'd just experienced would never leave him, as engrained on his memory as the taste of cold beer or the mac and cheese that was his favorite meal as a child. Preferably with a side order of burger and fries. Jay had never lacked an appetite, whether for food, beautiful women or the finer things in life. Like this woman and her delectable body.

When he came, he almost blacked out from the intensity of it. Holding his own orgasm back, maybe, or just the whole idea of not seeing—hah!—her again for a month or two. He didn't know. He didn't care. But he feared he'd miss it like he'd missed few other things in his life.

He started to leave the bed but she tugged on his hand, pulling him back. He wasn't averse to that.

With his arms around her, she said, "Thank you."

He could have wept. He kissed her instead.

"I don't know how good your English is, but you seem to understand everything I say. Or most of it." She paused and he felt her breasts swell against his chest as she took a deep breath. "We can't see each other for a while. I'm going away. Do you understand?"

"*Ne*." He kept his "yes" light, as if he didn't care. But he did. He cared that she wanted to tell him, instead of just disappearing. As Stranger, his only contact with Whitney was a special email address they'd set up and the PayPal account linked with it. She could have just gone and he'd have no way of contacting her.

"It will be a couple of months," she said. "I understand if you need to move on. You might already be doing this with any number of women."

"Only you," he said.

She understood that. Her voice lightened. "Really? Well the same goes. I mean, it's only you. But as I said, if you need to move on, you have to do that. We don't have any promises, that was the deal, right?"

He grunted his agreement.

"I want you to know these last weeks have meant a lot to me. I haven't, well, done it for a while, and I needed to. I was scared doing this, but I needed it."

He raised himself up on one elbow, as if he could see her face instead of a shadow against the white linen. He stroked back her hair, took the wayward strands off her face and kissed her cheek. "I will wait." He kept the Greek clear. He didn't want any confusion now. If he'd dared, he'd have told her in English, but she'd pick that up for sure if he tried to say too much. "Only you. Only me. Say it."

"Y-yes." He heard her voice lighten when she smiled. "It's been good, hasn't it?"

"*Ne.*"

"Will you wait?"

It wouldn't be good if she knew for sure he would wait. Stranger couldn't be tied down. Shit, his imagination was going off here. He'd already made up a slew of information about Stranger. He was an expatriate, came to L.A. to work with relatives already here. He was working for his green card and would get it soon. He worked at one of the studios as an electrician and he had joined the Stranger Danger site on a whim because he was doing well, but he was too uncommunicative as yet for regular dates. He found that he loved the whole darkness aspect and enjoyed exploring the fantasies of one woman. He'd take a day off work to do it.

Either that or he was a fabulously wealthy billionaire who flew here from all over the world when she called.

He liked the electrician best. Undereducated and unsure of himself. Mostly he played to that persona.

He couldn't risk the chance of her getting seriously hurt by one of the sickos who undoubtedly frequented that place.

He leaned down and kissed the tip of her nose. "Sleep." A concession. He didn't often do that, hold her until she slept. But this time could be the last time they met like this and he wanted to experience every minute with her. He'd leave when she slept, when he was sure she slept.

Doubts assailed him now. Was he doing the right thing, encouraging her to get the work done? What would she be when she came back? He was very fond of the woman he knew her to be. Of the bright, inquisitive, intelligent woman he knew as Whitney Carmichael and his incredibly arousing, exciting, inventive lover.

Fuck, he knew better. He was in love with her.

He didn't want her to come back as a mannequin, looking like so many other women he'd seen cruising down Rodeo Drive, there as much to be seen as to shop. The ones who thought so much of themselves there was no room for anyone else. He'd dated women like that, fallen for a couple before he'd learned better. Not that he thought that would happen straightaway. But maybe—fuck, what had he done?

Chapter Five

ᔌ

Whitney couldn't remember feeling so nervous at an interview before. She'd spoken to drug lords in Baltimore and military leaders in Afghanistan, both bristling with weapons and attitude, but meeting one old lady had her scared to death. Maybe because it impacted on her personal life too. She still hadn't decided to go ahead with the procedure, had lain awake thinking about it. Wishing Stranger could be there to help her forget, to help her get some rest. But he wasn't, and if she did this there was a chance he would never be there again. The procedure would take around six weeks from operation to full recovery, and he might not want to wait. He might find somebody else.

Just the thought brought a lump to her throat.

Now she sat in her car outside the wrought iron gates and waited for the impersonal tones to come through. "You may enter. Please drive to the right-hand side of the building, where you will find parking spaces."

She had expected something casually grand, but this modest house—modest by movie star standards—looked almost homey. A long building in an off-white stone set in a gated community, it didn't proclaim its status. Maybe Ms. Hawthorne didn't hold the elaborate parties that required the spectacular pools, open areas and the like. She'd seen them before when reporting on them. She'd shadowed a reporter in her early days before deciding the Hollywood beat wasn't for her, but it had been interesting. Most stars let reporters in for a certain time, then turned them out. In a way she could understand why so many reporters had turned and bitten the hands that fed them, because they'd been treated like the help. Worse.

She had the lurking suspicion that she might be heading back into that world, but not as a reporter. As a biographer, a recorder of old Hollywood and maybe the new, if it didn't involve kowtowing. This was certainly an interesting place to start.

A friendly-looking maid met her at the side door. "Will you come this way, please? Ms. Hawthorne is expecting you."

It was eleven o'clock and the May day was heading for fine, bordering on scorching. Whitney had donned a light summer sundress in dark blue with a pale blue shrug on top, and plastered herself with SPF 30, just to be safe. She didn't know if sunburn might affect the upcoming surgery, which she might or might not have.

The maid took her to a terrace at the back of the house that had a spectacular view over L.A. Two loungers were set on either side of a table with a large white parasol sprouting from its center. The city looked glorious from this distance. Not that Whitney spared it more than a mere glance. The lady sitting on one of the two loungers took all her attention.

Dressed all in crisp white, Ms. Hawthorne seemed like a legend come to life from Whitney's biased viewpoint. While Ms. Hawthorne studied her through her big, black sunglasses, Whitney froze. The woman was the star of some of her favorite films, had acted with legends, had loved one. When people said "living legend", they often meant her. Her hair was gray now, drawn into a loose, stylish knot on the top of her head. In her ears were tiny gold studs in the shape of four-leaf clovers, a gift from her lover. That had been his symbol, the way he'd signed his autographs, and the earrings had been the first public sign that they were together. Fuck, had she kicked research's ass on this one. Although her delicate hands were spotted with age, in all the ways that mattered, this woman was ageless.

Whitney had no idea what to say. "I've seen all your movies," maybe, or "I loved you in *Take Me to Dinner*." Both gauche but so true.

161

Luckily, Ms. Hawthorne took the lead. "Good morning."

"Good morning," Whitney managed. She gave an uncomfortable laugh. "You must be used to this, people staring at you. I'm sorry." Oh God, did she sound stupid.

Ms. Hawthorne motioned to the spare lounger. Whitney sat but didn't lean back or swing her legs up onto the footrest. It seemed wrong, somehow. She dumped her capacious bag on the tiled floor. "Thank you for seeing me."

Ms. Hawthorne slid her glasses down her nose and peered at her over the top of them. "Not at all. Your case intrigued me. So did this." She gestured to the table, drawing Whitney's attention. On it was the manuscript she'd sent at Ms. Hawthorne's request, the draft of her biography of Rock Hudson. "I worked with him a couple of times." She grimaced. "Awful man. Narcissistic to the extreme. Not entirely his fault though. The studio had him by the balls."

She grinned and Whitney remembered the exact same expression in one of her films. Startling to be so close to such a legend.

"Appropriate in the circumstances," Ms. Hawthorne added. "He could act straight though, I'll give him that. Sit back, dear. Have a drink. Non-alcoholic, I'm afraid. Once I'd have been breaking into the vodka at this time. Not these days. Help yourself, and you can pour me one at the same time, if you would." A smooth flow, covering Whitney's gaucheness. Fuck, was Ms. Hawthorne used to this kind of situation.

Whitney obeyed and put the iced fruit juice in its tall glass within easy reach for her hostess. "I still don't know about the surgery."

"It's your decision, dear. From this, I'd say you could make a career for yourself without going in front of the camera." She gestured to the untidy heap of paper. She'd obviously read it. Whitney saw a few penciled notes and longed to get a look at them.

Ms. Hawthorne pushed her glasses back up her nose and reached for her drink. "You write well and you have a readable style. You've discovered a few things about Rock Hudson that nobody has before, to my knowledge. You have a bestseller here, if your publishers want to make it one." She gave a cackling laugh, so typical of her. "Tell me about yourself. Just talk."

After a few hesitations, Whitney found it easy to talk to the lady, who listened, watched and occasionally slid her glasses down her nose in what Whitney came to recognize as a characteristic gesture. Her eyes were the same piercing blue Whitney remembered from the movies, if a little more watery. The lined face still held remarkable beauty and, despite her research, she wondered if Ms. Hawthorne had actually had a few discreet procedures done. Evelyn Durban was famous for having the surgery that turned her from a pretty starlet into an outrageously sexy, glamorous star, but that didn't mean her sister hadn't had a tweak here and there.

She didn't tell Ms. Hawthorne about Stranger. He was her secret, one she guarded jealously. But she told her everything else.

Ms. Hawthorne didn't interrupt her until the end. Then she said, "In my day, they'd have arranged the surgery and made the contract dependent on you having it done. Have the work done. It won't alter who you are. You have a strong sense of self and I don't think this will affect it. Look at it as a makeover, something you need to do to progress further in your career." She glanced at Whitney and put her empty glass down on the table. "You have to know when to compromise and when to hold out. It's as important a skill as anything else."

That last sentence hit Whitney hard, and put everything into perspective for her. "I see. Thank you." More than any other advice, this had helped her to make up her mind, not because of who Georgina Hawthorne was but because what she said had made sense. She wasn't doing it for her or for

Stranger. She was doing it for her career, to enable her to do something she really wanted to do. "How do you know when to compromise?"

"Trial and error." Ms. Hawthorne shrugged her still elegant shoulders. "Everyone makes mistakes. It's part of being human. But you can backtrack from some of them, and fudge over others. If you don't take the chance, you'll never know. You're about to be on the receiving end of a lot of egregious claptrap, because everyone wants to be sure. Just remember what you want to get out of this and you'll be fine." She glanced at Whitney and gave a most un-Hawthorne-like grin. "My sister never regretted what she had done, even though some of it was less than perfect. They'd always called her the clever one and I was the pretty one in our family. That surprises you, doesn't it? But when she found herself in the glamour part of the market, she went with it. Because she enjoyed it. Being a sex symbol gave her the power to break away and be herself. That's why she had it done." She grimaced.

"She looked a bit like a store mannequin at the end, and I used to joke with her that she used a sleep mask because she couldn't close her eyes, but she'd done it for a reason." She chuckled. "I had a little work done, you know. Just eye bag removal and a light facelift. I wanted to keep most of my lines. I'm an actress and I've always depended on mobility of expression. But I started to look too haggish too early. It gave me an extra ten years on my career. Are you shocked?"

Whitney laughed. "No. I've lived in this town long enough to know that the most successful people do what they have to." The rapidity of promotions at the Kodak Theater sometimes shocked even her. The way the setting for, say, a pirate film could be replaced by the setting for maybe a new gangster series in hours, and it was as if Hollywood had never heard of pirates.

"Up to a point."

"Yes." Suddenly she felt camaraderie with this woman who had risen so high and stayed there, despite the fall of the studios, the rise of TV, the highly publicized relationship with a married man, ageing. Georgina Hawthorne had done it on her own terms and ended here, in this lovely house with the view over her kingdom. "You have to know that point, don't you?"

"You do indeed. And you have to know that there's life outside Hollywood. They work to make you so dependent on them when really it's the other way around. At least some of the time." The lady cackled, a laugh she had deployed for great effect from time to time, notably in *Flawless*, a romantic comedy where she'd played a society queen cursed by an unacceptable laugh. When she moved, when she spoke, she reminded Whitney of one of her parts, but she was more than that, much more. She was herself.

"Did—did your sister go too far, have too much done?" Toward the end she looked grotesque, as if she were a mask rather than a human being. But by then Evelyn had retired to live her last days in comfort.

"No, she did not, as far as her career was concerned. We discussed her procedures and she went ahead. I paid for some of them and she paid me back later, precisely to stop the studio having that stranglehold on her. They hated that." She gave a reminiscent smile. "It cost her a couple of roles, but after she starred with Monroe they couldn't ignore her. She provided an earthiness and a frank pleasure in sex to contrast with Monroe's ethereal innocence. And no, that wasn't a critic talking, although they loved the film. They just worked so well. And in private, she understood a lot of Monroe's concerns because she shared a lot of them. They remained friends until she died."

"Do you know anything about—"

"Monroe's death? No. We knew about her affairs—most of Hollywood did—but Eve was away filming in Africa when Monroe died, and I was never that close to her. Just a very sad thing to happen to a troubled young woman." She sighed. "There are survivors, people who succeed and people who let Hollywood beat them down. Which are you?"

That was the question. Put that way, she had only one answer. "I want to succeed."

Ms. Hawthorne fixed her with a hard stare. "Not 'I want to'. I *will*. Tell yourself that ten times a day and you just might."

Half an hour later, Whitney got up to leave after Georgina — "Call me Georgina" — had declared herself tired. Only then had Whitney remembered she was talking to a woman in her eighties. As she rose, Georgina said casually, "It's about time I told my version of events. I find you easy to talk to and you don't seem entirely without good sense. After you've had the procedures, call my private number and make an appointment with my assistant. If you want to write my story, of course."

Whitney left with her head in the clouds. An authorized biography would make her career and lead her to other assignments. She had a way out. If she wanted it.

Chapter Six

✦

"Ready?"

Whitney could hardly believe she'd finally arrived at this point. Six weeks it had taken. Once she explained that she couldn't take more than a month's recuperation, they rushed the pre-op system for her. She'd been interviewed, talked at and signed enough documents to fill a whole bookshelf. She knew because she had copies of them and had to clear out some of her novels to make room. She'd read them all too, and had a lawyer look them over. Nothing she shouldn't sign. She hadn't, after all, signed her soul over to the Devil.

After the operation, she'd had so much swelling that it hadn't been worth looking in the mirror for long, and it had depressed her so much that she hadn't bothered after the first couple of times. But when Jay arrived to see her, he hadn't flinched. She joked that he'd grown so used to her looking bad that this couldn't be much worse. He'd lost it and walked out, but reappeared half an hour later, telling her he was so mad at her for saying that, he'd had to get away.

Then he'd helped her, joking, telling her the gossip from the station, and she'd forgotten that snap and his loss of control. At least he'd left. But for a moment he'd scared her, a wild look in his eyes she hadn't seen before.

Because of the amount of time she was away, Whitney had to tell her boss. Anyway, she suspected Nev had put her up for all this. Certainly he didn't seem surprised, only pleased that she was doing it. But he couldn't keep the anchor job open for her, and Whitney had spent a few nights brooding in front of the TV watching Jay set up a relationship with Carol, the new presenter, who was, she hated to admit, good at her job, and not an airhead bimbo. Mandarin speaker her ass. The job didn't require it any more than hers did.

Secretly she'd hoped that Carol would be hopeless so the network could fire her and she could apply for the job.

But today was the day. She'd resolutely kept the mirrors covered in her apartment and asked the hospital to do the same. She'd had the work done in one of the expensive clinics frequented by the rich and the famous, but the nondisclosure agreement she had to sign meant she couldn't tell anyone who she'd seen there. Shit. She could have a series of articles about the "natural beauties" she'd seen troop in and out of this place.

They'd sent her home a few days after the procedure, with strict instructions on how to behave and how to sleep even—not on her side for the first two weeks—something that had driven her crazy but she'd managed it with the help of two large pillows on either side of her.

Now she couldn't avoid looking anymore. The last bandage had been removed, she only waited for Jay to arrive. He'd been so supportive, she couldn't have done this without him.

The door to the private room opened quietly on a knock. And he stood there. She smiled, feeling absurdly shy, and then she knew she didn't need a mirror.

He smiled. "Wow." Reflected in his face she saw herself. He wasn't knocked out by her stunning beauty, something she'd half feared, half wanted, and he didn't look at her as if she were a stranger. No. He just looked, like he did when he perched on the end of her desk to say hello. Like one friend to another, and something deeper, something she'd always thought she'd imagined.

But she lifted the mirror anyway.

Wow was right. She recognized the person in the mirror but it looked like her sister, except that she didn't have one. They'd taken the shape of her father's nose as a model. She could see tiny marks where her moles had been but the doctor had warned her to expect those. Since they'd all been successfully removed with laser surgery, none of them deep enough to require incisions, she could expect even the marks to fade.

She touched her cheek, where the worst of her moles had been. They had been birthmarks rather than moles, the surgeon had explained, and might have faded over time, but it was better to have them removed now.

Now that she saw it, she agreed. And her nose no longer dominated her face. It wouldn't be the first and often the only thing people saw when they met her. They'd narrowed her flaring nostrils, shaved down its size, but it wasn't a tiny button nose or a blade, like one that had been worked on too much. She'd been afraid of that.

Her fingers trembled against her cheek. She swallowed. "It's me."

"It looks like you," Jay said, humor in his deep voice. "I'd recognize you anywhere."

"Now what do I do?"

"Live your life."

The surgeon cleared his throat. "Before you do, it's not entirely over yet. This being L.A., and it coming up on July, I want you out of the sun at all times. No SPF 30 for you, I'll prescribe you a total sunblock. Over all your face and your lips too."

She touched her mouth. "Did you do anything there?"

"No. I just want total cover. Understand?"

"Yes sir."

She forced a reluctant grin from the surgeon. "Back here for your checkups. By next year you should be healed enough to go into the sun, but the marks might not tan evenly."

"I've never been a big fan of deep tans." She hadn't. Her skin had never reacted well to the sun and she was already used to plastering on the cream and sunblock. "I can't believe it." She held the mirror up again. "Did you do anything else?"

"Just smoothed over your marks, did your nose. I don't think anything more was needed."

And that was all that was paid for. She'd asked Ms. Hawthorne—Georgina—to ensure that the Trust didn't pay for more than was actually needed. She'd heard of people addicted to cosmetic surgery who couldn't leave well alone, but went in for refinement after refinement—the latest figure, be it full breasted or flat chested, the bubble butt. They changed their shape like they changed their wardrobes. She'd never do that.

Without thinking, she stretched her hand out on the bed and Jay took it. Just like that, so natural, so real. Of course he would. They were friends, she thought, ignoring the flash of heat she always experienced when Jay touched her. Impossible. He was a friend and a work colleague. He'd brought in the decorative straws that had made her laugh when it was more comfortable for her to use them rather than to sip from a glass, he'd brought her the books she enjoyed, brought her Kindle in to her so she could download the other, more risqué books. All the things that friends do. Nothing else.

Besides, she had Stranger. She'd heard from him once via their special email. He'd just said, "Still waiting." So he hadn't found anyone else he preferred. She couldn't help but be pleased. The note sent a thrill through her, and she looked at it more than once while she was recovering.

Jay squeezed her hand, drawing her attention back to him. "Your parents are here."

She stared at him numbly. "What?"

"You told them not to come until you were well. They arrived yesterday. Did you send them an email?"

"Yes, just to let them know—" She broke off. "But it's the middle of the semester."

"And you're their only daughter." When she glanced away, he tugged on her hand. "Hey, don't look like that, like you've seen a ghost. Is there a problem? Should I tell them you're not ready to see them?"

She swallowed. "No."

"Then what is it?"

"Did you see my mom?"

"Yeah." He bit his lip. "Ah. I see. But she's—"

"I have to face them sometime. I just didn't know how to tell my mother. And I didn't say I was having a nose job, just that I was having the moles removed." She stared into space and, as she always did, took a deep breath and counted to ten. It helped a little. Not much. "Okay, I have to see them. I guess I was putting it off." She sat a little more upright and fixed her gaze on the door as Jay left and had a quick word with the people outside. She'd just had her mother's nose cut off. The one her mother was so proud of, the one she'd constantly tried to reconcile Whitney to.

Her parents came in, fixed expressions on their faces. She recognized them because she would have done the same. In case the surgeons had turned her into someone unrecognizable, or into a bimbo. Either could have happened. After all, she'd had the procedure done in L.A., the home of plastic surgery, where they'd perfected the plastic part.

Her mother's face relaxed just a little and her father's eased into a genuine grin. He scratched his head, his invariable habit when nervous, ruffling the tufts of hair he had left. A handsome man still, a shade shorter than her mother, but most people were, he was dressed in slacks and a shirt, open at the neck. He swept past her mother to take Whitney into his arms and give her a big hug. "Hi, sweetie. You look wonderful."

"You'd recognize me in the street then?" Her voice was shaky but she couldn't help that.

"In a crowd of lookalikes. I'd know you anywhere." His voice shook a little too.

171

"It's for my work, you know that?"

As her father drew back, she faced her mother. The two women stared at each other, her mother taking her new features in with a critical eye Whitney almost welcomed. Only her surgeon had looked at her like that, without emotion. But by the time she spoke, her mother's fine gray eyes glistened with unshed tears. "Very good," she said eventually. "The camera will love you. That's what they say, isn't it? Do you plan to appear as a reporter or a weather girl?"

"Neither." That last shot pierced her to the heart. "It's just to get the initial job. I might start as anchor, but I want to be the kind who interviews politicians, not the kind that reads from a teleprompter and looks pretty. I just want that start, and I wasn't getting it. They were passing me over in favor of prettier, equally qualified people." So hard to explain the competitive world of modern journalism to her parents.

"Your boyfriend is the pretty kind."

"He's also a great journalist." She couldn't let her mom denigrate Jay. "And he's not my boyfriend. Just a friend." Except that he'd come to mean so much more. She didn't dare admit it, even to herself. During the last six weeks, Jay had never intimated to her that he wanted to be anything more. She had to accept that he saw her as a trusted friend and colleague. That had to be enough. Even if she wanted more, it seemed he didn't. And in any case, it would complicate matters far too much. Sleeping with colleagues didn't work.

And she had Stranger. But he was her secret, her fantasy.

Her mother nodded. "He is. Unafraid of getting his hands dirty. I read one of his books."

She was talking about Jay as if he weren't here. Glancing around the room, Whitney belatedly realized he had gone, along with the surgeon, leaving her alone with her parents. "What did you think?" Where had he gone, why had he gone? She felt alone, bereft.

"It was amusing. I'd have thought the people he works with might have objected though."

She grinned. "They encouraged him. They thought it was funny. The details are accurate enough, just the super-brave heroes he writes about couldn't exist. The ones that go against orders and still win out."

"I don't have time for modern fiction normally, but I thought his prose was good." From her mother, that was high praise. She'd have to tell him.

A smile flickered across her mother's fine lips. "I'm relieved by your appearance, to tell you the truth. I thought you'd go over the top. So what are your plans now?" That would be all she'd get. A casual "okay", in her mother's more formal words. She couldn't ask about The Nose. That was the end.

A flash of understanding shot through her. No wonder she'd never felt entirely secure about herself or her background. A series of "okays" with no "greats" or "superbs" or even "dreadfuls" didn't help in the long run. Guidance would have worked better, especially the kind of focused guidance she only found at school or in college. Ironic that her mother had probably helped her students more than she'd helped her own daughter. But to drag that up now might ruin the tenuous bridge they were busy building. One day she might talk to her about it.

But she knew she wouldn't. She didn't need her parents' approval anymore. There would be no point risking what they had for something they might never have.

She shrugged. "To go back to work. The job I wanted is gone, but there'll be another one soon. They're expanding the network, employing more journalists. I'll get the next job." She paused. "And I'll brush up on my Mandarin. That was what lost me the last job, or rather, gave them the excuse to give it to someone else. I've been practicing."

"You want to go to China?" her father asked.

"There could be some exciting developments there."

"And your boyfriend's headed for Russia."

Jay? Why hadn't he told her? Pain spread through her but she'd known this might happen. He couldn't put his career on hold for her. But it hurt that she'd heard from someone else first. "Yes, intrepid reporters rarely stay in the same place," she said with a wry smile. Loss racked her while she spoke, acted as if she knew.

"How about you, dear?"

"My life's about to change for the better." So why didn't she feel happier?

Chapter Seven

80

Jay took her home and left her to settle in. He offered to come back later with a meal but she said no, claiming she was tired. He left after she promised to call him if she wanted him. They didn't speak about Russia. The air between them was so tense she could feel it. She wanted to know how he really felt but she couldn't ask him, still too unsure about her new self to ask something she wouldn't have hesitated about a couple of months ago.

Conflicted, that was how she felt. Jay was her friend, her best friend. She couldn't imagine being without him. In the last few months they'd grown closer, almost like brother and sister. Sometimes she thought he might be thinking of something else when she caught his blue gaze on her lost in contemplation, and once or twice he'd moved closer, almost as if he wanted to kiss her, but he never had.

And Stranger. Was it just sex? She didn't think so. He held her afterward that last time, and she'd enjoyed sleeping in his arms. She'd missed him. But when she'd written to their email address, he hadn't replied until that one, brief message.

They'd taught her how to do her makeup to cover the small marks. Not that she'd have to do it for long. She went through to her bathroom, got out the cosmetics and sat at her vanity. It wasn't covering the marks so much as getting used to not using shaders and blushers to reduce the effect her nose had. She had a whole new face.

When the phone rang, she dropped the lipstick she'd decided to try, startled by the shrill sound in the silence. She grabbed her cell from the table and checked the caller. A number but no ID. She almost hung up but on a whim, she answered. "Hello?"

"Whitney? Hi, sweetheart. Sorry to startle you. This is my private phone, I don't often use it at work."

"Oh." But he'd called her now. He had to know she'd keep it in her contacts folder.

"Are you okay?" Neville sounded truly concerned, not just a boss making a routine inquiry.

"Yeah, yes, I'm fine." She injected a little more liveliness into her voice. "Great, actually."

"I wondered. I know where you've been, and you tell me Jay does, but you can't just stroll back into work as if nothing had happened. I want to talk to you about how to handle this."

"Probably not the best idea."

"How about dinner? If you're not too tired, we could meet tonight."

She checked the time. Barely seven. If she didn't accept his offer, she'd probably watch TV, bathe, have an early night. Brood. "Sure. Where and what time?"

"Eight? And don't worry about where. I'll pick you up."

It was on the tip of her tongue to tell him where she lived but of course he'd know. He had access to her employment records.

She found some black pants and a pale-pink shell top, one she'd deemed too fine for the office, and added a string of glittery black beads and matching earrings. She had a black leather jacket that was in good shape. It looked odd next to the denim and leather jackets she'd used in the field. They were battered and well-used but she'd bought the black one recently. Maybe in the near future she could wear that one to death too. But for now it looked reasonably good. As long as Nev wasn't taking her anywhere too fancy.

Nev arrived in his Porsche. She heard the roar as it turned into her street and then the pause when he stopped outside her building. Smiling, she grabbed her purse and left her apartment.

He stood outside the car, leaning against the polished black surface, looking like something out of *GQ* magazine.

She stopped as he straightened, tugging on his jacket with a gesture she doubted he was aware of. His eyes widened and fixed on her face. "Fuck."

"Suave as always." She walked toward him and she felt different. Always before she'd felt slightly inadequate in his presence but now she felt a subtle shift in the power balance. She'd taken him off guard. That had never happened before. "It's just me, Nev."

He gave a long, low whistle and stepped aside to open the car door. "Madame, your carriage awaits."

She laughed.

He took her to a restaurant downtown where he'd booked a table in one of the dining rooms. This place had a string of them, instead of one big room. At least it wasn't the Four Seasons hotel restaurant, or somewhere really swanky. She'd eaten there, gone there to see and be seen, but only with work. When an African politician had visited to attend the film awards ceremony, she'd worn something dark and nondescript and done her best to shrink into the background, telling herself it was her job. She hadn't gotten anything out of the wily bastard either. A waste of the company's money.

Here she strode through the restaurant to their table, head high, noting the way people glanced at her—and didn't look away. One or two men looked again, and she reveled in it, knowing it wasn't because she startled them. It felt really good. It was worth it, just for the minute it took to reach the table for two.

She ordered the fish, Dover sole, and he ordered steak. She leaned back in her chair and watched him. "Typical."

"What?" He flicked that heavy swathe of hair off his forehead.

"Raw meat."

"Rare. Not raw. Not even blue."

The waiter arrived with the wine and Nev waved at him to serve it, not to bother with the tasting ritual. She liked him for that. They chatted about the newsroom since her absence and, as their starter arrived, he abruptly asked her the question she knew he must have wanted to ask all along. "Are you ready to come back?"

"Whenever you say."

"Tomorrow."

She caught her breath. "Sure."

He grinned, his mouth tilting in the one-sided way women found so attractive. She could see why. She always could, but she'd never held his attention like this before. "Probably best if you come back on Monday. Start the new week. It'll give me a chance to explain." He took a bite of his salad, watching her as he chewed.

Whitney dug in, mildly surprised at how hungry she felt. He cleared his mouth, took a sip of the crisp white wine he'd ordered. "So what do you want me to tell them?"

"The truth. That's all you can tell them. Unless you want to start a story about fairies and magic wands."

"I'll tell you something, Whitney. It's like magic to see the change in you. You're confident as well as beautiful."

"I always was." She grimaced. "Confident, that is."

"Yes, when you knew nobody could see you. Now you've completed the circle. This is the reporter I want. This is how you always should have been."

She shrugged. "It's not easy. Wasn't."

"It was part of your problem. You'd hang your head forward and that would make it all so much worse. If you'd walked with that sway before, held your head up like that, it wouldn't have looked half so bad."

She bit her lip, then looked away and down at her plate. "Would you have put me on the screen?"

He tipped his head back then dropped it again and met her gaze. "No."

"Why not?"

"You know why."

She gave a wry grin. "He who must be obeyed."

He shrugged. "Something like that." He forked up another bite of salad, then pushed his plate away.

The waiter arrived, took their plates and replaced them in short order with their entrees.

For the first time in days, she was hungry. The delicate scent of the fish wreathed around her senses, blending with the earthier scent of Nev's steak, and her mouth watered. She tucked in, only to glance up to see Nev's amused smile. "What?" she demanded once she'd cleared her mouth.

"How do you keep your figure, eating like that?"

"Exercise."

A vision of precisely what exercise flashed into her brain and she heated, her pussy warming into life. The thought of Stranger bending her over an anonymous hotel bed, ramming into her as if he couldn't help himself, made her close her eyes for a second to regain control.

When she opened them, Nev was watching her, one brown eyebrow cocked and a gentle smile curling his fine lips. "I would love to know what's brought that look to your face. If I'd seen that pre-operation I'd have been tempted to defy Mattson and put you on the screen anyway."

She latched on to the thing he'd inadvertently told her. "You mean Mattson didn't want you to do it?"

Now it was his turn to close his eyes, but he groaned. "Shit. I don't suppose there's any chance of you ignoring that?" He reached for the wine and poured them a new glassful each. She'd kept with the white but he'd gone on to water after the second glass. She'd never driven a performance car, but she guessed it took a great deal of concentration and sobriety.

"Nope," she said cheerfully. "Would you have put me up for the job anyway?"

He leaned back, studying her, a wry expression in his eyes. "Truth? No, I wouldn't. You know what the media is like, none better. They'd have eviscerated you. You could have expected to see yourself on SNL and the other shows. They might say they admire you, give lip service to my 'courage' in putting you up there, but they'd have torn you apart. As anchor. As a correspondent, maybe. But I don't think that's your real forte."

That intrigued her, and she knew he knew it. He was leading her away from the sensitive area of who gave the orders at NewsInc these days. But she let him have his way for now. "What is my forte then?"

"You can put complex world situations in a nutshell. And you have decided opinions about them. Jay, now, he works best under fire. He can convey what it's like in a situation, can make the average man in his armchair feel like he's in the field, hiding in a muddy bunker getting shot at. You're cooler, more analytical. You'd be best in the studio or maybe abroad behind the lines. In fact, I can see you working well with Jay in that capacity. If you're patient and you want it, I'll see what I can do to make it happen. The new girl is working out well, so her position is filled, but another one will turn up."

Working with Jay as a team? Her heart leaped at the thought, but she couldn't make a career decision on the basis of her libido.

"He's expanding."

He didn't pretend to misunderstand her. "Mattson? In more ways than one. He wants to grow the show, make it five nights a week instead of three."

She laughed when she thought of the media mogul's expanding waistline. But she wouldn't let him distract her. "New media as well?"

He moved closer, touched her hand. "Maybe." So he was, and Nev knew it. But she saw something else in his eyes too, a wariness she didn't understand, mingled with warmth he never allowed through in the office. "I think I know what he's trying. Do me a favor, Whitney. Don't ask more. I happen to think that a smaller, more closer-knit team is the way to go, but I don't call the shots anymore."

He didn't have to say any more. Mattson wanted to dazzle Nev with talk of expansion but in reality the man was trying to squeeze Nev out, make him less important. Then he'd hire somebody young and hungry to do the nights Nev didn't cover. But Nev wasn't buying it.

Nev was planning a breakout. He couldn't poach her or Jay, their contracts bound them, but if they waited the six months required, they could move to whatever Nev was thinking of doing. He had a private fortune, inherited from some uncle or other, and he knew people, was related to some movers and shakers in L.A., so he could do it. His show was worth a fortune and if he moved to a different network, kept his team, Mattson wouldn't be able to touch them.

"Okay, I won't ask anything else. But you have to know that Mattson suspects whatever it is you might or might not be planning. He's on top of the world right now. He knows everything."

Nev smiled and picked up his fork. "So do I, honey. So do I."

So he had something on Mattson, did he? Intriguing.

After their totally delicious meal, Nev curved an arm around her waist and led her outside to where the valet had his car waiting. He took the keys and passed a note in a practiced gesture, then helped her in, lingering a little at the curve of her waist, his fingers delivering a gentle stroke before he released her.

She'd become aware of his increased interest in her throughout the meal. She knew, he knew. Body language was part of their stock in trade. But she found herself enjoying the game as she never had before. Before this, when a man had hit on her he was either desperate or recalling the adage that her grandfather used to tell her, "They don't look at the mantelpiece when they're poking the fire. Watch yourself, girlie." They wanted the body. Like Stranger. If her mother had known her grandfather had spoken to her like that, she'd have creamed him. But his advice proved a welcome counterpoint to her mother's more ladylike approach to child-rearing.

No, not like Stranger. She guessed he had a fetish for sex in the dark, but he'd never treated her badly, never more than she'd asked for or wanted. And toward the end of their relationship, he'd been tender, held her after sex until she'd fallen asleep and left early so she could use the bathroom and put herself to rights before she left. And he always paid the bill. She'd checked the PayPal account recently. He hadn't touched it.

She'd have been lying if she said she didn't enjoy the drive back to her house. With their cards on the table, the atmosphere felt more relaxed. They understood each other. Nev was under Mattson's thumb right now. Nev's first priority was always NewsInc, but he treated his staff with a fair hand. Then Mattson's dawn raid had put the company in his hands. She also knew that Nev was planning to get out from under that thumb. If Mattson ever started to dictate policy directly, he'd be gone, but otherwise he'd stick it out and choose his time. And he wanted Jay and her to form a team and join him. Lots to think about. Not least of which was wondering if Jay knew.

Nev pulled up outside her apartment building and, before she could get the door open, he'd rounded the car and held out his hand to assist her. Nev knew she was capable of far more than climbing out of a car on her own, so the old-fashioned gesture made her smile, but she took his hand.

He hauled her out of the car and into his arms. And by the look on his face, it wasn't accidental. Before she could pull back, he cinched her closer and kissed her.

Nice, real nice. Nev kissed well. She opened her mouth a little but he didn't plunge in to half choke her. Instead, he tasted gently, touched his tongue to her inner lips, her teeth, and met her tongue with a touch of welcome. It teased her into tasting him back, sliding her tongue alongside his.

But good though he was, it didn't compare with Stranger. When *he* kissed her, he brought her alive, made her want things, want more.

Nev released her but she didn't move back immediately. He gazed down into her face. "Let's call it a kiss between friends, shall we? Seeing you in the car, I couldn't resist, but it's all kinds of inappropriate. I didn't mean for this to happen." He took a deep breath and let it out again in a sigh that gusted over her hair. "If you ever leave the company, or I do, we are so going to pick this up where we left off."

Whitney wasn't so sure but she knew one thing. She had to see Stranger, and soon.

Chapter Eight

ℬ

He kept her waiting nearly a week. Three days after she'd walked into the office to a chorus of whistles and applause, she finally got to meet with the person who meant most to her, who was beginning to mean far too much. She needed to know so many things, not least if it was him or the situation, the sex-in-the-dark-with-a-stranger setup. Either way she was fucked.

She could see only one way out. So she emailed him and he replied with a date, a hotel and a room number.

She stared at the emails, hers and his, and felt the chills of anticipation. Tonight it could be different. Tonight she'd open up. Maybe.

Jay stared at Whitney as she typed up her latest article. Still gorgeous but still the same. He let out a sigh of relief. After the office staff had gasped and laughed and had her buy a round of coffees to celebrate, she'd settled right back in. She worked just the same, did her assignments, looked for other stuff, called her contacts to tell them she was back. His only moment of concern came when Neville had strolled through the big room on the way to his office on that first morning. He'd paused at her desk and they'd exchanged a smile. An intimate smile. He'd have thought Whitney hated him still for not giving her the job, but they seemed to have made their peace with each other. His investigative antennae went on alert. When had they done that?

He couldn't help it, every bone in his body yearned to walk over to her desk and just take her away. She was his, dammit. He could fight the urge as much as he wanted, but it was still there, still as strong as ever. He had no right, he knew that, but tell that to his cock, which came to alert every time she walked past his desk, smiled at him, chatted with him. Agony. Thank Christ she'd contacted him last night.

He'd run out of excuses. She didn't need him close anymore, didn't need the support of a friend. He had no idea if she'd want to continue or if she'd want to confess. He'd already decided he had to tell her, but maybe not tomorrow...

No, cowards never had clear consciences, and she was bound to find him out eventually, if not sooner.

* * * * *

He arrived at the hotel an hour early and, since it was early evening in midsummer, was startled to find the drapes drawn. He stood in the open doorway before he closed the door behind him and reached for the light switch.

"Leave it."

She was here. She'd gotten here even earlier. His eyes not yet accustomed to the gloom, he felt for the wall and leaned against it, trying to get his bearings.

"Strip," she said.

He tried to muffle his laughter but he couldn't help but release a single chuckle. Silence, then he covered it up. She knew his—Jay's—laugh, and she wouldn't be slow putting it together. Unless he distracted her. "How did you know?" he asked, as usual in gruff Greek.

"I saw your silhouette." She spoke English. She'd already figured out that he could understand. She no longer spoke slowly and clearly. And she used big words now too, assuming he knew them. He wasn't sure what that meant yet.

"Are you naked?"

"Find out."

Heat rose in his cock and he took a quick breath, trying to control the surge in his libido. These commands, turning the tables, really did it for him. He loved controlling her, but it seemed it was her turn with that. *Well, okay, ma'am. Here we go.*

He took his time, undoing the buttons on his shirt and cuffs slowly, letting her hear the rustle. He'd worn a good button-down tonight, wondering if she'd want to see him first, wanting to look his best. To dress for her. But he was undressing for her instead.

A shadow to his left outlined the presence of a chair. He tossed his shirt over it and started on his pants. A shame, he'd worn the pants to his Armani suit. But maybe she'd get to see them another time. The thought lingered and his anticipation rose even more. He had to ease the zipper down carefully over his erect cock and then slide the pants down his legs. He paused to unfasten his shoes so he could take them off at the same time. Women didn't go for the bare legs with socks look.

As he was fumbling to get his left shoelace to loosen, a hand grabbed his ass. He couldn't prevent his gasp of shock. "Stay there."

Heart in his mouth, he waited for her to make a move. He had his right leg unencumbered, but his pants were still wrapped around his left ankle and his shoe was only half off. He managed the shoe, but didn't dare move any farther.

"Mmm, nice." She groped both buttocks and drew her pinkie over the crack between, as if by accident. But he knew better. He shivered, not hiding his reaction. She'd had a manicure before she came back to work and those nails made for great teasing. He could hardly wait to feel them score his back.

"Anybody ever tell you what a great ass you have? Firm, the muscles hard, but there's still a great curve." She slid her hands over it again.

He shuddered. "Good."

"No." A pause. She hadn't meant to say that. If he didn't know her, if he really were a stranger, he wouldn't know how inexperienced she was. He knew Whitney tended to piss off her boyfriends after a couple of dates, and he knew why. Afraid of competition, or afraid they'd talk about her. Or just plain scared of getting involved. Well, not this time. She was his. He'd give her all the time she wanted to explore the boundaries of sexual pleasure. If there were any boundaries. Together they'd take the journey. If he could only persuade her.

She ran one fingernail down his balls through the cotton of his boxers. He cried out, tingles filtering through him at her touch. She withdrew and slid her hands down again, under the elastic, over his taut buttocks. "Good," he repeated, retaining the Greek by sheer willpower.

He felt exposed, even more so when she shoved his boxers down his legs. And then she ran her nails over him again, but this time she slid her fingers back, dragging them over his ass crack, over the sensitive skin there. He swore. "*Gamoto!*"

"What's that mean?"

"Damn." He didn't know many really good Greek curses. The person he'd learned the language from never used them, and he could hardly ask her. But it was the best he could do until he could use English.

She laughed. "You don't curse? Want me to make you?"

A cold substance landed on his left butt cheek. "Sorry. Not on target."

Jesus, shit, no—oh yeah. She smoothed the gel over his ass. "I want to put something there. Are you okay with that?"

Nobody had ever messed with him there before, but it felt good when she did it. And here he was thinking about her inexperience. Well, she'd sure turned the tables on him. And he was loving every minute of it. "*Ne,*" he managed. But it sounded needy even to him. His cock strained, leaked fluid he badly wanted her to claim with her mouth or her fingers. But she didn't.

She slid something that felt like a smooth rod over each cheek, and only when he was quivering in anticipation did she slide just the tip inside, although it felt like a fuck of a lot more. After the first feeling of discomfort and tightness, he felt his ass ease to accommodate whatever it was, the tight muscles relaxing. When he moved, he could feel it, rubbing inside, touching places he never dreamed would stimulate him so much. He'd read about it and dismissed it as not for him. Fuck, was he wrong.

"Stand up."

He bent to kick out of his shoe and the rest of his clothes. Even that made the rod resonate inside him, made the strangeness even more strange.

He took his time, savoring the sensation.

"Are you okay? You have to tell me if you're not. Say it in Greek, tell me to stop and I will, I promise."

"*Ne.*" Accustoming himself to the feeling, he realized that the huge stick she'd jammed up his ass was actually quite slender probably something the average ass-fucker would sneer at. "It's good."

"I wanted to try it." She paused. They faced each other in the darkness, only their breaths and the muffled sounds of the ever-present traffic stirring the air in the room. This being a good hotel, the air-conditioning hardly made a sound, but in the silence he became aware of the gentle purr. "It might be our last time, so I wanted to try things I'd read about."

"Anything else?"

"Yes. Do you want to tie me up? Spank me?"

No, that didn't appeal. But he wanted her and if he didn't have her soon, he'd explode. "I want to watch you." He held his breath. He rarely spoke much. Would she discover his identity now?

"Watch me?" She sounded uncertain. "Now?"

He let out a long breath. "Later." Without warning, he seized her arms, turned her around and pushed her toward the chair where he'd left his clothes. "Bend over." That rod was killing him. Every time he moved he felt it, stroking the place inside, driving him further toward coming. Jesus, he'd have to get one of those things. Try it on her, if she'd let him. He grinned into the darkness. His and hers. He liked that idea.

"You must not take it out," she said. "I'll stop." Her voice wavered but she sounded determined. What a darling.

"No you won't." He wouldn't let her, but he had no intention of taking it out. "Do it." He'd never sheathed his cock so fast but he let her hear the crackle when he tore open the packet so she'd know he was still thinking of her protection.

He nudged her feet apart with his knees and stepped between them, feeling for her pussy. Beautifully wet, soft and so inviting. He slid his fingers along the crease, down again, and tweaked her clit, enough to make her give a sharp cry. Then down, making sure he wouldn't hurt her when he —

Ah yes, that was it. He bathed the head of his cock in her hot juices, let it find its own way home. He gripped her hip in one hand, put the other over her stomach to hold her steady while he filled her. He didn't stop until his balls touched her ass. She stuck that beautiful ass in the air as she bent over the back of the chair. He risked a few more words. "Are you holding on?"

"Yes." She definitely sounded strained now. Good. He wanted her needing him.

He rotated his hips, savoring the lush, wet depths. She moaned and pushed her ass back against him, into his groin. The rod tightened in his ass as he tightened his buttock muscles and he loved it. Withdrawing, he stroked her stomach, then went lower to take her clit between his thumb and forefinger. "No mercy," he promised, and drove back in.

Every time he thrust, the rod caressed him inside, the feeling so strange but so fucking good. It drove him to push harder, fiercer, and he forgot all his determination to seduce

189

her, to persuade her that she'd want to keep him. He wanted this woman to come before he did, preferably more than once, but if he couldn't hold on that long then he'd make it the best she'd ever had. He'd suck her to a climax if he had to. The chair jarred as he moved and he wondered if it would hold steady. He'd risk it.

The chair hit something firm, a dresser perhaps, and gave him a sure surface so he could fuck her without mercy as promised. And he did. Drove into her with hard, deep thrusts, withdrawing nearly all the way and then plunging back in again, right to the hilt, his balls bouncing with every stroke, that rod driving him crazy, pushing him toward the inevitable climax. Every time, that delve into her soft, lush depths urged him that bit further toward his orgasm, however hard he fought to retain control. It was no good. He was lost in her.

Her cries mingled with his grunts as she pushed her ass against his groin. He ground into her, stopping to alter his rhythm, to bend a little more so he could change his angle. By rights his knees should be trembling with fatigue, especially after his recent recovery from a broken leg, but he felt nothing except her, nothing but his cock deep inside her, possessing her, becoming a part of her.

And then she must have done something because that rod in his ass purred and hummed into life. *Fuck, it's a vibrator.*

He couldn't hold on any longer. He cried out and shot into her, losing all but a tiny piece of his mind as she enveloped him, took him on the ride of his life.

He fell over her, panting, trying to move, but he was already losing it.

She hadn't come.

He withdrew and fell to his knees thankfully because he was sure he couldn't stay on his feet any longer. Scenting her, he knew what he'd do. When she would have risen, he pressed her down, one hand on her back. He found her clit again with the other. Then, guided by her aroma, he planted kisses on her thigh, then higher, then he found her pussy.

Whitney let the remote fall from her hand. The satisfaction she felt when he came, so hard, so deep, had made up for her lack of orgasm, but he wasn't about to let her go. He closed his arms around her, urged her back down and kissed her. He licked and she shivered. So close she could hardly bear it. When he found her pussy he pushed inside, licked her out. Oh God, that was good. He had a great tongue. A fucking wonderful tongue. She'd take Greek lessons until she could tell him precisely what to do with it. Not that he needed telling.

He found her clit, twisted it, and she moaned. "Stranger, oh Stranger." She wouldn't call him Nicos. She knew that wasn't his real name, just knew.

He chuckled, muffled because of what he was doing, and murmured something she didn't catch. In that low voice again. He attacked her again, licked her. She wanted him to suck her dry, keep on doing it until she couldn't stay here any longer, until she couldn't hold her legs straight for him. So good.

"Ohhh…" Inside, her muscles tightened and he sensed it, licked further. She concentrated on keeping straight, holding on.

Then she exploded and he pushed something inside her. His fingers. Two fingers. Her inner muscles clamped around them and she cried out, cried his name again. Oh so good.

"Enough," he muttered.

She didn't know how much time had passed, how long they'd been there, him on the floor, her draped over the chair, his clothes under her. She pushed on the chair seat to get upright. The world spun and she went dizzy, but held on to the chair as the spell passed.

Dim shapes suggested the layout of the room, which, for a change, she'd seen first and been able to memorize as well as she could before he'd arrived.

She cleared her throat. "I want to talk to you." She took the necessary steps to get to the bed. "But go and make yourself comfortable first."

He huffed a laugh and hauled himself to his feet, using the chair to support himself. "Bath," he said.

It took her a few minutes to process what he meant. "In the dark?"

"No."

She swallowed. She'd been about to suggest switching the light on, but his idea was so much better. Except she didn't know if he'd go for it. "You want to see me?"

"*Ne.*"

"I thought this situation turned you on. This whole stranger danger in the dark thing."

A low grunt.

"You go in first."

"Do not leave."

She frowned into the dark. Something familiar echoed in that tone.

He slowly got to his feet and she leaned back on the bed, resting and waiting. Her heartbeat quickened, anticipating what might happen next. What would he look like? The toilet flushed, probably him disposing of the condom, then water poured in the sink. He'd want to remove the vibrator. She wondered if she'd have the courage to do things like that in the light and decided what the hell, it wouldn't matter anyway.

Was he, as she'd guessed, a construction worker, or someone who worked in the Bay? Maybe driving a tourist boat, or even research. His powerful muscles indicated some kind of physical work on a regular basis. She hadn't felt the carefully designed muscular structure of someone who worked out regularly. Perhaps he was in the military or the navy, even a SEAL — or the Greek equivalent.

More water poured, the sound deeper. He was filling a bath. Lines of light gleamed in the gaps around the door. Whitney swallowed, not sure if they were doing the right thing. This would either make or break them, but they had to progress. They had a relationship of some kind, and she wanted to find out what kind it was. If they were to remain fuck buddies, so be it. It might even play better with how her life was right now, give her time to develop her career before she concentrated on private matters.

Yes, that would work. But deep down she knew she was lying to herself. She had very little experience of love, but she'd missed Stranger while she'd been away, it was like an ache in her heart. It couldn't be love, surely. But his tenderness, his consideration and his breathtaking lovemaking had her and she didn't want him to let go.

"Come." The single word spoken through a crack in the door was her only warning. As she climbed off the bed and headed for the bathroom, the light snapped off but she felt safe because his hand was there, ready to hold hers and guide her to the tub. A splash told her he'd stepped in and the crisp hiss of foam told her he'd added bubbles. Heavenly scent wreathed around them, a mixture of lavender and other, subtler aromas. Not a standard hotel bubble bath, even one provided by a four-star.

She hesitated. Getting into a filled bath in the dark with someone she didn't know... But he'd proven so much to her. His voice sliced through the silence. "Trust me?"

Yes, she trusted him. Sometimes a person had to let go of reason and trust their instincts. If she couldn't trust Stranger with this, she couldn't trust anyone or anything. And wasn't that a pissy way to live?

So she let him tug her in. She got in facing him but he pressed on one shoulder and turned her so her back was to him. Only then did he sink down, his legs wide so she could sit between them and rest her back against his powerful chest. He curved his arms around her waist. Bubbles caressed her

193

skin, silky and luxurious. She'd never felt so cared for, so wanted. So—loved.

Not possible. She'd already decided that. But this might be the start of it, if they let their relationship progress out of the dark.

He murmured in her ear, slowly, in luscious Greek. "There is a light switch here. Shall I pull it now?" That voice, softer now. She knew it. She didn't dare think it.

"Yes." She hadn't realized she could use such a tiny voice, barely a breath.

One arm left her waist and her heart seemed to double its beat. She could hardly get her breath. He pressed a kiss to her shoulder. "Here we go."

Light flooded the room. Startled, Whitney looked down to shade her eyes until she'd gotten used to the change. Then she blinked and sat upright. Looked down. Two strong arms, liberally sprinkled with black hair, encircled her waist.

Stranger sat very still, his cock already half erect, pressing against her back. She swallowed. Her breasts skimmed the bubbles in the large corner tub. Ivory, she noted, with shiny chrome fittings. A big room, with a rough-surfaced tile floor. A mirror above the sink. In its surface she saw a head of black hair. His. And a forehead, one she'd kissed in the past. She couldn't see his legs but felt them embracing her own. He bent his head to kiss her shoulder again and a heavy lock of hair fell forward to caress her sensitive skin. "Do you speak any English?" she asked. "Or was that a disguise?"

Questions flooded her mind in the next instant, all the things she'd wondered about him. Of course he could remain anonymous. She had little hope of finding him, even if he lived here in L.A. Millions thronged the sprawling city, or cities, and it would take years to comb Hollywood, Beverly Hills, Burbank and all the other places.

"I speak English."

His voice had softened, enriched with a melodious tone she'd never before heard in Stranger. Because he'd been careful. But she had heard it before somewhere. Almost afraid to turn around, she leaned back into his warmth. It might be the last time she touched him this way, without history, without blame. "No shame," she murmured.

His low voice whispered into her ear in English. "Look at me, Whitney."

No. It couldn't be. "You know my name...?" Her voice trailed off as she turned around, shock galvanizing her into action.

"Jay?"

Chapter Nine

ॐ

Hurt and shock glazed her mind. Jay kept his arms around her but loosened his hold.

"Yeah."

"The Greek?"

He forced a grin and shook his hair back. "My grandmother. She married an Irishman. Her family disowned her for it but they came around later. Greek Irish is some combination. People assume, but they don't usually ask. When I was a child, my mom caught glandular fever and my grandmother took care of me for six months. I learned Greek then, because she was always more comfortable in the language. That's why it's a bit rough. And it's why I don't know any real dirty words in Greek. I trained as a singer when I was a kid. They teach you to use different timbres and tones. That helped me with the voice but I kept it short. You'd have got there if I didn't get you worked up so fast." He snapped his words off. "Sorry. I'm babbling. Nervous. This is worse than facing a division of Afghanis, all armed to the teeth."

Her eyes opened wide and she stared at his face, those dark eyes she'd looked into so many times before. But not here, not naked in a hot bath. She felt numb, her mind scrambling to catch up with reality. "Why, Jay? Why didn't you just ask?"

"I did, remember?"

Yes, she did, now. When he'd first arrived home with his broken leg and orders to rest for at least two months, if not three. When Nev had taken him off rotation and put him behind a desk. When the network had discovered Jay attracted the female viewers and decided to delay his return to the field.

"So you decided to do it this way?" She glanced down, flushed when she realized her nipples were on display, then tossed back her hair and stared up at him defiantly.

"No. It wasn't that." He sighed and leaned back. "I needed to use your terminal one evening. It was late and the internet was down, so I rebooted and my laptop still refused to connect. So I tried yours. Yours connected okay. You'd left the URL on your desktop. I'm sorry, but when I booted up, I hit it and your browser opened on the page. That was honestly what happened. What was I supposed to do?"

"Talk to me about it. Why didn't you do that?"

He gave a bitter laugh. "And tell you that I'd snooped around your computer? Knowing you, you'd have made an appointment at Stranger Danger just to show me you didn't care. No, don't say no. You know you would." He sighed. "So I set up an identity there and contacted you. I had an advantage over you — I knew your persona."

"I remember," she said suddenly. "I remember that night. I'd come across the web address and put it on my desktop. The next day I made a paper note of it, took it off my desktop and deleted my web history. You did a number on me." She jerked in his arms, trying to pull away, tears in her voice. She hated that he saw her so vulnerable. She'd always presented a hard surface to the outside world. She'd had to.

She turned to face him, the water swirling against her skin.

"No. Listen, just listen, please. You scared me. That site scared me. You must have been desperate. Or something. I didn't know, but I wanted to try to help. So I set up the meeting and arrived that night with some of the stuff I'd collected abroad. Handcuffs, an unloaded firearm, a blindfold and some other things. I laid it all out on the table by the door. I planned to scare you, that was all, make you see how dangerous it was."

The bastard. She'd tell him the truth now, make sure he understood how badly he'd acted. Although from the grim expression on his face and the hurt in his eyes, he might be realizing that already. "I didn't care," she said, her voice low. "By that time I didn't care. I wanted something that wasn't a pity fuck. Something where the man avoided looking at my face. When he had doggie-style sex with me because he liked my butt, not because he didn't want to look at my face."

He reached for her then dropped his hand into the water. "I cared. And I never would have done any of that. I liked your face. You've always put yourself down. I can understand it, especially with the career you chose. But something happened that first time, Whitney. Once I had you in my arms I got so hot, so fast, I couldn't stop what happened next. I wanted it so much, I'd have died rather than stop. And then it just snowballed. I should have stopped, I know that." From the expression in his eyes, he meant it, but Jay had lied about things before, professionally, lied about his position to protect the troops he was with. And he'd lied about Stranger Danger. Or had he? No, she had to be fair. She hadn't given him the chance.

She shook her head. "So sex in the dark does it for you?" She bit her lip and blinked away the betraying sheen of tears in her eyes. "It doesn't really matter what I look like, does it? Maybe we should just keep going, because you were the best fuck I ever had."

Her attempt at hardness was belied by the tender expression that came to his eyes now. "You were mine. And more."

She forced her face to remain clear. She'd had enough practice at that. "I didn't know you were capable of this, Jay."

"Me either. I shocked myself." He shook his head. "I know I should have stopped, should have told you, but it was so fucking exciting."

"And you were bored to death in the office. Once your leg got better, Nev kept you as anchor. But you're okay now," she added brightly. "You're going to Russia."

He stared at her. "You know?"

She'd wrong-footed him. "Sure I know. But someone else told me. Not you."

He made an impatient gesture with one hand. "That has nothing to do with us. You know I've been dying to get back in the field. Anchor doesn't suit me."

"It suits other people though, doesn't it?" At his questioning look, she explained. "All those women who want you to anchor them." She bit her lip and looked away. Now wasn't the time for laughter, but when she'd seen that particular fan letter, she'd grinned and joked with him. It hurt that she'd enjoyed that moment, remembered it with pleasure. "I told you I wouldn't forget that one."

"You did. But you're the only person I want to anchor." He reached out and took her hand. "Now and for the foreseeable future."

"Yet you're going to Russia?"

"Only to cover the conference in Moscow."

She heard his words with relief. A special assignment that would take two weeks, or three if he stayed behind to interview the important people who would be attending. Then her heart plummeted. Russia was too close to a major field of conflict right now. Would he go on to Afghanistan instead of coming home? Jay chased danger. His performance before had been so stellar he'd won awards for it. He could choose the company he worked for, write his own check for it. And if she gave him nothing to come back for, that was where he'd go.

"So you'll come back to me?" She had to do it. Couldn't bear to think of him going back to that hellhole.

"You know what I want, don't you? Where I want to be."

"But it's getting worse. And you'll be a target. You're high profile now."

He frowned. "That's what's stopping me. I'd be a danger to any unit I joined."

So he'd thought about it then. "I can understand that." And she wasn't stopping him, unlike his comrades. He didn't seem to mind leaving her behind.

"But I could take a different approach. I don't want to make a war into a soap opera."

Her breath caught. "What kind of approach?" She dreaded to think. He hurtled into danger, uncaring for himself. She didn't want that for him.

"I'll tell you when I know." He squeezed her hand. "Come here, let me hold you. Please. Let's forget all that for now."

If she got out of the tub and left now, he'd sign up. She couldn't leave him with no choice. She had to give him something to stay for. Some reason not to go.

That would be her. She didn't even know if she loved him, only that he'd been the best of friends and an amazing lover, but she hadn't yet linked the two personas. Neither was enough.

But if he asked her, she'd say she loved him.

Jay knew he hadn't played fair. He couldn't bear to see that look of naked vulnerability on her face, that look he'd seen for the first time just now, when she realized he could go on to 'Stan from Russia. He didn't need her to tell him what she'd thought because he'd considered it himself. She'd masked her reaction quickly but he'd seen it all the same. She didn't want him to go. Fuck, *he* didn't want to go now. Because of her. She was making him reassess all his preconceived ideas, his plans for the next few years. Right now he didn't want anything else. He just wanted her. He'd make it right for her, somehow.

A lone tear tipped out of the corner of her eye and trickled down the side of her face. He wanted that tear, wanted to capture it in a crystal bottle and wear it, wanted to ensure it was the last tear she ever shed.

In his dreams.

He'd known who she was all along. She hadn't. So while he was as sure as he could be that he loved her, wanted to commit to her, she'd only just discovered that her midnight lover and her friend and colleague were the same person. Time, she needed time. A commodity they didn't have.

Her breasts, breasts he'd caressed, sucked and kissed, skimmed the frothy white bubbles, making him yearn to do it again, sweep her into passion, make her forget everything except his name. He shifted, easing his arousal. What was it about that fucker? It had a mind of its own.

He had to let her go now, if she wanted to go. If she came back, she had to do it of her own accord. Not because he made her. But he'd do everything in his power to make her come back. How could he persuade her that he didn't give a fuck about her face, except it was the one he wanted to see on the pillow next to his? She might look different, more acceptable for the camera, but inside she felt the same. He knew because something similar had happened to him.

After his first book had hit the big time, and again when he'd started the anchor job, people recognized him in the street, and he was always sure it was somebody else. Whitney had to reconcile the woman inside with the one in the mirror. He wanted to help her do it. Stranger was a constant between the old Whitney and the new one. He had to persuade her to keep it that way.

He lifted his hands, relieved when she didn't brush away his gentle strokes on her upper arms. Raising the stakes, he bent and pressed a gentle kiss on her lips. They opened and he rejoiced. This time he didn't linger, but drew away enough to murmur to her, "Close your eyes. Just go with it."

With a sigh, she gave in. He felt it heat his lips and then he moved in again and urged her closer. She tensed and then relaxed before she allowed him to tug her between his open thighs, the movement made easier by the silky water. The bubbles were bursting fast but the water was still warm. They'd heat it a little more.

Loving the way she nestled close to him, he groaned when her body met his, all the way down to their thighs. His cock finished hardening against her stomach, coming to full, rampant life, the sensitive skin on the head getting the treat of its life. He ravaged her mouth, his tongue plunging deep to taste and take, and she allowed that too. So exhilarating to have a strong woman allow these intimacies, so much more than a soft, yielding woman. This woman had stood in battlefields and calmly described her situation into a handheld camera; she'd stood outside embassies under siege, under the eyes of baying mobs, and not one of them had touched her. And now she was allowing him to touch her, to caress her, to feel her nipples harden into tight berries against his chest. Oh fuck, but he wanted her.

But this was too awkward and there wasn't enough room. "Bed," he said, and got to his feet, tugging her up. She came gladly, smiling now, and let him lead her into the bedroom. They fell on to the bed together, their bodies slip-sliding against each other, rolling over the cover.

He reached out, blindly grabbed one of the condoms he'd optimistically left handy and then shifted her away just enough for him to roll it on. When she tried to help him he brushed her hands aside. "I won't last if you do that. I'm not kidding, Whitney, I want you like I want my next breath."

When he lifted her, she helped, pressing her knees against the mattress, seemingly as eager as he. Sliding inside was as easy as a hot blade going into butter. But much, much better feeling. So she wanted it for real, her juices flowing for him. Still, he took it slowly, savoring the deep plunge into her body, knowing he'd never get enough of this. If she let him. Silky wetness enveloped him, so much warmer than the water that had surrounded them a moment ago, so much more welcome.

She moved and her inner muscles rippled down his shaft, making him take a sharp breath. "So good," he murmured. "You feel wonderful."

"Hmm." She lifted as he withdrew to drive in again, but this time they made it long and languid. He'd taken her with passion, with anger tingeing his actions, with hopeless need, but he thought he liked this way best. Maybe. Until the next time. But right now he was loving the hell out of this. And her.

He slid inside her, memorizing every tiny part of her flesh, every flinch she made when he touched the most sensitive part of her. He paused, grasped her hips to hold her steady halfway down, and then rotated. Gave a wicked grin when she responded with a sharp cry but she didn't see it because she kept her eyes closed. As if she were afraid to look. He wouldn't force it. Not now. She'd taken enough already, and maybe she wanted Stranger back.

He murmured to her in Greek but didn't disguise his voice. That was gone for good. But she could have the rest. "Remember that I kissed you here." He kissed the tip of her new nose—"and here"—he dotted kisses over her cheeks, her chin, where her moles had been, where tiny, fading marks still remained. "Remember that I did it before and after. This doesn't change who you are, Whitney, or what you are. It makes you marketable. But you were always lovely to me. You always will be. It makes no difference in the way I feel about you." He kissed her tears away but he didn't stop making love to her.

He held her, worked her and watched her shudder, felt her muscles spasm and clench around his cock. If not for that he wouldn't have known, because this climax was quieter than he usually experienced with her, almost frighteningly controlled. He wanted to give her everything, show her what she meant to him. That would come. He was too impatient, always had been. *Wait, you fucker, wait.* He had to use all the patience he could drag up from his sorry soul. She needed it—she deserved it.

When his own orgasm began to tighten his balls and heat his body, he released her slowly so she sank down on him, making him groan in pleasure. She brushed the sides of the bath, found the rim, gripped it and eased her body up and down on his. He slid his hands up her body to her breasts, cupped them, caressed them, pinched her nipples. She liked that, he knew she did and the small sound she made at the back of her throat told him she did.

He cried her name when he came, when he poured his essence into that condom, and took only a few minutes' rest until he realized the cover was not only wet, but cold. He pushed it away and pulled back the bedcovers, snuggling them in to the sheets and blankets.

* * * * *

Unable to sleep once more, he left her in bed an hour later, letting himself soundlessly out of the hotel room, preparing for one of his middle-of-the-night walks. He needed to think. If he slept with her he might scare her, waking up with one of those fucking nightmares. He'd been lucky to get away with it once before. Worse, he might hurt her. He couldn't risk that. Better this way.

Chapter Ten

೧

Nev leaned back in his chair and stretched. "Thanks for coming in, Whitney. Can you close the door?"

He wore his poker face. She couldn't read a thing. His desk was tidy, only a manila folder lying on the shiny glass surface, and his laptop was open and running. But she couldn't see what was on the screen.

Every time, every fucking time she had to face the boss like this, all her insecurities leaped up to swamp her. Was this it then? Was he going to let her go? They'd claim they were cutting down on staff, or he'd send her out to the sticks to cover local events. Oh yes, she could see that happening. She could face the camera now, so they'd send her to head up some god-awful small town in the middle of the country. Whitney had never done small towns, and had done her best to get out of the one she was born and reared in. They'd find some excuse, she just knew it. Perhaps they'd decided they wanted a correspondent in Iceland. She didn't speak Icelandic either. *Oh fuck, stop it, Whitney.*

"How's your French?" he asked abruptly, as soon as she'd sat down.

"Fine." Her mind raced and quickly came up with an answer. The Russian conference was the small precursor to the peace talks in Paris. It would be complex, meaty and important.

Neville grinned. "Yes, that's it. Paris. Those talks are vital, and if anyone can explain it and not make people fall asleep, it's you."

"You want me to do it?"

He leaned forward. "Whitney, you went the extra mile. You're more than presentable now, and don't pretend you don't know what I'm talking about. I'm impressed. I'm also—" He cleared his throat. "Never mind. I've gone the extra mile for you. Mr. Mattson doesn't know about your—"

"Surgery," she suggested.

He grinned. "Yes, sorry about that. But I told him you could do it better than anyone else I have on staff. He suggested radio coverage or off-camera stuff." He grimaced. "I said it wouldn't work."

"It might have," she said softly.

"You don't deserve that." He paused. "I told him about the surgery after he agreed."

"Well done." That would have taken guts. Likely he'd put his job on the line. So why wasn't she leaping in joy? It was what she wanted, wasn't it?

But she'd have to do this. Even if she agreed to the relationship that Jay wanted, their jobs meant they'd have to be apart sometimes. A vision flashed before her. For the first time, at the moment of his orgasm, she'd seen Jay come. She couldn't get the sight out of her head and it returned at the most inappropriate times. Like now. His dark head thrown back, his lips stretched tight, his eyes half closed and unfocused. The bliss she'd given him swept over her once more, heating her blood.

She also rejoiced at the words he'd whispered to her. That he wanted her anyway. He'd known who she was all along and it hadn't deterred him. The dark had been her choice, not his. So surely he hadn't put her name forward to the Trust. She was beginning to believe what he'd told her. Every time he'd glanced her way in the office today, she'd heated and blushed like a girl.

And she realized something else. If Jay hadn't put her name forward to the Durban Trust, then someone else had.

Nev. He'd done what he thought was right, and he'd done it because he thought she was being treated unfairly. "Thanks, Nev."

"Glad you accepted. You'll do a great job."

She smiled. "I meant pushing me to get the work done. I'd never have done it on my own. I got caught up with being true to myself, moles and all, and I didn't see further than the end of my nose. You were right. I had to do this. We don't live in Cloud Cuckoo Land, after all." It almost choked her to say it, but he'd been right. And he'd left the final choice to her, just smoothed the way, made it possible.

He gave her a one-sided grin. "You know Greek?"

Shocked, she stared at him, recalling the light Greek endearments Jay murmured in her ear, fancying for one moment that Nev had been there instead. No, that didn't work. Not a twinge. "Yeah. You know I do." Of course, Cloud Cuckoo Land came from an Aristophanes play. Stupid even to think that Neville had been her stranger. But he had put her name forward to the Durban Trust and got her a scoop with Georgina Hawthorne. Once she'd done the work on the biography, she'd ask her for an interview for the TV station.

"I thought that was Jay who knew Greek." He opened the folder and riffled through it. "Ah yes. Just that I haven't had any reason to use your Greek yet. And you say here that it's only basic."

She shrugged. It was certainly better than it had been. "I could work it up if you needed it."

"Not right now, but you are a clever one, aren't you? Five languages fluently and several others you can get by in."

"I like languages. They come naturally to me. It was an easy degree."

"Good for you. More useful than journalism, that's for sure." He snorted and closed the folder. "Anyway. We'll want you there in three weeks. You'll be away at least a week, probably two if you can snag some extended interviews. I'll send Ritchie with you." A great cameraman. "You'll have more, but Ritchie will be your main man." He smiled, his eyes friendly. "Okay?"

"Sure. Thanks." She got to her feet. "And thanks for writing to the Durban Trust."

She glanced back to see him frown. "Is that who did your work? Why didn't you say? You could have done a feature on it."

"I signed a confidentiality clause," she said. "I asked them if they wanted publicity and they said no." She shuddered at the kind of exposé reality program that might have resulted. The kind that had made old man Mattson rich.

Then it hit her. He hadn't sent the letter. He hadn't known who'd done the surgery, or who had paid for it. He didn't know.

That only left one person.

* * * * *

Apart from a curt "My place, ten tonight", Whitney had hardly spoken to Jay all day. He could take it. Maybe she wanted to keep it all business and she was finding it as hard as he was. Speaking of hard, just looking at her brought back memories of the night before. He had only one ambition left. To see the desire in her eyes when she looked at him, to know she wanted him, Jay Preston O'Neill, and nobody else.

Now, arriving at her apartment with the single red rose he'd managed to collect from a florist on the way, he felt like a walking cliché. But maybe she'd like it. She never cracked on the job, but maybe she'd like him to treat her like a gentle, sweet woman sometimes, when they were alone together.

He'd soon find out.

She opened her door and glared at him, then folded her arms across her chest. "Come in." She backed up, letting him enter the place. It was better than his city apartment, one he was considering giving up. He only kept a studio apartment here because he was out in the field so much, but recently it had driven him crazy. One largish room had seemed enough for his stopovers between assignments, but months doing the anchor job had him wanting to pace around like a caged tiger. He couldn't even do that because of his bad leg until recently.

He followed Whitney into her living room and when she gestured for him to sit, sank into one of the large sofas facing each other on either side of the fireplace. He left plenty of room for her but unfortunately she chose the other one instead of coming closer so he could greet her with the kiss he ached for.

He gave her the rose with a mock flourish. "For you."

Her mouth twitched in a smile. "Thanks." She put the rose aside.

Oh well, not everything was going to work. "What did you have planned for tonight?" He knew what he wanted, but it had to be her decision. At least initially.

"I just want to talk to you, Jay. Out of the office. Without anyone listening."

So she'd chosen safe territory. Tension gripped his lower stomach. This didn't sound good. Or perhaps she wanted time out. It would hurt but he'd give her that, as long as she came back to him. His jaw tightened. "So talk."

"Did you send the letter to the Durban Trust?"

Whatever he'd expected, it wasn't that. "Why do you ask?"

"Because if it was you, Jay, it changes everything." She leaned back, her face carefully schooled into an unemotional mask, but he knew her better now. Her eyes glittered with a different emotion. Anger? Arousal? For all the times he'd made love to her, he couldn't tell that. Because they'd done it in the dark.

"Why?"

"Answer my question."

Lynne Connolly

He made an impatient gesture, nearly catching a crystal
lamp resting on the table next to the sofa. "Yes, I did. What of
it? You were never going to do it yourself."

Hurt. It was hurt he could see. And anger, rising to make
her dark eyes flash and obscure her pain.

"I had enough respect for myself. I was better than that."

"Bullshit! You know the world as well as I do. You lost
the anchor job to Carol." He sprang to his feet, glaring down at
her. "You're no fool, Whitney. You know that to stay on top in
our world you have to be beautiful as well as good at your job.
Don't pretend you don't." What was she saying, and why?
She'd been happy to accept the surgery. He hadn't forced her
into it, just pointed her in the right direction.

"It was for you. You fucked me, liked it, and you wanted
the pretty face to go with the body. Didn't you?" She almost
spat the last two words at him.

"No. I told you. I wanted you anyway."

"And I was easy. So easy."

He couldn't believe her. "I didn't make you do it. Did I?"

Her eyes glittered with more than anger, and moisture
dampened the corners. Jay resisted his violent desire to drag
her close and kiss it all better. She wouldn't want that and if
she pushed him away, it would kill him. "But you gave me
hope. You made me think that my face didn't matter that much.
Do you know what I'd thought about before I got that letter? I
even considered meeting my Stranger for a regular date. He'd
asked for one. Do you remember?"

He nodded. "And I meant it. I wanted a real
relationship."

"What, fucking in the light?"

He couldn't deny that part, but he wanted so much more
too. "And the rest. I wanted to look deep into your eyes, watch
your arousal, watch you come. I wanted to see your reactions,
not just feel them." He paused, hands clenched by his sides,

210

anger and frustration coursing through him. "Oh, what's the use?"

He strode to the other side of the room and growled. If it had been his apartment, he'd have punched a wall, just to feel the pain. But he'd leave a mark on her pristine white paintwork. So he couldn't. He spun back to face her, fury spiraling out of control, and inside it all, bewilderment forming the core. "You're determined to be a martyr, aren't you?" She'd suffered, sure, but she seemed to want to keep on suffering. Cause herself pain, if nobody else would do it for her. "So be one, Whitney. But not with me. I won't be your punching bag."

"Did I say you were?"

"I can see it happening. You'll whine that I made you have the work done, won't you? You'll hold it between us, use it as a weapon. Well, no more, baby. This isn't happening. I thought this would be a romantic evening before I have to leave for Moscow. You know I'm leaving in a couple of days, don't you? But no. You had to do this."

She stared at him, mouth agape. He didn't give her a chance. "Don't bother to see me out."

He strode down the street and walked, just walked. It must have taken some time, and he must have instinctively walked in the general direction of his own place in West Hollywood, because he looked up to find himself outside Grauman's Chinese Theater, with crowds of people walking around as they always did. Day and night, they were there.

Jay rarely found himself in this district, especially when there was no special event planned. He hadn't covered the social desk for a long time, so he'd never been one of the unfortunates dressed in an off-the-rack tuxedo waiting for the celebrities to arrive on the red carpet. Even in his younger, poorer days, he'd avoided that grisly fate. Nothing short of a miracle, considering he'd based his career in L.A.

Lookalikes thronged the sidewalk, posing for photos with the tourists, and people walked erratically, stopping abruptly to take pictures of their favorite celebrities' stars on the Walk of Fame.

He nearly fell over one group, and two of them turned and then did double-takes. *Shit.*

"You're Jay O'Brien!" one exclaimed in absolute delight.

Not tonight, please, not tonight. He'd walked miles in a daze, but now he was forced to snap his attention back. Only it wouldn't snap, wouldn't come. He stared at the girl. A teen or early twenties, pretty, blonde, with pretty blonde friends. Interesting that they'd all used the same shade of blonde, so they looked like weird copies of an original.

Bethany. That was who they'd copied. Except her shade was done with more expertise and soldered into place every night with nearly a whole can of hairspray. He knew because she'd complained to him bitterly about it. How the fuck did news anchors get groupies? "You're more gorgeous in real life!" one of them squealed. "Will you sign this?" She thrust a piece of paper at him, a paper bag from one of the nearby stores. They'd been shopping, he registered dully. They didn't sound Californian, but he couldn't place their accents. Everything seemed to be moving in slow motion and his mind even slower, so he couldn't catch up. Something was badly wrong.

"We came here to see you. We have tickets for the studio tour. Will you be there?"

He lifted his hand, his fist clenched, and they drew back, their gasps audible even in this crowded place. The moment seemed to last forever.

Jay unclenched his hand, signed the paper bag and shoved it back at her, staring as if she held the answer to his problem. What was this shit, when the people reading the news were given more importance than the news?

When he moved on he'd made his decision. Easy as that, the fork in the road opened and he left it behind. He knew what he had to do. He found his cell and hit speed dial.

Whitney listened to the door slam, sitting back in absolute astonishment. She'd wanted to talk to him, to get the subject aired and out of the way. But he'd blown up like a firecracker, accusing her of things she'd never done. Had she? She dashed her tears away with an angry hand. It wasn't her fault, fuck it, and if they were supposed to dance around the fact that he'd applied for her surgery for the rest of their lives, then perhaps it was better she knew now.

Knew what? She had no idea. That he was touchy, that he would blow up like that.

But something didn't ring true. She'd noticed Jay's volatility on more than one occasion in the office. Never as Stranger. But he'd been spikier than she remembered. Come to think of it, he'd always left first when they'd used a hotel room. She'd put it down to chivalry before now, but what if there was another reason? Like him not being able to sleep for long?

Forcing back her instinctive hurt, Whitney sat and thought. She thought while she tidied her apartment, while she showered and got ready for bed. It was half an hour before she picked up her phone and hit speed dial. "Nev? About that job..."

* * * * *

Today Whitney wasn't surprised when Nev called her into his office and asked her to shut the door, but what he said shocked her to the core. "I need you in Russia next week. Can you handle both conferences, or should I assign someone else?"

She stared at him, jolted out of her shock only when he snapped his fingers. "Come on, wake up."

Whitney cleared her throat. "Where's Jay?"

"Gone."

"Gone where?"

"I'm not at liberty to say."

She stared at him. "Why not?" she managed.

He shrugged. "I can't say. Truly I can't."

"You've sent him back to the battlefields, haven't you?" An awful thought grabbed her. "Even worse. Covert? You've sent him in with the SEALs?" That was the only reason she could think of right now why Nev wouldn't tell her where he was, or even what he was doing. "After what I told you last night?" She'd shared her concerns, and look what he'd done. "He's not fit to go, Nev. He could kill himself out there!"

"That was always a possibility." Nev didn't look happy. "He called me before you did and asked to be reassigned in the field. He didn't want the Russia job, he wanted you to have it. Wanted you to have a good run at the whole conference season. I have to say, I think it's a good idea. You get to go to the Moscow conference, then the Paris. You'll see what the themes are going forward, you'll be able to gauge the mood and how it changes. I can't make him do it."

"I didn't want him to go because he'd have gone straight to Afghanistan from Moscow." She frowned. "Has something happened? Something you can't tell me about? A new development in terrorism?" Bile rose to her throat. "If they get their hands on Jay, he's done for. He'll never survive. Nev, I think he's ill." Now it made sense, the way he'd exploded in her apartment, the way he'd turned into someone different.

Nev frowned. "You could be right. But short of kidnapping him and forcing him to get help, I can't do much about it."

"Aren't you worried?"

"He's a grown man. I'm his boss, not his nursemaid." He spread his hands in a gesture of helplessness. "Truly, Whitney, I'm bound to secrecy. I can't tell you. I'm sorry."

She spun around and stormed out, slamming the door so she didn't see Nev sink his head into his hands and utter a colorful string of curses, in all the languages he could think of.

Chapter Eleven

❧

Four months later, Whitney still had no idea where Jay was, but Nev had contacted her regularly with the news that he was still alive and at liberty. That was all she had. She'd done her best to forget him, but no dice. Nobody else would do, it seemed. She'd even dated a couple of men, and influential, powerful, good-looking ones they were. But they stirred nothing in her. Unfortunately they were perspicacious enough to know it too, and one questioned her about the man she'd left at home, suggesting he could help her to forget him. She gave him a chance but left him at her hotel room door. No comparison.

She bought new clothes, ones that didn't make her slide into the background, helped by the generous wardrobe allowance she received from NewsInc. She should have been in heaven. But every solitary night she found it hard to get to sleep, and when she did, she dreamed she lay in his arms, protected and warmed by his big body.

She sent messages to him, via Nev, and received brief ones back, messages she treasured, containing snippets of things only she could understand.

Sitting in her living room after what seemed like years away, she opened her laptop and read through the messages he'd sent. She didn't have to read them. She knew them by heart, but when she saw them it set up a link. One she increasingly needed.

Strangers meet in the night and connect.
I miss our collisions in the dark.
My soul is dark without you.

I'll keep a rose for you.

I'm here, you're there, like strangers communicating in the night.

Be well.

The last one worried her, because it could have come from anyone, but she'd received one more after that.

I'll see you when you get home. I'll come in the light this time.

He hadn't come yet and she'd been back a week. She planned to visit Ms. Hawthorne the next day. Georgina had responded warmly, with an invitation to call at two in the afternoon. Whitney's life was resuming. All but one part.

A knock at the door sent her heart leaping and she choked on a breath as her throat tightened. But it was nighttime. He said he'd come in the light, so she'd spent every day this last week on tenterhooks.

She was pathetic. She could have had an affair with a multimillionaire, a man with a quiet, authoritative style who'd have fascinated her in the old days. She could have stayed in Europe, worked for almost anyone she wanted. And here she was, back where she began, as if nothing had changed.

She checked her watch and wondered who was calling. She hadn't ordered pizza, she'd eaten an hour before. Seven p.m. Maybe Nev. He'd said he might drop by, to discuss something he didn't want to talk about in the office. Maybe he wanted a date, although he hadn't given her any indication that he was interested recently and she wouldn't date her boss.

Maybe she ought to think about moving on.

She went quietly to the door and glanced through the peephole. She'd had special one-way glass installed, but it was all she had right now, as her security camera needed a battery. The little screen showed nothing. The peephole did.

Instead of glancing, she stood and stared. Standing in the glare of her security light, there he was. As if he'd never been away. Except he seemed a little broader, more—powerful, somehow. Or something.

He glanced at the peephole and smiled.

She opened the door.

"Hello." He shifted from one foot to the other.

She smiled and pushed the door wider. "Come in," she said.

They didn't speak until they were sitting in the same sofas as before, facing each other. She didn't offer him a drink or food, not yet.

"Where have you been?" If he lied, she'd kick his ass out and never see him again.

"In this country," he said. His voice thrummed through her, touching every part of her being. "In a hospital."

Whatever she'd expected, it wasn't that. Shock reverberated through her. "You've been ill?" He didn't look ill. If anything, he looked stronger.

He leaned back, the muscles in his chest straining his navy T-shirt. "Yes."

"I find that hard to believe," she said, staring pointedly at his abs and moving her gaze to his pecs. No lower. Not yet.

"Not every illness leaves a scar." He sighed. "One you can see, at any rate." He dropped his head and stared at his hands, as if gathering courage. Then he lifted his chin and met her stare. "I've been in a mental institution. I lived there for a couple of months, then I moved back to my apartment but attended the place every day. I finally got my release papers. So to speak."

"Rehab?" She'd never seen any evidence of it, but functioning addicts were common in this town.

"No."

She came up with an answer, the one that had been lurking at the back of her mind for months. She closed her eyes and leaned her head back against the cushions of the sofa, staring at the ceiling. "You had PTSD."

"When you say it, it doesn't sound so bad."

She didn't look at him. Not until she'd blinked the pesky tears away. "I thought I had it once. Perhaps I did but it passed, so maybe it was just getting used to so-called civilization again after six months in the field." She lowered her chin and their gazes met.

His blue eyes appeared darker than usual, or perhaps the ambient lighting she preferred made them seem that way. A self-deprecating smile flickered across his lips and then disappeared. "It took me awhile to admit it. It'll pass, I told myself. Until that night I yelled at you and then left. I nearly hit you, Whitney. That terrified me as nothing else ever has. I had to leave and I couldn't trust myself to explain. I wasn't clear-headed. I walked for hours and ended up on Hollywood Boulevard. That place never sleeps. Ever. I nearly hit a woman there. I was violent, everything pent-up, but I didn't know *why*. That was when I knew something was badly wrong. That moment. The walk, and the shock of what I'd done to you, and then not remembering that walk…" He shrugged.

"You called Neville, didn't you?"

"Yeah. He'd been trying to get me to see a shrink for a while. That was why he kept me from going back in the field."

"And he didn't tell me." At that moment, she hated the manipulative bastard. "He knew if he told me, I'd never have gone to Russia, much less Paris. So he didn't tell me. I'd have come to you instead."

"I know. That's why I told him not to tell you. Told him I'd fucking shoot him dead if he even hinted at where I was. I wanted you to get that break. And you did it." The smile returned and she basked in it. "You did real good. Better than I would have done. You got them to tell you things they wouldn't have told their mothers. Fucking A."

"Thanks." His praise affected her more deeply than the raise Nev had given her or the emails she got from fans. He was damn good at his job, and he never praised unless he felt it was due. "I did my best. I'd have done it better with you."

"Not possible." He bit his lip. "It wasn't nice, Whitney. I didn't want you involved because there was nothing you could have done. I didn't want to hold you back. No." He gave an angry slash of his hand. "I needed to do this on my own. Rediscover myself. I slept most of the first month away. They gave me heavy narcotics, ones that meant I wouldn't dream, and I talked to a bunch of shrinks. They put me with soldiers, men who'd been in the thick of it, and I felt like a fraud but they were good. They always are.

"That helped, to share how I felt and to see men stronger than me collapse and then walk out of that place more or less intact." He paused and gave a self-conscious laugh. "I've got enough material for the next book. I managed to finish one and get it to my publisher, and now I have enough material for the next one. I must be a real writer. Using everything, good, bad and unpleasant."

"Have you used us?"

He gave her a wry smile. "I'm trying not to. I want to hug that to myself."

He got to his feet in one smooth movement. "Knowing you were there making a success of yourself was what helped me the most. I watched you on TV and cheered you on. So thanks. And thanks for the experience."

"You're going?"

"Don't want to get in your way." He moved around her sofa, careful not to touch it, as if he'd be able to feel her through it.

"What way?"

He shrugged. "You seemed friendly with Blaine." The millionaire she'd dated. She'd attended the opera with him in Paris, hoping to make more contacts. They must have been photographed plenty of times.

She shook her head. "It wasn't like that."

"Not by the way he was looking at you. You were all over the gossip blogs." He held up a hand when she would have gotten to her feet. "Hey, I wish you all the best. I'm just grateful you were there for me when I needed someone."

Truth time. Warmed by the fact that he couldn't hide the hurt he felt when he mentioned Blaine gave her the courage to tell him. "It really wasn't like that. He was interested but I wasn't. He took me to places I couldn't get into on my own, even with a press card. You know, restaurants, parties, the opera opening nights, that kind of place. With him, I wasn't the important one and I heard plenty. He was a sport, that was all. After I told him I didn't want to date him for real I expected him to disappear into the ether, but he didn't."

He gave a sound that was half laugh, half choke. "I might have known. You were very thorough with your information. Watching you and critiquing you kept me sane at times. Not that there was much to critique."

"Made you use that formidable brain." She got to her feet slowly, quietly.

He didn't move away. "I guess."

She took a small step. He stayed where he was. "I couldn't forget you. I wanted to. You made it clear you weren't available." Another step. "I've lost my sense of perspective where you're concerned. Lost everything. If you want to move on, then I guess I could cope." She'd arrived in front of him, barely half a step between them. Her breasts only just missed skimming his chest. Now it was up to him. "I want you. Do you want me?"

With a catch in her breath, she watched him, watched the flat broadcaster's face dissolve into sheer, unadulterated

221

want—eyes darkening, mouth softening. In a move so fast she didn't register it until he'd done it, he grabbed her waist and hauled her close, a groan reverberating through her mouth as her lips met his for their first kiss in months.

He made it swift, fierce and totally devastating, stopping to murmur, "Want is a poor word for it." Then he attacked again, taking her in a ravaging expertise that she surrendered to with only a slight whimper.

He took her mouth with a power that made her gasp when he lifted his lips away, then kissed her nose, her chin and began to work his way down before he paused. "Bedroom or here? I don't care but I need you now. Don't say no."

"No" hadn't crossed her mind for a minute. She took his hand and led him to her bedroom, not stopping until they reached the bed, where he took her in a hold she didn't have a hope of breaking, pressing her against him so their bodies met from mouths down to thighs. Heat seared through her, a mixture of arousal and need. He ground his erect cock against her, the insistent shaft heating her through his jeans and her clothes, as if they didn't exist. At her shudder, he paused. "Too much?"

It warmed her that he still thought of her well-being. "No. Not fast enough." Before his mouth descended onto hers again she added, "I'm still on the Pill. I'm game if you are."

He groaned against her lips. "Oh God, I won't last."

She touched his jaw. "Then don't. We have all night."

"More than that. Longer."

Maybe, but right now she didn't care about the future. Only now.

They helped each other out of their clothes, tossing them without looking, intent on getting each other naked. That was all that mattered now. She ran her hands over his broad chest, sliding up to his shoulders and gripping them to bring his head down to hers. He cupped her breasts, pinched her nipples, sending a delicious shot of pleasure-pain down to her pussy, and moved down before curving his arms around her waist and dragging her close. Her breasts mashed against his chest and she shifted against him to feel the delicious abrasion of the hairs sprinkled over it and his firm, male flesh. He closed his eyes and groaned. "Fuck, I've missed this. And there's one thing that's new, that I need more than my next breath."

She gazed up at him, loving the fraught moment of expectation, the lull before the storm. "What? You can have anything."

A wry grin curved his mouth. "That's more than I deserve, sweetheart. I want you to keep your eyes open. I want to see your orgasm build."

"The same goes for you. I want to see the desire in your eyes, to know you want me."

"You could have seen that anytime. I always wanted you. I always knew it was you."

It didn't hurt anymore, that he knew her. She'd caught up, come to terms with her surgery, her new life, recognized that she'd turned that big nose into an excuse. Her mom hadn't minded, not really, cared only that she was happy, and Jay had wanted her before and after.

Now she wanted him the same way. Before and after.

They fell onto the bed, so it was a good thing it was a sturdy piece of furniture. As it was, the wooden base creaked a little, but it held. Not that the mere collapse of a bed would have stopped them now. It probably would have passed unnoticed. He rolled her under him and kneed her legs apart, then paused to stare down at her, smiling. "Beautiful," he said. "Mine."

Before she could protest his chauvinist claim, he'd slid his cock against the wet crease, pausing at her clit, and she groaned, her eyes fluttering closed.

He stopped and she realized why. She opened her eyes.

Grinning, he touched the corner of one eye. "Make sure they stay that way."

"And you," she managed before he slid down and inside her. Even at this level of arousal, he had to push to gain entrance. She loved that, loved how the smooth head of his unencumbered cock moved past the tight ring of muscle at the entrance to her vagina to the wet depths inside. She cried out when he plunged deep, filled her for the first time in months.

He stared into her eyes, his arms braced on either side of her, his hands cupping her head so she couldn't look away. She stared up, felt the sensations below and gazed into the depths of his eyes, bright with arousal, the dark circle in the center expanded with the darkness of desire.

She saw it, the desire in his eyes, her need reflected back at her and increased tenfold by his own.

He began a rhythm, thrusting deeply, and she braced her body, pushed back. Slowly she slid her feet up his calves, his thighs, and up to his buttocks and waist, curving them around, feeling him sink deep, and then deeper still. His angle of entry changed and she gasped, pushing her head deep into the pillows.

But she didn't close her eyes.

Their visual connection enhanced what they were doing, their bodies combining, straining to bring each other pleasure. She forgot herself in him, let her body serve his, any way he wanted it, and he did the same. She didn't need him to tell her. She could see it.

Who could have imagined that simple missionary position could be so incendiary, more arousing than anything they'd done before?

He drove into her without mercy and she pushed back, raising her hips off the bed with her eagerness to meet him, to feel his cock slide past that spot inside her with each powerful thrust. They didn't speak, not finding the need for words, their communication deeper and more complete. Their gasps and groans were the only sounds in the room except for the creaking of the bed, and that didn't affect either of them.

Slowly her excitement rose and he saw it, watched it, nurtured it to a full flowering. When she cried his name as the first spasm racked her body, he reminded her. "Keep — them — open."

She forced her eyes wide, stared at him. He stared back so she saw his reaction, his wince when he started to come. They came together, gasps and cries punctuating the spasms that rocked them below. She cinched her legs tight, holding him inside her for every last drop of his semen. She wanted it all, and he gave it.

She blew his mind. Just fucking incinerated him. He held her close to his chest, felt her soft breaths ease then quicken as she woke. A pause, then she kissed his nipple. "I love you," she said.

"I love you too." He didn't have to think about it. He'd murmured it to her while she slept, hoped she heard. Now she heard for sure.

She lifted her head, her dark hair catching on his heated skin. "You don't have to say it."

"I know. I said it because I wanted to. Because I needed to tell you."

"Where do we go from here?" She rolled onto her stomach and he pulled her back. Propping her chin on one hand, she smiled at him. "What next?"

"Who knows? What do you want to do?"

"Want?" She frowned, then smiled, the sun breaking out after a squall. "I don't want to work for NewsInc anymore."

"After your success? I bet the offers are pouring in. Is that it? You're going to move for the money?"

She shook her head. "Not for the money, no. Nev's done his best, but Mattson keeps contacting us, telling us what slant to put on the stories. 'Don't forget who you're representing', stuff like that. Having long conversations, trying to wear us down. Not just me but my co-presenter and the others. I got it out of Nev last week, and he gets it worse than we do."

"What's he planning?"

She shrugged. "He won't tell me directly but I can guess. He'll resign. If he leaves and then I join him right away, he could be accused of poaching. So I won't ask. But I don't want this gig anymore. Mattson's the definition of dumbing down and I don't want it."

"Do you have anything else in mind?" He lifted a hand and stroked her hair, now in a sexy, tousled mane. "Or do you expect me to keep you?" He'd asked that to get the reaction he did.

Her eyes sparked and she thumped his chest with her free hand. "The fuck I do. I have a contract from Georgina Hawthorne for an authorized biography, so that'll keep me busy for a while. And now I've cracked old Hollywood, I can get a few more contracts like that, if I want them."

"You worked so hard to get in front of the camera." He cupped her cheek. "Do you really want to stop?"

"I loved doing the job. But I can give it a rest while I work on the biography. I have enough to keep me in bread and rent and then some, so I can stop and think. I can join Nev after six months if I resign now. And let the other offers dangle. My agent can do that for me."

"Ha. He won't be happy about that."

"She. I'm switching agents too." She grinned at him. "Your turn. What next?" A cloud crossed her features. "Are you well enough? Do you have to go back? You know I'll be there for you, whatever, however. Always."

He hauled her up for a kiss. He made it long and sweet and afterward, pulled her onto his chest. "I'm fine. Or I will be. A bit more therapy and I'm done. Cured. Or as cured as I'll ever be."

"Was it bad?"

"Yes."

She winced. "I can guess. I had nightmares for a while, when I got back from 'Stan. But they passed."

"Mine didn't." He smiled. "But they're nearly gone now, and I know how to cope with them. They taught me a technique." His smile deepened, his eyes crinkling at the corners. "I know a better way now. If I hold you all night, you'll keep them at bay."

"Will you go back to work?"

"Maybe. Probably. I don't know yet. Not for another six months, at least. I have a book to write." He paused. "And a screenplay."

She put her hands on the mattress and pushed up, giving him a delicious view of her breasts. "Really? They optioned it?"

"Top drawer. Signed Tom Vernon for the main role."

She laughed. "The latest action hero. He can't compete with you though, you're the real thing."

He couldn't stand any more. He hauled her up, letting his cock find its way between her legs. "Shut up and fuck me, love of my life."

BEDHEAD

Shoshanna Evers

ഔ

Dedication

ഌ

*Dedicated to a childhood friend whose wedding invitation
in the mail sparked my imagination.*

Chapter One

ഇ

Michele Peterson looked up at the ceiling fan, which seemed to just waft the stifling hot air around her tiny one-bedroom apartment rather than do its job. Beads of perspiration covered her upper lip, and she knew without glancing in the mirror that her face was bright pink, flushed with heat.

"I need a beer," she announced to no one.

An image of an icy cold bottle settled into her mind, straight out of a beer commercial. Snow-capped mountains and whatnot. Michele sighed with pleasure at the thought. All right—she'd have to make herself decent to go out, even if she just went down to 107th and Broadway to the corner market.

She grabbed the heavy blonde wig off the mannequin head and pulled it on, the scratchy weight of it already making her feel about twenty degrees hotter. She may as well be wearing a wool hat in the middle of a New York summer.

The synthetic wig's bangs hung low across her forehead, hiding the fact that her eyebrows, like her eyelashes and the hair on her head, were almost completely gone. Her hair had fallen out a few months after her seventh birthday and, after running a bunch of tests that proved she was completely healthy, her doctors gave her and her mom the diagnosis—alopecia areata. Not much she could do about it, though god knows they both tried. Almost twenty years later, and her hair had never grown back to its former glory. Some bits stuck out of her head in patches—short crinkly hairs, almost like the scant hair she was too embarrassed to have a bikini-waxer remove.

231

I can't go outside without the damn wig. When she went out bald, everyone treated her as if she were a cancer patient or something. As if she were sick and suffering through chemotherapy. Perhaps if she'd lost her hair from chemo she'd be able to look at her lack of hair as a battle scar from a war she'd fought and won. She wished she could go back in time and make child-Michele a T-shirt that said *I'm not sick — I'm bald.* And then another T-shirt that said *If you're reading this shirt, congratulations — you're not staring at my head.*

Michele sighed. If she ever had a kid with alopecia, she'd make her snarky shirts at one of those design-your-own-shirt places online. Not like that would ever happen. She'd need to have sex to have a kid, and what man would want to screw a bald chick? A twenty-six-year-old *virgin* bald chick. That was just bad mojo right there.

Brushing the wig into place, she grabbed her keys and walked down the four flights to the street. Just for now she decided to forgo the false eyelashes she usually applied, although her lashless eyes also made her look, well...off, somehow. At least to her.

The dirty city air outside hit her thick and heavy, covering her body with a fine layer of yuck she'd have to shower off later. She walked toward the corner market, barely noticing the other people brushing past her on the crowded sidewalk.

"Hi, Mr. Patel," she called as she stepped into the store.

The owner smiled and waved back before returning his attention to the long line of customers. Michele went straight to the refrigerated wall stocked with beer and milk and grabbed a six-pack of Amstel Light. A tall guy — with a thick head of gorgeous brown hair — reached over next to her and grabbed the same thing.

"Great minds think alike," he said, smiling at her.

He had a five-o'clock shadow. Lucky bastard. He was probably covered in hair. He wore a simple T-shirt but an expensive watch, an enticing combination.

She smiled back at him. *He's cute.* But she wasn't wearing her eyelashes. She looked awful. Turning away, she took a deep breath. *Chill out.*

"Oh, yuck," the cute guy exclaimed. "That couldn't feel good on your head."

Oh. My. God.

She turned back to him, horrified. Usually people had at least some semblance of manners and didn't point out the wig.

Holy fucking shit.

"Wh-what?" she stammered.

"The air conditioner," the guy said, pointing straight up above them. "It looked like it dripped nasty runoff water right on your head. You didn't feel that?"

Michele reached up and patted the top of her wig experimentally. Wet.

"Eww," she said, laughing nervously.

Of course she couldn't feel anything falling on the wig, it wasn't really her scalp or her hair. But he didn't know that.

He pulled out a clean handkerchief and reached out to touch her head.

"No!" she cried, pulling away.

"I'm sorry," the guy said, taking a step back. He put his hands in the air, like *I surrender.* "I just moved here from Ohio—I keep forgetting that New Yorkers don't want to talk to strangers."

"What? That's not true. I don't want you...groping me, that's all." He'd hardly been groping her, and now she felt a bit silly.

"Of course," he said, looking suitably embarrassed, although he hadn't actually done anything wrong. "I'm Andrew Calhoun, by the way. I swear I'm not as weird as I seem."

Michele laughed. "I believe you. I'm Michele." She stuck her hand out and he gripped it, his hand large and surprisingly cool compared to her heated, sweaty palm. Maybe from holding the beer.

"So, are you a native New Yorker?" Andrew asked. "You've got a bit of an accent."

"Really? This is nothing compared to some of my friends," she said. "But yeah, born and raised." She hefted her six-pack and joined the long line of customers waiting for Mr. Patel to ring them up.

Andrew stood behind her, holding his beer and a bag of chips.

"Long line," he commented.

"Uh huh."

"You know, there's a bar across the street," he said. "I mean, of course you know. You live here. You think it's air-conditioned?"

"Should be," she said. Could the hot guy be flirting with her?

"Can I buy you a drink? I bet we'll get served ten minutes before this guy ever gets to us."

He just asked her out. Definitely. Even though she wasn't wearing her eyelashes and she had nasty runoff water on her wig. Should she go? No, definitely not. Well, what the hell. This kind of thing didn't happen every day...or any day, really. "Sure!"

Too desperate. Chill.

Shrugging as if she didn't really care too much either way, she took his six-pack and set it next to hers back in the fridge area of the store and left his chips. They walked out together, and Michele wanted everyone to see her with the cute guy—to know they were going to get a drink together. *Look at me, Mr. Patel,* she thought. She'd been shopping there for two years, but never with a guy.

Someday I'm gonna come in here and buy condoms from behind the counter. And I won't even blush.

234

She sighed. *Yeah, right.*

Andrew's large hand touched the small of her back, gently guiding her off the curb and across the street. She reveled in his touch, feeling the heat of his hand through her light tank top.

It took a moment for her eyes to adjust to the dim light in the blissfully air-conditioned bar. Andrew led her to the bar, where a few guys sat entranced by a game on the overhead television.

"Two Amstel Lights," Andrew asked the bartender and patted an empty barstool. She sat, balancing precariously on the wobbly seat, but Andrew just stood there next to her, leaning his elbow on the bar counter. "Thanks for coming with me," he said. "This is the first Sunday I've had in New York since I finished unpacking stuff."

"Wow, you really are fresh off the bus," she said, laughing.

"Yeah. Don't mug me." He grinned and slipped a tip to the bartender when their drinks showed up, thick drops of cold condensation on the bottle. "Just like a beer commercial," he said, taking a long gulp.

"I was just thinking that!" she said, doing the same and, remembering what he'd said earlier added, "Great minds think alike."

"Oh, this is weird. I was just thinking *that.*"

She giggled, feeling tipsy even though she'd barely drunk half her beer.

"Sorry I groped you before. It's not my style."

"Oh come on, you didn't really grope me and you know it," Michele said. "I just get uncomfortable when someone grabs at my head."

"Why?"

Um. Really?

Did Andrew really not recognize she wore a wig? That she had no eyelashes or eyebrows?

Tell him. You have to tell him or it's just wrong.

And if she didn't, when he found out he'd feel as though she lied to him.

Just tell him now and get it over with.

But sitting there in the dim bar, feeling desirable for the first time in a long time, she couldn't do it. Couldn't tell him that under the wig, she was bald.

If only I had hair.

If she had her own real hair she could finally feel comfortable having sex with a man, she just knew it. She even wrote an email to the Durban Trust to see if she could be a beneficiary of one of their generous cosmetic surgery grants. She attached a picture of herself without the wig on and everything, and told the truth for the first time in writing — that she needed hair so she could lose her virginity. Feel a man's hands tangled in her hair, tugging on her ponytail, smoothing the sweat-covered strands from her forehead after a night of lusty sex.

She must've scared the hell out of them because the Trust retained a psychotherapist who called and gave her a phone consultation about the whole thing. That was two weeks ago, and she never heard from them again. She'd avoided checking on the status of her query because she really didn't feel like hearing the rejection. And she certainly couldn't afford to pay for hair transplant surgery on her own.

So if this was her only chance to feel beautiful, right now in this bar with this hot guy, then she had to just go for it.

Michele shrugged and took another sip of her beer to avoid answering Andrew's question about why she didn't want him going near her head. Why wasn't she over this by now? Twenty years of being bald hadn't really gotten easier with time. Especially when she met someone new. *The woman who won Miss Delaware that time — she has alopecia too,* Michele reminded herself. *She's not ashamed to go out bald or with a wig, she feels beautiful either way.*

Andrew gazed into her eyes and all her thoughts of wigs and baldness and feeling uncomfortable dissolved. "You're gorgeous," he said.

Michele laughed. "Okay, I think you've had enough to drink."

"I'm serious. And you have such beautiful long hair. I love blondes."

Michele felt her excitement wash away as suddenly as if he had dumped a whole bucket of water on her.

"I said something wrong," he said, reaching out for her hand as she turned to get off the barstool. "I'm sorry, I put my foot in my mouth. You probably get hit on all the time. I didn't mean to upset you."

Is this guy blind or what?

"No, you didn't upset me," she lied. "I just realized what time it was. I have to go. Thanks for the beer."

She slid off the barstool, flashed what she hoped was a friendly smile, and walked outside. The thick city heat hit her and she took a shaky breath. She really had to talk to her landlord about the broken air-conditioning. If it hadn't been so hot in her apartment, she'd never have come out and met Andrew—and never gotten her hopes up for nothing.

"Hey!"

Michele turned at Andrew's voice behind her.

"Here's my card," he said, handing her a white business card. *Andrew Calhoun, Advertising Executive*, it read.

So he knew all about the importance of packaging and image. And he liked blondes.

"Thanks," she said, plucking the card from his hand. The walk light hadn't changed yet but Michele just wanted to get away so he wouldn't see her cheeks burning with embarrassment. She stepped into the street, a yellow cab honking as she came within inches of its tires.

She half walked, half ran all the way back to her four-story walk-up with the broken air conditioner. Bolting the door behind her, Michele sat on the threadbare couch in the middle of the apartment and fought back tears of frustration.

If I had hair, this wouldn't have happened, she thought miserably. They'd still be at the bar, talking, flirting and maybe getting a little tipsy. Then she'd invite him back to her place and they'd fuck each other silly.

She tore the wig off her head, relishing in the feel of air on her sweaty scalp. Grime from the runoff water that had fallen on her wig coated a few of the synthetic strands. She stood with a sigh and carried the wig to the sink, where she washed and combed it before setting it back on the mannequin head.

He loves blondes. God she was a moron. Why'd she even accept Andrew's invitation in the first place? She'd already known where it would go—nowhere. It certainly wouldn't have ended up in bed, which was where she most wanted to see Andrew.

An image of his impressive physique showing through his T-shirt flitted through her mind. She should have just told him she was bald immediately, as soon as the water hit her head. She could've just said, "Oh, I didn't notice the nasty water hitting my head because this is a wig. Obviously." But apparently it hadn't been so obvious to Andrew.

She should call him and explain herself. Maybe he'd still want to see her, just as friends. He was new to Manhattan, after all. Pulling his now sweat-rumpled business card out of her pocket, she sighed. Now or never.

Checking the number on the card carefully, she sent a text that took ten minutes to word properly but that she hoped sounded off-the-cuff.

Sorry bout that, no hard feelings? -Michele

He texted back quickly.

No prob, drinks tonight, same bar @ 8p?

Whoa. Okay. No, wait. She had to work tomorrow. But…all the other customer service reps came into the office hungover on Monday mornings. Why shouldn't she? It was about time she got a life. It's not as though she had to do brain surgery.

Just one more text to tell him the truth.

I'm not really blonde, this is a wig. I'm bald.

But she couldn't hit send. Sighing, she pressed erase and wrote *See you at 8.*

* * * * *

The sun started to go down as she got ready to go out with Andrew. Michele carefully applied her false eyelashes, which looked pretty natural all things considered. With a fine-point, smudge-proof eyebrow pencil, she drew on eyebrows and then let her long-banged wig cover them. Not bad. She just hoped he didn't try to touch her hair when they kissed.

Yup, she'd already decided to kiss him. All she wanted was a taste of him, really, before he found out the truth and she went from being his date to his platonic friend.

She walked slowly down the street to the bar, relishing the break from the stifling heat in the mild summer night air. Andrew was already waiting at the bar, nursing something amber-colored on the rocks.

He stood when she stepped through the door.

"Thanks for meeting me," he said, smiling.

Damn, he looked hot. He'd changed into a dark, fitted button-down shirt and jeans that probably cost him two hundred bucks.

"Sure." Michele smiled back and resisted the urge to smooth her wig, not wanting to draw attention to it.

"I promise not to hit on you again," he said, "since that seemed to have the opposite effect I meant it to have this afternoon. But can I at least buy you a drink?"

Michele laughed and nodded. "I'm in the mood for a frozen margarita."

The bartender handed her the frosty drink a few moments later and she took a big sip, trying to gain some liquid courage.

"You don't have to worry about hitting on me," she told Andrew, resting her hand on his knee. "I won't mind."

Andrew chuckled and placed his hand over hers. His looked so huge compared to hers. She lifted his hand and pressed hers flat against it, sizing up the difference.

"Big ugly hands, I know," he said.

"No, these are great hands."

"I got a paper cut today on a cardboard box when I was getting them all ready for recycling," he said, pointing to a red mark on the side of his palm.

"Ouch."

"Yeah, ouch."

With the ice broken, Michele was amazed at how quickly they both got into the groove of conversation. The next half hour flew by.

This guy was so sweet—certainly nicer and funnier than any guy she'd ever gone out with before. Not that she had much experience in the dating department. She giggled to herself, the tequila in the frozen margarita making her feel especially easygoing.

She asked him all sorts of questions about advertising, both to keep the conversation flowing and to ascertain just how important he thought looks were. He seemed passionate about his career, and he didn't even seem bothered by her rather lame job as a telephone customer service representative.

"I'm taking some time off to reevaluate my priorities," she said, even though he hadn't asked. For some reason she always felt she had to defend living a non-workaholic lifestyle.

"That sounds awesome." He took a sip of his drink. "I did the same thing before I went to grad school."

"Really?" He seemed so pulled together, she couldn't imagine him working a dead-end job while he sorted through his options.

"Really. It's worth it." He smiled and then pulled her hand toward him so she was only an inch away from his face. "If I kiss you will you run away again?"

This is it.

Her taste before it all fell apart. She shook her head and kissed him, reveling in the softness of his lips and the roughness of his cheek against hers. He slipped his tongue into her mouth and she welcomed it, tasting scotch.

He touched her face, cradling it, and it felt so...right. So nice that she even forgot to be worried about his hands being so close to her wig.

And then he tangled his hands in her wig, probably thinking it was her hair. She gasped against his mouth as she felt the wig shift back across her forehead and pulled away quickly.

"Shit," Andrew said. "I did something wrong again. Was it slipping you the tongue? Too soon?"

Michele straightened her wig discreetly. "No, not too soon."

Tell him, tell him, tell him, tell him!

She opened her mouth but no words came out. Instead, she stood and kissed him fiercely, grabbing his hands so they'd stay out off her head and pulling them tight around her waist.

"Come back to my place," he murmured against her lips.

No way. Yes way. No way. "Okay. Yes."

They walked out of the bar holding hands. Could she really do this? She'd just met Andrew. She made it this far without ever having sex—could she really go through with it tonight?

Yes. She could do it...because Andrew was a stranger. He didn't know she was bald, and since she'd only just met him today then it shouldn't matter to her if she scared him off and never saw him again. Right?

She'd just have to figure out a way to have sex without him discovering her hair wasn't real. But he was bound to try to touch her wig again. That's what people did during sex, or so she imagined.

Andrew also lived in a building with no elevator, but fortunately he was on only the second floor. By the time he unlocked his apartment door, she was ready to call the whole thing off, despite her damp panties and her undeniable lust for him.

He kissed her deeply the moment the door closed, lifting her up against the wall so she could straddle his hips with her thighs. *Oh god, this is all happening so fast.*

He supported her easily, as if she weighed nothing at all. The bulge in his jeans poked against her mound and she moaned, grinding against him, forgetting all about her hair or lack thereof and focusing completely on Andrew's hands on her body.

"Show me the bedroom," she whispered.

He groaned in response, kissing her harder, and then...her wig slid off. Completely, utterly off her head and onto the floor. She felt it immediately but it took him an agonizing two seconds to realize what he'd done with his wandering hands.

Michele gasped in surprise and a sudden burst of anger toward him. She pushed against him, forcing his muscular torso out of her way so she could get down on her own two feet and pick up the damn wig.

Hot tears of embarrassment slid down her cheeks and she swiped at her eyes as she struggled to put the wig back on.

Chapter Two

Andrew stared at Michele in surprise. Her long blonde hair was a wig? He'd never have guessed, perhaps because it just never would have occurred to him to think it might be. Some brown, short crinkly hairs stood out on her mostly bald head in patches. Her eyes were red and weepy as she quickly pulled the wig on.

"Michele?"

He didn't know what to say, what to do. It wasn't fair — he'd finally found a woman he could talk to and laugh with, a woman who turned him on like crazy, and she was sick. Had to be. Chemo made people lose their hair.

"Oh god, Michele," he whispered, pulling her in close despite her stiffness in his arms. "You have cancer."

"I do not have cancer," she spat. "I'm perfectly healthy."

"But, why — "

"It's called alopecia, okay? I'm bald, that's all. Don't worry, I won't make this any more awkward than it already is. I'll leave now." She squirmed in his arms and he released her.

"Wait," he said, touching her arm. "Why do you have to leave?"

"Are you serious?"

"I'm so sorry I upset you. I know I'm not smooth and I'm so embarrassed — "

"You?" she asked incredulously. "You're embarrassed? How do you think I feel?"

Andrew shook his head. "As long as you're not sick, that's all that matters. I don't care that you're wearing a wig."

244

He paused, thinking about what he'd just said. Was it true? Did he really not care Michele was bald?

She was still a beautiful woman, even without the wig. And now that he knew her baldness wasn't indicative of cancer, he felt so relieved that she probably could have been missing a limb and he wouldn't have been turned-off.

"You're still hot," he said finally.

She snorted and folded her arms over her chest.

"I mean it."

Michele glanced pointedly down at his groin. He'd lost his erection. Sighing, he dropped his arms from her waist.

"That's what I thought," she whispered, her voice sounding raw and hurt.

"Gimme a break," Andrew said. "I literally thought you were dying. Of course that made me go limp. But now that I know you're okay, I can easily prove to you that you still turn me on."

"If I lost my hair from chemo, it would mean I was getting treatment, not that I was dying anyway. I would be a survivor. Instead I'm just—"

"Beautiful," he interrupted.

Michele raised her drawn-on eyebrows. "Yeah, right."

Damn it.

Andrew pulled her against him and kissed her, forcing away the last two minutes from his memory so he could concentrate on the feel of her sweet lips on his. She let out a small sigh of pleasure and he ran his hands up over her breasts, dipping one finger below her neckline to touch the lacy bra beneath her shirt.

He started to pull her shirt up over her head but stopped himself. If he did that her wig would end up on the floor again and Michele would never forgive him twice for the same stupid mistake.

"I have an idea," she whispered.

245

"Okay." He held her tight against him, letting her feel his thick cock hard against her thigh. She really did still turn him on. There was something about her that made all his hormones go into overdrive. He felt like a horny teenager again.

"I'll go into the bathroom and get naked," she said. "Then I won't have to worry about you tearing my ugly wig off again."

"Or you could just leave it off so we don't have to worry about it," he suggested. "Either way. And it's not ugly."

"I may be about to fuck you, but I don't know you well enough to be with you without my hair on. I can only be one kind of naked with you."

"You have to stop saying the word naked if you want me to keep my hands to myself," he said.

She smiled doubtfully and walked toward the bathroom. He smacked her ass as she went, eliciting a delightful yelp.

Michele closed the bathroom door behind her and took a deep breath. Her worst nightmare had just come true. She stared at herself in the mirror and grabbed some toilet paper to wipe her eyes, being careful not to dislodge the fake eyelashes.

Her wig came off in front of the one man she wanted to be totally sexy and desirable in front of. But...the world didn't come to a crashing halt, as she'd always sort of imagined it would. He did go soft though, and he'd stared at her with a look of pure horror that she'd never forget.

Why, why did he have to be so damn sweet? What if he was really grossed out, and just didn't want to hurt her feelings? Was this—her very first time having sex—going to be a pity fuck? Or something that he'd laugh about later with his buddies?

She could imagine the conversation.

So get this, guys. I bring this chick back to my place to bang, and her hair plops right off her head onto the floor! And I still banged her.

246

Yeah, they'd probably all lose their shit over that one. Big fucking joke.

Forget it. Straightening her wig, she stepped out of the bathroom. Andrew's face fell when he saw her still fully dressed.

"I'm sorry," she said. "I can't do this."

"Okay," he said. "I don't want to pressure you into anything you don't want to do."

Ha. More like he didn't want to be stuck pity-fucking a bald chick. Michele forced a smile on to her face and shrugged. But he really did look dejected. Could he really want to be with her, even after seeing her without her wig?

"Look, Andrew, you're a stranger, so I'm going to be straight with you. I'm a virgin." She felt herself blush at the words but she pushed on. If she didn't tell him everything now she never would, and then she'd never see him again. "I've never felt comfortable enough about the whole alopecia thing to have sex with a man, and having you take my wig off was probably one of the most embarrassing things that's ever happened to me."

"Oh god, I am so sorry, Michele, I really am," he said, grasping her hands in his. His hands felt so large and warm and comforting. "And if I'd known you were a virgin I would have probably not come on so strong. And now I've completely scared you off."

Hearing the sincerity in Andrew's voice, Michele found herself smiling. "Actually, I'm pretty sure that I've completely scared *you* off."

"Great minds think alike," he said.

She laughed at what had quickly become their inside joke. "I'm not so easily scared."

"Me neither." He leaned in and kissed her tentatively, pausing as if to ask her implicit permission. She responded by kissing him back, running her hands along his broad shoulders.

"I'm not ready to have sex with you," she admitted.

"That's fine, I understand," he said. "We just met."

"For some reason I thought it'd be easier with a stranger."

Andrew shrugged. "Let me play with you. We don't have to have sex."

"Promise me you won't go anywhere near my wig."

Andrew looked chagrined but he nodded, pulling her toward him by her waist, his fingers on her waistband. "Someday you'll let me touch of all you," he said, unzipping her fly. He slid his hand into her panties, running his thumb over her clit. Michele gasped, loving the sensation.

Forget what happened with the wig. Just have fun.

Andrew knelt on the floor in front of her and tugged her pants down around her ankles. She stumbled trying to spread her legs as her feet tangled in her clothes. Andrew laughed and steadied her. "You only had one drink," he said, pulling her panties down.

"I'm not drunk," she assured him, gasping when he spread her labia with his large hand. "Oh my god. I can't believe I'm doing this."

He looked up at her, pausing. "Is it okay?"

"Don't stop."

He grinned. "Baby, I haven't even gotten started." He licked her pussy, spreading her folds with his tongue.

Michele moaned, running her fingers through his thick hair, pulling the strands the way she wished he could do to her. If only she could afford the hair transplant surgery she so desperately needed.

Andrew flicked her clit with his tongue in a pulsating rhythm and suddenly she couldn't think about her self-conscious worries or her hair or even the fiasco with the wig falling off.

She couldn't think—just feel. Michele moaned, holding Andrew's face to keep him where she needed him as she crested on the edge of orgasm. He gave her a little nibble and she moaned in pleasure, her head snapping forward to her chest as she came hard.

He lapped at her cream, kissing all the way down her inner thighs, holding her ass in his hands.

"Thank you," she whispered, feeling winded. He stood, still fully clothed. "I've made a mess of your hair," she giggled.

"I liked how you ran your fingernails over my scalp," he said, kissing her. "Someday maybe you'll let me return the favor."

She could taste her own musk on his lips and she kissed him deeper, loving the naughty taste of her own pussy.

"Stop talking about someday, Andrew," she whispered. "Please, please don't push me. Just being here after what happened is a huge deal for me, do you understand that?" She smiled to soften her words.

"I'm glad you stayed."

"I'd like to suck your cock," she said. He grinned and started to unzip his fly. "Wait."

"What's wrong?"

"I don't want to kneel in front of you. I won't be able to do this if I'm worried you're going to touch my hair like I did to you before."

Andrew groaned inwardly, but he understood where she was coming from. "Michele, maybe it's not my place to say this, but do you make all of your decisions based on your alopecia?"

She looked offended. "No." She sighed and kicked her pants off from her around her ankles so she could stand straighter.

The sight of her in her blouse with no panties or pants on made his erection throb.

249

"I told you, I'm a virgin. So I've probably made every sexual decision in my life based on alopecia. But that's it. Just sex."

"Sex is a big deal."

"Not if you're not having any," she countered.

"You're wrong, Michele," he said softly. "Then it's an even bigger deal. I don't want to do anything you're not ready for. But I've already seen you without the wig, and I'm still here, still hard and ready for you. That has to count for something, right?"

Michele tilted her head to one side as if considering his response. "Enough talk about the wig. Pretend you don't know, please, Andrew, for my sake."

"Pretend I don't know you're really...bald?"

The look of need in her eyes swayed him.

"Okay," he said. "If that's what you want."

"What I want," she said, her voice low and seductive, "is for you to strip."

Andrew laughed, nodding. He slowly unbuttoned his shirt, taking it off, enjoying the look of anticipation in her eyes. He worked out every day at lunch in his office, and he was proud of the physique he'd built. He rarely had the opportunity to see the look of appreciation on a woman's face though, that Michele gave him.

She ran her hands over his chest, lightly touching his nipple, hardening it into a tight pebble. "Take off your pants, Andrew," she whispered.

"Anyone ever tell you that you don't sound much like a virgin?" he teased, but he did as she requested. His cock stuck out, thick and erect, a drop of pre-cum clinging to his tip.

Michele turned around, giving him a fabulous view of the pale white globes of her ass. He ran his fingers over her smooth skin, noting for the first time that she was completely hairless, without even a hint of fine hairs or stubble.

"Would you get me one of your neckties?" she asked, looking toward his bedroom.

"Is this a formal event?" he joked.

"If you want me to suck your cock," she said, turning back toward him sweetly, "you have to go sit on the couch. And then you have to let me tie your hands behind your back."

Andrew's cock twitched at her words. *Holy shit.* "Done." He grabbed the first tie he saw from his closet and walked across the living room, picking up his cotton undershirt to cover the leather couch before he sat down. He didn't want his sweaty ass-print on it.

Hers, on the other hand, he'd be happy to have on his couch.

Michele grinned and straddled his thighs, carefully holding herself up by her thighs, keeping her wet pussy inches away from his aching cock. She reached around behind him as if to hug him, and he felt his tie binding his wrists together. The whisper of silk on his wrists made another drop of pre-cum drip out of his cock. He could feel it rolling down the side of his shaft.

Michele got off his lap and eyed him, studying her handiwork. Damn, he looked good, his broad, muscular body sprawled on his leather couch, his legs spread lewdly. And best of all, his hands bound behind his back with his own silk tie. Michele felt her pussy clench in anticipation.

Now she felt in control of the situation Now she could focus on pleasure, and not on worrying about what his busy hands were doing near her wig. Maybe someday, if she ever got her hair transplant, she'd never have to worry about that again.

In the meantime, some light bondage did the trick nicely.

She'd fantasized about doing this for years. Played it all out in her mind. Of course, in her fantasy the man she'd been with had never accidentally pulled off her wig, had never even known about her wig. In her fantasy she met a stranger and tied him up right away so he'd never have the chance to find out. Then he'd be at her complete mercy.

"I may be a virgin," she said, kneeling in front of him, stroking his thighs, "but I have a very active imagination."

"Oh yeah?" Andrew responded, his voice throaty.

Michele licked the trail of pre-cum from the tip of his cock to his balls. "I've imagined doing this for so long."

She'd imagined doing it so many times, in fact, that as nervous as she was on the inside, she was still managing to act as boldly as she'd always fantasized she would.

Nice.

He groaned as she swirled her tongue around the head of his cock, licking the slit, bringing forth another glistening jewel of moisture. His arms flexed as if he made a move to reach for her and then remembered he was tied up.

Laughing, Michele sucked his cock into her mouth, swallowing as she took him in, inch by inch, before pulling her head back and plunging onto him once more.

"Holy shit, baby, where'd you learn to do that?" he groaned.

She ignored him, sucking harder, loving his salty taste. No reason he needed to know she learned how to suck cock by reading a how-to book. 'Cause that was pretty lame.

Let him think whatever he wanted. She swallowed around his cock and gently fondled his balls, weighing them in her hands.

His cock pulsed in her mouth and suddenly he moaned. "I'm coming."

A hot jet of cum hit the back of her throat and she swallowed hungrily, pulling every last drop from him. When she finished, she stood and smiled at him. He'd laid his head back on the couch cushion and was breathing heavily, his eyes closed.

"I had a great time," she whispered, giving him a peck on the cheek. She reached around behind him and undid the slipknot easily. "But I'm really not ready to have, you know, actual intercourse."

"I understand," he said, his eyes glazed with satisfaction. "Give me a moment to recover and I'll walk you home," he paused, "Unless you want to sleep over, in which case I'd love that."

She couldn't sleep over though, surely he knew that. She didn't sleep in her wig, and she wasn't about to spend the night with Andrew bald. Maybe she really did make important decisions based on her alopecia.

Sighing, she shook her head. "I have to go to work tomorrow morning."

"Okay. I don't want to pressure you."

"Thanks for not running away screaming about the alopecia thing," she said finally, pulling on her clothes.

"I know it's probably a big deal to you," Andrew said. "But it's really not that big of a deal to me. You're still beautiful."

Despite the sincerity in his tone, Michele couldn't bring herself to believe him. Would she ever feel whole, even without hair?

Chapter Three

ॐ

Michele stood in her shower, washing away the sweat from the hot day. Her pussy still felt swollen from Andrew's earlier attentions. She grinned as she lathered up her body and scalp, feeling the patchy areas of hair that grew on her head. She used a volumizing conditioner on the little hair she did have, not that it helped.

She'd had such an amazing time with Andrew. Thank goodness he'd let her tie him up. Otherwise she wouldn't have been able to blow him and really get into it the way she'd done. She loved the feeling of power she had, eliciting those sexy groans from him as she sucked his cock.

Tonight could have gone really badly. He could have been angry with her for lying about the wig, or he could have been disgusted and thrown her out. Neither response would have surprised her. In fact, the only thing that could have surprised her when her wig fell off was his actual response.

He didn't mind. He still thought she was hot. And he still gave her a mind-blowing orgasm and let her tie him up and have her way with him. Her!

Michele stepped out of the shower and wrapped herself in a towel. She slipped on a thin cotton tank top and boxer shorts. She was too amped up to fall asleep, even though it was after midnight.

She turned on her laptop and scanned the twenty-plus emails she'd gotten since that morning. Her gaze landed on an email from the Durban Trust.

Shit. The official rejection, no doubt. Not that she expected anyone to pay for her hair transplant—she just hoped, that's all. Hoped enough she'd been more than willing to spend the several hours it had taken her to write the email to the Durban Trust in the first place, detailing her dream. Not that the email had been very long. Most of the time she put into it revolved around gathering up the guts to put her true feelings into words.

Now as she saw the email in her inbox and clicked on it, the fact she'd actually told a complete stranger online she was a bald virgin and needed money for hair made her blush. No wonder their psychologist called and spoke to her. She probably sounded nuts to them.

Congratulations, she read. *The Durban Trust is happy to inform you you'll receive a grant for the full cost of your hair transplant.*

Oh. My. God.

Michele read the entire email through again twice to make sure it was the real deal. She'd heard of other women getting their plastic surgery paid for through the Durban Trust, but she never thought she'd be one of them. Hair transplants cost thousands of dollars.

Oh my god. A well of excitement rushed through her. Excitement, disbelief...gratitude. Intense gratitude. This was going to change her life.

According to the email, she could see a surgeon next week for an evaluation to determine her suitability for the procedure. *It's real, it's going to happen!* Michele closed her eyes for a moment and pictured herself diving into a hotel pool, perhaps splashing in the water with Andrew, her own natural hair soaking wet, the long strands covering her entire head with no bald spots whatsoever.

The thought of Andrew spurred her imagination. How incredible would it be to have him run his fingers through her hair? To be able to sleep with him without worrying about being bald.

She could barely wait to see the surgeon next week.

* * * * *

Andrew assessed the logo designs presented to him at the board meeting the previous week, barely able to focus on work despite the importance of the new account. He took an early lunch and retreated to the Starbucks down the street. Memories of last night ran through his mind and he texted Michele before he could overthink it.

How r u?

Lame, he knew. But he wanted to make her aware he was definitely still interested in her, despite the fiasco with the wig. He'd been thinking about her all day. For some reason, he wanted to see her without the wig again. It wasn't like a fetish thing, he just wanted to see the real her, completely naked.

Like she said, she was even more naked without the wig on. Somehow, that turned him on. For her to be even more naked with him than she'd been with anyone. And she was a virgin—which kind of scared him a bit. Everyone remembered the person they lost their virginity to forever. What if he screwed up the experience for her?

She probably wouldn't sleep with him anyway. The woman got to the age of twenty-six without losing her virginity, so what made him think he'd be the one to change her mind?

Then again, she didn't seem to be averse to having sex— just to the idea of her wig falling off during sex. Or so it seemed. He loved how she bound his hands behind his back when she blew him so he wouldn't try to tangle his hands in her hair. Fucking hot.

But knowing her head and hair were off-limits made them forbidden fruit. Now all he wanted was to see her naked head and touch it. He laughed softly to himself and stared at his phone, willing her to text him back.

Then the phone rang. Michele!

"Hey there," he said, unable to keep the smile out of his voice. "I was just thinking about you."

"I have incredible news," she said. "I'm going to get a hair transplant!"

Not what he'd been expecting her to say. "You mean...surgery?"

"Yup—it's going to be fully paid for by a grant. I'm seeing the surgeon next week, it was the earliest he could fit me in."

"That seems pretty drastic," he said, setting his cup down on a nearby table. "Surgery is a big deal."

"Not *that* big a deal," she muttered.

"I'm not trying to be a buzz kill, but when I was in high school I knew a girl whose cousin died from a bad reaction to anesthesia. They tried to sue the doctor but couldn't because, as it turns out, that sort of thing happens often enough that they make you sign a consent form saying you understand you might actually die. And...she did."

"But you're not trying to be a buzz kill."

"I'm just..." He sighed into the phone. "Surgery seems unwise."

There was silence on the other end of the line. Then, "I thought you'd be excited for me. This is my dream come true—I'm going to have my own natural hair."

Andrew frowned. He'd never convince her not to endanger herself in a two-minute phone call. "Let me take you to dinner tonight."

"To celebrate?"

He shook his head, even though she couldn't see him. "I'll pick you up at eight, is that okay?"

"Can't wait," she said and hung up.

He didn't want to scare her. Didn't want to take away her excitement. But damn it, she was talking about undergoing real surgery, probably going under general anesthesia, which people had *died* from, for what? Hair? He wished he could prove to her she was completely desirable, bald or not.

If he could convince Michele she didn't need hair to be comfortable having sex, then he'd be one step ahead of the game. Tonight, if she'd let him, he wanted to initiate her into the wonderful pleasure of lovemaking. As much fun as last night had been, he wanted to slip inside her wet heat and become one with her, if only for a short time.

Maybe once she realized she could have sex and not even think about her wig, she'd change her mind about wanting to have a hair transplant.

* * * * *

Michele answered her door with a grin. She'd have hair soon, real hair! And when she did, the first thing she'd do is jump Andrew's bones. 'Cause damn, he looked hot.

"Hey there," he said, kissing her cheek, careful not to pull on her wig's blonde strands. "You look gorgeous."

"I know you said you love blondes," she replied, stepping out the door with him, "but after the hair transplant I'll be a brunette. That's my natural color, or at least it was when I was seven before I lost my hair."

They walked down the four flights of stairs and out into the humid summer night. Andrew took her hand in his and she smiled, enjoying the feel of his large, warm hand on hers.

"I told you I love blondes, but I think if you were wearing a red wig I'd have said I love redheads. Or brunettes. Or whatever. I don't actually have a preference about hair, I really don't."

Interesting. Michele raised her drawn-on eyebrow at him. "So why you'd you say it?"

"I wanted to tell you I'm attracted to you, and I'm not very original."

She laughed. "Okay, that actually makes me feel better."

"In fact, if you weren't wearing your wig I'd have said I loved bald chicks."

"No," she said quietly. "I don't think you'd have asked me out at all. You'd have seen me and assumed I was sick and dying, just like you thought when my wig fell off. You wouldn't have asked me out."

Andrew looked uncomfortable and she knew she'd hit the nail on the head. It wasn't fair for him to say she shouldn't get the surgery when he didn't understand how she'd be treated on a regular basis if she went out *au naturel*. How amazing would it be if *au naturel* for her included her own hair from the transplant?

They stopped in front of an Indian restaurant and glanced up at the red awning.

"Let's eat here," Michele said at the same time Andrew announced how great Indian food was.

"Great minds think alike," they said in unison.

"Okay," she laughed. "This is getting out of control. You need to stop reading my mind."

Andrew pulled her in close and kissed her. His tongue slipped past her lips and she moaned against his mouth. She desired him so intensely. And now that she was going to have a hair transplant, she'd finally be able to sleep with a man — with Andrew.

The hostess of the restaurant cleared her throat and Michele realized they'd stepped inside the open door and had been kissing in the entranceway.

"Sorry," she mumbled, her face flushed.

Andrew looked at her and grinned. "Let's get takeout and bring it back to your place."

Oh, hell yes.

Fifteen minutes later they carried their boxes of takeout chicken tikka masala and samosas back up the street to Michele's apartment. They practically sprinted up the four flights of stairs.

"I don't want to pressure you," Andrew said, setting the food on the counter in her kitchen, "but I've been thinking about seeing you naked all day."

"Yeah, no pressure," she laughed. Her pussy got wet at his words. Now that she knew she'd have real hair soon, she felt more comfortable around him somehow. As if just knowing her baldness was temporary made it matter less.

Maybe tonight would be the night she'd finally lose her virginity. Because even if her wig *did* fall off, well, it was as though it wouldn't matter. She unbuttoned her blouse slowly, staring directly into his eyes.

"Ooh, a button shirt," he murmured, kissing the cleavage revealed by the two open buttons. "May I? I really want to undress you, and this way you don't have to worry about..."

He didn't finish his sentence, but she knew what he was thinking. She wouldn't have to worry about him pulling her wig off by pulling a shirt up over her head. "Yes," she whispered.

His nimble fingers made quick work of her blouse as he kissed a trail down her breasts and across her abdomen. She unbuttoned him at the same time with much less finesse, until she reached his fly. "You're killing me," he said, grinding against her so she could feel exactly what he meant.

"I definitely don't want to kill you. I sorta like you." She freed his cock, holding his thick length in her hand. Groaning, he placed his hand over hers, guiding her. A bead of pre-cum wet his slit and she used it to lube his shaft.

"Please, can we go into the bedroom?" he asked. "I want to do this right. On a bed."

"Is it wrong to do it up against a wall?"

He laughed and she led him into her bedroom and turned off the light. The room sank into darkness.

"What about the Indian food?" he asked. "Are you still hungry?"

"Starving." She dropped to her knees and licked his cock.

"I like the way you think." His hands rested on her head and she stiffened, pausing. "I'm sorry." He moved his hands off her head carefully so her wig didn't budge.

"No, don't worry about it. It's so dark in here even if my wig slipped you wouldn't see. I...sort of did that on purpose. Cut the lights, I mean."

He pulled her to standing and hugged her against his muscular chest. Now that her eyes had adjusted to the near-complete darkness, she could see only the faint outline of him.

"Someday maybe we can have sex with the lights on," he said.

"As soon as I get my hair transplant."

"You don't need surgery." He kissed her, preventing her from protesting.

Fuck it—she didn't want to protest anything at all right now anyway. She just wanted to feel...everything.

"So is that what we're doing?" she whispered against his lips. "Having sex tonight?"

"Only if you want to."

Oh yes. She wanted to. And she knew exactly why tonight, after waiting 'til the age of twenty-six, she was ready to lose her virginity.

The hair transplant. Knowing the Durban Trust would pay for her surgery and that soon she'd have her own natural hair made her feel more comfortable in her skin. Even though she still had no hair, still wore a wig, she could fuck Andrew senseless and feel good about it.

She stripped her pants off, shimmying them down her legs the way she imagined a stripper would and willed herself to stop thinking about hair for just a moment.

He slid his hand between her legs, rubbing her clit with his thumb. Oh yes, she could definitely feel good about this.

"So?" he whispered, his thumb moving so expertly across her slick pussy she had no idea what he was asking about.

"So…what?" she asked, breathless, dropping her head back, ignoring the feel of the wig slipping slightly at the motion. The lights were out. Fuck the wig.

"Do you want to have sex?"

"Yes, please."

He grinned at her, his white teeth glinting in the low light, and kissed her again. "I want you naked, Michele. Completely naked."

She fumbled with her bra and tossed it on the floor, her nipples pebbling as the air hit them. "Better?"

"Take off the wig, baby," he whispered, his thumb still flicking her clit, making every rational thought flee her mind. But his words stopped her desire cold.

Her wig? Oh god. He wanted her to be bald? Why on earth would he want that?

She stared at him in the darkness, suspicion filling her. "Why?"

"So we don't have to worry about it. So I can touch your head and really *be* with you. All of you."

"I suppose…I suppose since me being bald is temporary, it will be okay."

He stopped playing with her clit and she arched toward him, her body already missing his touch. "Temporary?"

"You know, it's just until I get the hair transplant—which should happen soon, right?" Michele smiled at the thought of herself with her own natural hair. If Andrew really wanted her to take the wig off, she'd do it. For him.

Andrew had to force himself to keep his mouth shut. If thinking a hair transplant was going to change everything made her feel ready to take off the wig, then so be it. It wasn't his place to disillusion her.

No, his place was right here, kissing her…showing her how incredible sex could be, hair or no hair.

"May I?" he whispered, touching the synthetic strands of her wig, feeling their unique texture as they flowed over his hand.

Michele nodded, her eyes wide in the darkness. Andrew gently slid her wig off her head and placed it carefully on the dresser before turning his full attention back to her. She stood naked before him, her full breasts heaving, her head bare and strangely erotic.

"Thank you," he said softly, touching her scalp, running his fingers over the sensitive nerve endings on her naked head. Short tufts of wiry hair grew randomly, sticking out like an untended garden overrun by wildflowers, with no rhyme or reason to their placement.

She moaned at his touch and he kissed the nape of her neck and along her ear, relishing the nearness she'd been denying him.

"You're not...turned-off?" she asked, her voice shaky.

Andrew chuckled, pulling her against him so his hard cock pressed into her thigh. "You tell me."

She giggled but shook her head, the movement surprisingly different-looking without the wig swaying back and forth. "I need to hear you say it."

"You're beautiful, Michele. All of you. You could probably wear a garbage bag and I wouldn't be turned-off."

He pulled his pants off, stepping out of them as they fell on the floor. He wished they could make love with the lights on, but he understood her concerns. At least in the dark she could feel more at ease.

"I can't believe I'm going to have sex," she said finally. "This is so weird."

"Is it weird? I don't want to weird you out."

Michele sat on the bed, then stood and pulled the comforter back before sitting again. "You're not the one being weird. It's me. I feel all...discombobulated."

"I think you need some distraction," he said, sitting next to her on the soft mattress. "Lie back."

Michele lay back on the bed, the pillowcase cool on the overheated skin of her head. She definitely could use some distraction. She'd never had a man take her wig off before. He may as well have torn her panties off, that's how naked it made her feel.

Which, interestingly enough, wasn't necessarily a bad thing. Just a weird thing. And that's how she felt— *Oh my.*

Andrew ran his hands up her thighs, spreading them lewdly. The warm night air caressed her bare pussy and she closed her eyes in anticipation. He kissed her nether lips, licking her wet folds up and down before sucking her clit into his mouth with a ferocity that belied his gentle approach.

"You have an incredible pussy. I could eat it all night," he murmured, locking his mouth on her clit.

"Good." She gasped as he sucked harder, the sensations rushing through her body, electrifying her senses.

She reached down and grabbed his head, holding him in place as he brought her higher and higher, licking her mercilessly until she shattered, coming so hard she scratched his shoulders as she rode over the edge.

"Wow," she breathed, lying back on the pillow, panting. "Sorry about scratching you."

"No, I like it," he laughed. He propped himself up on his elbows, looking at her. "Are you ready?"

Michele watched as he sheathed himself with a latex condom, rolling it carefully up his thick, pulsing shaft. "Definitely ready," she whispered, wetting her dry lips with her tongue.

Andrew covered her with his muscular body, holding his weight off her. He positioned his cock at the opening to her wet, swollen cunt, sliding inside just a couple of inches.

She gasped and he froze, letting her accommodate herself to the new sensation.

"You okay?" he asked, concern — and restraint — creasing his forehead.

"I'm fine."

He slid all the way inside, filling her pussy, shocking her with just how damn different it was than masturbating with a dildo. He was warm and wet and throbbing, literally pulsating inside her, while the dildos and vibrators she'd used in the past paled in comparison.

"Does it hurt?" he asked, still not thrusting.

"I'm fine," she repeated. His concern for her well-being was really sweet, but her hymen must have torn years ago, when she first started experimenting on her own.

He kissed her, slipping his tongue deep into her mouth as he slowly moved within her, sliding almost all the way out of her pussy, his cock rubbing along her clit, then thrusting in until the hairs on his balls tickled her sensitive flesh.

She moaned in pleasure as he fucked her ever so sweetly, bringing her hips up to meet him thrust for thrust. Why had she waited so long to do this?

"Are you okay?" he asked again.

"God, yes," she breathed, gyrating her hips beneath him as if to spur him on. His hands, she suddenly realized, had been touching her bald head this whole time. She hadn't even noticed, she was so distracted by the whole losing-her-virginity thing.

Now all she could focus on was his hands on her naked scalp, his fingers toying with the little hair she did have.

It's just temporary, she reminded herself. *Soon I'll have the hair transplant and the alopecia will be like a bad memory.*

So why not enjoy his hands on her head while she still had a bald head?

She kissed him back, nibbling on his lower lip. He groaned and she bit harder, until he pounded his cock into her with passion to match her own.

Grabbing his firm, muscular ass with both her hands, she guided him, making him thrust hard but slow, enjoying the sharp inhalation of breath he took through pursed lips as he fought to control himself for her pleasure.

Each stroke nudged against her swollen G-spot deep inside until she melted around his cock, moaning his name.

Andrew picked up his pace in response, fucking her harder, faster, until he stiffened in her arms and held his breath, his cock pulsing inside her as he ejaculated into the condom. He collapsed on top of her and she welcomed the weight of his sweat-covered body.

"That was incredible," he whispered, rolling off her. "Are you okay?"

She laughed. "You keep asking me that. I promise, I'm fine. If I wasn't you'd hear about it."

"Thanks for letting me be your first."

"Thanks for making me feel desirable even without my wig on," she said, resting her bare head on his chest, feeling his heart thud against her ear.

"About that," he said. His voice reverberated through his body and she had to lift her head so she could hear him properly.

"Oh god. You changed your mind. You want me to put the wig back on?"

"No! Hell no. I don't want you getting any surgery. You don't need that hair transplant, Michele. It's silly to think you do."

"Silly? You really have no idea what you're talking about, Andrew."

"Don't go to that appointment, baby. Please. This is crazy. Didn't I just prove to you that you don't need to get surgery?"

Michele looked at his clenched jaw and sighed. He didn't get it, and unless she could send him back in time and have all his hair fall out he never would. In fact, since he was a man he'd never truly understand what she'd gone through her whole life as a bald woman.

He'd never understand what high school was like for her. How difficult it was for her when she met new people. How could he? Men could shave their heads and walk around without a second glance.

"I'm going to that appointment whether you support me or not, Andrew. I just met you—but having my own hair has been my lifelong dream. I'm not going to just give that up for you."

"Fine." Andrew rolled over, his back to her. "Then I'm coming with you to meet the doctor."

Chapter Four

ॐ

Michele sat on the thin white paper on the examination table at Dr. Goodman's office. She still wore her street clothes and her wig.

Andrew stood in the corner of the exam room, playing with an invisible thread on his suit. She knew he'd taken a long lunch to join her today, despite her protests that he didn't need to bother.

He looked so handsome standing there...and so worried.

"It's just a consultation," she said, trying to soothe his nerves.

"You don't need a hair transplant."

Enough already, damn it! This was getting ridiculous. "Get out."

Andrew's thick black eyebrows shot up in surprise. "What? Why?"

"Because you are a buzz kill and you're ruining what should be the happiest moment in my life."

Andrew let out a sigh. "I rearranged a big client so I could be here for you."

"That's sweet. Can you be here for me...someplace else? Like the waiting room?"

He stepped in close to her and kissed her nose as she looked up at him from her perch on the exam table. "I'm trying to be supportive," he said. "I just think that you need support for being the real you, not for having unnecessary, potentially dangerous cosmetic surgery."

"I appreciate that."

"So I can stay?"

She shook her head. While she truly did appreciate his concern for her well-being, she wasn't ready for Andrew to see her with her wig off in the bright fluorescent lights of the doctor's office. The thought made her palms sweat. "I'll see you in a few minutes."

Andrew pressed his lips against hers and she let out a little mewl of pleasure as he slipped his tongue past her lips.

Someone coughed. *Uh oh.*

Michele pulled away from Andrew in embarrassment, warmth spreading over her cheeks.

An older man with a trim build and a receding hairline, the doctor looked nothing like the polished plastic surgeons she was used to seeing on television.

"I'm Dr. Goodman," he said warmly, sticking out his hand. "You must be Ms. Peterson."

"Michele," she corrected, suddenly feeling shy. "And this is my…" *What is he?* "Friend. Andrew."

Andrew shook the doctor's hand. "I'll be in the waiting room, reading about Dysport versus Botox, I guess."

Michele laughed nervously and waited until the door closed behind him to look back at Dr. Goodman.

"Thanks for seeing me so quickly," she said. "I know you're very booked."

"Well, you were referred by the Durban Trust. I love their work, and I feel honored to be able to be a part of it. Now," he said, placing his hands on her head. "Let's see what we have to work with."

She stiffened as he methodically removed her wig, setting it aside. An air-conditioning vent she hadn't noticed before now blew uncomfortably on her naked scalp.

The doctor examined her head, rolling her scant patchy areas of hair through his fingers as if testing their durability.

He took a comb and combed through her entire scalp as she sat like a mannequin, awaiting his verdict.

"I read your file," he said, continuing with his assessment. "My understanding is you first lost your hair at the age of seven?"

"Yes."

"That must have been very traumatic for you."

She remembered being a kid, having to give her teacher a note from her mom so she could be the only kid in school allowed to wear a hat in class. Eventually the hat made her stick out more, and she felt as if it just drew even more attention to her. She spent her childhood school years without hair and without covering up.

The doctor stood behind her now so she didn't have to speak directly to his face. That made it a bit easier somehow. "Yeah, it was," she said. "But it was more traumatic when it just never grew back."

"Never?"

"Well," she amended, "maybe a little. And sometimes in different areas of my head. But it never grew back to like it was before. I had a full head of long, dark hair. It felt different too, then. Softer."

"That's common with your form of alopecia, whereas other patients may have different forms that have different outcomes."

"So what about my outcome? Can you help me?"

"Here's the thing," he said finally. He sat on a rolling stool in the corner of the office and looked at her, his lips tight.

"What's wrong?" she asked, but her stomach was already in knots.

"I'm sorry to have to tell you this, Ms. Peterson —"

"Michele," she interrupted automatically.

"You're not a candidate for a hair transplant."

She felt as if he'd just kicked her in the gut. "But...but the Durban Trust will pay for it. They'll pay for the whole thing."

"I know they would," he said. "But a successful hair transplant relies on the suitability of the donor site. You don't have enough donor hair—that is, the patches of natural hair already on your scalp—to transplant around the rest of your head."

"But...I do have some hair, you said so yourself. Can't you at least try using those as the donor sites?" Her eyes filled with tears and she brushed at them with the back of her hand.

"It wouldn't be ethical of me to do that. I've been doing this for a long time, Michele. I know that you are not a candidate for a hair transplant. Even if I could do it, your type of alopecia could mean the transplanted hair would fall out, just like the rest of your hair does."

"So that's it? I'm just going to be bald forever?"

"I'm going to email the Durban Trust tonight, with your permission. I can refer you to a top-notch wig maker, someone who will custom-make you a human hair wig."

"That's it then? Another wig?"

"There are also excellent tattoo artists available who can tattoo on permanent eyebrows and eyeliner, so that you can wake up in the morning and go out and not have to worry about drawing on eyebrows or putting on fake lashes."

"Please," she begged. "Please do the hair transplant on me. At least try."

Dr. Goodman shook his head. "I'm sorry."

Andrew knocked on the door to the exam room. "Can I come in?"

No answer, just muffled sobs. He opened the door slowly. Michele sat on the exam table, her wig in her lap, her bald head making her look so vulnerable in the bright lights.

He put his arm around her, pulling her in close for a hug. "Are you okay?"

She looked up at him, her eyes flashing angrily. "Well, the doctor said I'm not a candidate, but I bet you're happy about that."

"I was worried about your well-being, but I never wanted the choice to be taken from you. I'm so sorry, baby."

She looked down at the rumpled wig in her hands and gasped, touching her naked scalp. "Oh god."

"What's wrong?"

"I didn't mean for you to see me without my wig on. Not in this…this lighting."

He laughed softly, holding her trembling hands. She really had no idea how beautiful she was, with or without hair. "Then I'm honored I got the chance."

She pulled her wig on, smoothing back the synthetic blonde strands. "Does it look okay?"

"You look gorgeous," he said.

"Dr. Goodman mentioned I might want to get eyebrow tattoos and tattooed eyeliner."

Andrew shrugged. "I don't know anything about fashion or beauty treatments. What you do is your business. I was really just worried about the surgery because of that girl I knew in high school's cousin, that's all. You do whatever it is you want to do. I promise I'll support you."

Michele smiled up at him and hopped off the exam table, wrapping her arms around his neck. "Thank you."

A thick tear rolled down her cheek and she sniffled, turning her head.

"Wait, why are you crying again?" he asked, confused.

"This was supposed to fix everything. The hair transplant, I mean." She sniffled and reached for a tissue from a tiny box on the counter. "And now it's not going to happen. It's like I won the lottery and then found out...I didn't really win after all."

* * * * *

Michele sat on her couch, barely watching the mindless reality television Andrew had turned on for her. It was sweet of him to take off the rest of the day to comfort her, but she hated feeling so emotionally bare in front of him. She wasn't scheduled to work until tomorrow morning, thank goodness. There was no way she could deal with being friendly to customers right now.

Her lifelong dream to have her own natural hair — shattered. It had never really occurred to her that the doctor would actually refuse to do the surgery. She figured if he was going to get paid either way then he'd probably at least want to try.

Damn Dr. Goodman and his ethics. Didn't she deserve at least a half-assed try?

The fact that she'd made love to Andrew with her wig off, thinking it was just temporary and therefore didn't really count as being truly bald anymore, struck her as ridiculous now. And horribly embarrassing. And then he saw her in the doctor's office with her wig off. How could she have let that happen?

And how was he still here, still sitting on the couch with her, taking the day off work to watch reality TV with her?

Andrew looked over at her and smiled. "I'm enjoying vegging out with you, but I need to check my email real quick and make sure my client got my message."

"Go ahead," she said, waving him toward her laptop in her bedroom. She waited until he walked out of the living room before pulling her wig off. Her air conditioner was on the fritz again and it was hotter than it should be. Useless landlord.

She sighed with pleasure as the breeze from her fan hit the sweat drying on her scalp. As nice as it was to have Andrew here, she didn't know if she'd ever feel comfortable enough around him to hang out without her wig on — and in this heat, wearing a wig was like wearing a heavy hat.

But if she sent him home just so she could sit around being bald, then she was letting her alopecia run her life.

And if she had no hope of ever having her own hair again, then she really needed to stop making so many decisions about her life based on her hair — or her lack of it. She sighed and pulled the wig back on.

She just wasn't ready to be around him without it.

* * * * *

Michele ducked into work late the next day, cursing under her breath as she slid her time card through the machine. She'd probably be docked fifteen minutes pay. At some point she'd need to go get a better job — a more exciting job. There was nothing exciting about being a customer service representative.

At least her job hadn't been outsourced to India. Yet.

The coworker who sat in the cubicle across from her in the large call center lifted his coffee cup in greeting as Michele slipped into her cubicle and turned on her phone. Michele waved her fingers back, forcing herself to get into a friendly mood. Not that she was a fan of her coworker — a superficial, looks-obsessed tail-chaser. If he knew about her alopecia, she doubted he'd even give her the time of day.

The first call came in immediately and Michele flipped her headset on carefully, quickly rearranging her wig as it slipped slightly. She looked at the index card she'd written as a reminder to herself on her very first day on the job, two years ago. Not the one with the script on it — she'd long since memorized that one. The card she looked at now for guidance simply said "Smile!"

274

Somehow just smiling, even when she didn't feel like it, made her voice sound nicer and more helpful over the phone. Callers responded to that nice tone, and Michele had gotten a rep as being able to soothe even the angriest customer.

The trick, she'd discovered, was to listen to the person's complaint and immediately apologize, even if the problem wasn't her or the company's fault. Most people called expecting a fight, and it never failed to amaze her how many other representatives gave them that fight. How on earth did it help to goad someone?

Then she tried to find out what the customer wanted done, and she over-delivered whenever possible. So if the person called because they were annoyed about a fee they were charged, she'd remove the fee and then give them a discount or something.

That's probably one of the reasons she was so upset about her experience at the doctor's office. She'd gone in expecting the world—a hair transplant—and had been offered a tiny country—the wig and tattoos. It was her own high expectations that led to her depression about the whole thing now.

In fact, if she'd never thought about the hair transplant, and instead the Durban Trust had told her "Hey, guess what? We're going to buy you an expensive custom-made human hair wig and pay for you to get cosmetic tattoos!" she would have been absolutely thrilled. Beyond thrilled.

So obviously what she needed was an attitude adjustment. And…just in case…a second opinion about that hair transplant. She felt her hope soaring once more and struggled to keep it in check.

But what if another doctor would be willing to give the hair transplant a shot?

* * * * *

The following week Michele sat in another doctor's office, rearranging her wig after the doctor examined her to give a second opinion on her suitability for a hair transplant. Having the surgery was so important to her that she couldn't just take one doctor's word on it.

"Well?" Michele asked hopefully. The doctor was a beautiful older woman with short red hair who probably never had to worry about baldness in her life. Still, Michele could tell by the look in the doctor's eyes that she seemed to empathize with her situation.

"I'm sorry, Michele," she replied. "It's just not going to work. Not with your type of alopecia and your scarcity of donor sites for the hair transplant."

Michele shook her head, willing herself not to cry. Despite her best intentions she'd let herself get her hopes up all over again, only to have them dashed once more.

"I know this isn't want you want to hear, honey," the doctor said, handing her a tissue, "but I'm going to recommend cosmetic tattoos and a human hair wig. I think they will do wonders for your appearance."

"I'm very excited about the tattoos," she admitted. "I imagine I would have gotten those even if I was a candidate for the hair transplant. I've already got an appointment set for later today."

"That's wonderful," the doctor replied, eyeing her carefully. "I assume the tattoo artist has been vetted and approved by the Trust?"

"Of course." The Durban Trust had already emailed her back saying they'd pay for the work and for a custom-made human hair wig and sent her a list of suggested places.

"Good," she said, straightening her lab coat as she reached for the examination room door. "Because cosmetic facial tattoos are quite permanent."

Thanks for that, doc. Because I need to be more terrified.

But the cosmetic tattoo specialist she'd be seeing in a few hours came highly recommended, and she mainly worked on alopecia patients. The whole needles in her face thing scared Michele—but what really scared her was exactly what the doctor said—knowing that this was permanent. What if she thought the tattoos looked ugly? They'd be there forever.

She'd gone to the wig fitting days ago, but the whole experience felt miserable, not like the excitement she knew she would have felt if she were getting a real hair transplant. All her plans on adjusting her attitude fell flat when she had to come face-to-face with the reality that it didn't matter if the Trust would pay for the surgery if she wasn't going to be a good candidate for it.

Getting the fitting for the custom wig made her realize she was settling for being bald for the rest of her life. She could go pick the wig up next week at her next appointment, where the wig-maker would show her how to wear and style the wig to make it look completely natural. No one, he had promised, would ever know it was a wig unless she told them.

Andrew would know, of course. Could she ever be okay being bald around him?

* * * * *

Andrew smiled at Michele and held her trembling hand as she sat under the bright lights of the sterile-looking cosmetic tattoo artist's office.

"We should have found you some Valium or something first," he joked, although she really did look as if she was about to faint.

"Honey," the tattoo artist said. The matronly older woman didn't look anything like the tatted-up punk rocker Andrew had been expecting. "I want you to take a look at my Before and After photo album. If this doesn't ease your mind, nothing will."

"Except Valium," Michele said.

277

The woman laughed, the deep throaty sound betraying what was probably a pack-a-day habit. "This girl has a similar facial structure to you," she noted, pointing to the album.

Michele flipped through the album slowly, and Andrew wondered if she was doing it mainly to buy herself some time before she'd get jabbed in the face with needles. Permanent marking needles. There was a reason Andrew never got a tattoo, and that was that the process of getting one seemed a bit like torture. Not that he'd dare let on his nervousness to Michele. She needed a rock right now, not someone just as freaked out as she was. So he'd hold her hand and be there for her.

The Before and After pictures really were inspiring. It was amazing what a difference the tattooed eyebrows and eyeliner made to a hairless face. And it would be so nice for Michele to be able to just get up and go in the morning without fretting about drawing on eyebrows and putting on false eyelashes.

"Okay," she said resolutely. "I'm ready. Do me now, before I lose my nerve."

Andrew laughed and squeezed her hand. "She's still got to draw the eyebrows on with marker so you can give your vote of approval first, remember?"

Michele took a deep breath. "Yes. Go for it."

The tattoo artist carefully drew a guide on Michele's skin so she could see how her eyebrows would look before she made them permanent.

"What do you think?" Michele asked, looking at the penned-on eyebrows in a handheld mirror. "Much nicer than the ones I usually draw on, don't you think?"

"You look great," he said truthfully. "And the eyeliner she's going to tattoo on really makes your eyes look incredible."

She looked over at the tattoo artist and nodded. "Let's do it."

Andrew squeezed her hand as the first micro-dot of color, a neutral brown, was applied. Michele had her eyes closed and seemed to be struggling not to wince to avoid jarring the tattoo needle unnecessarily.

It didn't seem fair how Michele had to go through this much drama and pain just to look like a regular "normal" woman. He wouldn't have minded if she never got the tattoos, but he could already tell after looking at the Before and After pictures in that book that the end result was going to be breathtaking.

Just like Michele.

* * * * *

Back at Michele's apartment, Andrew popped a bottle of Amstel Light and handed it to her.

"Thanks," she said, taking a gulp. She wiped the sweat off her forehead with the back of her hand and winced. "Ow. Damn tattoo."

"Are you okay?" he asked.

"I'm fine. I think I just need to get a bit tipsy and take a nap. My eyes feel tight and weird from the tattoo eyeliner."

He frowned. "She said it would take a couple weeks to totally heal."

"Be honest with me. Does it look okay?"

He viewed her appraisingly for the tenth time since they'd walked out of the tattoo artist's office an hour ago. "It looks incredible. *You* look incredible. The tattoos are even more natural-looking than I ever would have guessed they could be. She truly was an artist."

Michele smiled and drained the rest of her beer. "Thank you. And thanks for coming with me."

He stepped forward and kissed her, careful not to touch her tender new eyebrows or eyes. "If you want to put on the

TV I'll join you on the couch in a minute. I just need to check my email real quick."

"You're always working," she scoffed, but she smiled. At least he liked his job, unlike hers, which she couldn't care less about. Skipping work to get the tattoos was easy for her. "I'm going to watch something terribly girly, since I probably won't see your face for another half hour. You get sucked into the internet."

Andrew laughed and handed her another beer. "I'll be right back. You get started on getting tipsy."

He sat at Michele's desk in her bedroom and finished checking his work email before closing the window he'd opened on her laptop.

A Word doc sat on her desktop, titled "Why I Need Surgery_v1". It was most likely the rough draft of the letter she'd sent to the Durban Trust—the letter that got them to agree to pay for her hair transplant.

Don't snoop. It's not right.

Oh hell. She'd been so upset with him for not understanding in the first place why she wanted the surgery. And he really didn't get it. Why would a beautiful, healthy woman want to go through a painful and potentially dangerous cosmetic surgery?

This letter, this document on her desktop, held the answer.

He clicked it open, cursing under his breath. *Way to go with the willpower, man.* But now that the document was open, he had to read it. He couldn't look away if he tried.

To The Durban Trust:

I've heard of the amazing things your trust has done for other women, and I'm hoping that maybe I could be one of those lucky few.

When I was seven all my hair fell out and grew back in patches. Sometimes the patches would fall out and grow back. My whole childhood, middle school years, and high school I went to school terribly self-conscious about my lack of hair.

I didn't wear a wig back then because by the time I was old enough to want a boyfriend, all of my high school friends already knew I was bald and were used to it. But I never had a boyfriend.

When I went to college I started wearing a wig. It's hot and uncomfortable in the summer, and I'm always nervous about it slipping off, or about someone realizing it's a wig. I know most people know it's a wig. My lack of eyebrows and eyelashes usually clues people in.

Everyone thinks I have cancer.

I'm twenty-six years old, and I've never been able to be comfortable enough with myself and my baldness to date a guy for more than a few dates. So...I'm a virgin.

I can't believe I'm admitting this to a committee of strangers, but I need to get a hair transplant so I can have a sex life.

I want a man to tangle his hands in my hair in the throes of passion.

Please, please consider me for hair transplant surgery so I can fulfill my dream of having an incredible sexual experience, for the first time in my life.

Yours truly,
Michele Peterson

Andrew closed the document, clicking the little X in the upper right corner. Michele's letter to the Durban Trust disappeared from view.

So that was her dream? To be comfortable enough about her hair so she could have sex?

Well, they'd had sex—she was no longer a virgin. But she hadn't truly let herself go for him. He wanted to make love with the lights on and to have her revel in her sexuality—even when she was bald. Could he make that happen for her now that she'd lost her only chance to have hair?

Now that being bald was a forever state instead of just temporary, as she had thought when she agreed to make love before, would she even let him near her again?

He logged out of his email and walked back into the living room. Michele lay on the couch, dozing, the fan blowing what little hair she had on her uncovered head, the wig on the cushion next to her. She looked so vulnerable like that. It was all he could do not to take her up in his arms and hug her right then and there.

And now that he'd read her letter to the Durban Trust, he understood.

Her dream had been crushed.

But damn it, he could help. If he could make her feel desirable as a bald woman in bed, then she would have accomplished her dream—even without the hair transplant.

He sat next to her. Her lips parted slightly and she rolled her head back on the couch, apparently oblivious to his presence. But her cherry lips looked too delicious to ignore. He dipped his head to hers and kissed her softly, feeling as if he were awakening Sleeping Beauty.

Her eyes opened and she smiled dreamily, returning his kiss. Suddenly her tiny hands pushed hard against his chest.

He froze. "What's wrong?"

"I-I'm not wearing my wig. It was hot... I didn't know how long you'd be in there."

"I don't care, I really don't."

She sat up, pulling her wig back on. "But I do."

Andrew took her hand in his. "Listen, I understand now. I read your letter."

Recognition dawned on her face. "You *what*?"

Shit. He'd instinctively known he shouldn't have snooped, but he honestly just wanted to learn more about her. "I'm sorry. I should've asked your permission first."

"That letter was private! God, I told them everything—it wasn't meant for your eyes."

His cheeks burned with embarrassment. "I acted like an idiot. I'm sorry."

"I just… I want to hang out alone. Without my wig on. And without you."

Andrew stood, feeling shaky on his legs, as if he'd suddenly stepped off dry land and onto a boat. "I'll call you later."

She mumbled something under her breath. Something that sounded like "Don't bother."

Fuck.

Chapter Five

❧

Michele avoided Andrew's phone calls and texts the following day, just to get a little space and try to sort through her feelings. He shouldn't have read her letter—her very private letter.

Warmth spread over her cheeks as she thought about how she'd laid her soul bare in it. Told them she was a virgin. How she wanted to feel a man's hands tangled in her hair in the throes of passion, but she couldn't because she was bald.

God, she'd actually written all that stuff down, in black and white. And he'd read it. She wanted to scrub his memory like in that movie, just erase everything he thought he knew about her.

He shouldn't have read my letter. The thought had been repeating itself in her mind like a mantra ever since he woke her up.

But he had, and as of yet she possessed no special memory-erasing super powers.

Someone knocked at the door. She peered through the peephole, already knowing it would be Andrew. And it was.

She opened the door and he stepped inside, handing her a large bouquet of some sort of yellow flower mixed with those little white buds—baby's breath.

Awww. That's sweet. He knows he fucked up.

"Thanks," she said, taking the flowers. "These are nice."

"I'm sorry I read your private letter," he said, "but I'm not sorry about what I learned."

"Just to give you a heads up—you're ruining your apology."

284

"Damn it, Michele, you want to be comfortable having sex? Then you need to let go of your inhibitions with me."

"It's not that easy," she said softly.

"Take off your wig."

She gasped. "No."

"Take it off. I want you to get rid of any insecurity you have around me. You're not a candidate for a hair transplant — so you need to get on board with a new life plan."

"Get on board?"

"Yeah," he said, taking the flowers from her and tossing them unceremoniously on the kitchen counter. "I like you a lot, Michele. More than I've ever liked anyone else I've dated in years. But I can't be with someone who can't — no, *won't* — be herself around me."

Michele felt hot tears fill her eyes, burning her sensitive, newly tattooed eyeliner. "Fine, asshole." She tore her wig off, not bothering to smooth the little patches of hair left on her head.

He kissed her, his thigh pressing between her legs, right up against her clit. She moaned as he ran his large hands over the back of her neck and over her naked scalp.

"That's what I like," he murmured against her lips. "I don't want to fuck in the dark anymore. I want to see you — all of you."

She pulled his suit jacket off him, not bothering to hang it up. It lay pooled on the floor next to her wig.

"Take off your shirt," he said, his voice low and rough as he undressed himself.

She pulled her shirt off slowly, enjoying not having to worry about keeping her wig on straight. "Since when did you get so bossy?"

"Since you started acting like a brat," he laughed, his hands encircling her waist. She inhaled sharply as his thigh ground into her clit again.

"You...you're really not turned-off by the whole bald thing?"

"Honestly, it's not a 'bald thing' to me anymore. It's a 'Michele thing'. And now it's become a question of trust." He picked her up, carried her into her bedroom and laid her on the bed.

"Trust?" she repeated, but she could barely focus on the conversation, even though she knew it was important. Lust overpowered her ability to focus. She could hardly hear over the roar of her libido.

He tugged her jeans off, pulling her cotton panties, shimmying them down past her hips. With one long finger he touched her labia, slowly spreading them. She was so wet, so ready for him—even though daylight poured in through her bedroom windows and she was totally wigless and vulnerable.

But under Andrew's caress, she didn't feel vulnerable. No...she felt stronger. More alive than ever before.

"I need you to trust me enough to not worry about wearing a damn wig when you're with me in private," he whispered, circling her clit with his fingers, sending sparks of passion through her.

"Okay," she moaned, urging him to move faster, thrusting her hips up to his hand.

"Your dream is to have an incredible sexual experience," he said, rubbing faster, making her moan in ecstasy. "I'm going to prove to you that you don't need hair to make that happen."

"Don't stop," she gasped, her head snapping toward her chest as she came hard, creaming over his fingers.

"Baby," he said, quickly sheathing his cock and sliding deep inside her, "I'm just getting started."

He filled her completely, his cock hitting her G-spot as he rocked back and forth, grinding his pelvic bone over her overstimulated clit with every thrust. She melted around him, feeling her body turn into a quivering mass of nerve endings when he brought her to a second intense orgasm.

She kissed him, needing his lips on hers, needing to taste him. Even one day without him had felt like an eternity. His hands crept up to her head and she stiffened as he caressed the tufts of crinkly hair growing on her mostly bald head.

"Relax," he said, still running his hands over her scalp. "Just feel the sensation. Don't worry about anything."

She tried to do just that. His fingernails lightly dancing across her naked flesh, the gentle tugs and pulls on what little hair she did have, felt incredible. Absolutely amazing.

He picked up the pace, fucking her deeper, harder. Every thrust brought her to a dizzying new height as he grabbed her ass, angling her so his cock slid against her clit with each stroke. His lips brushed across her face and nuzzled against her bare head, but it didn't bother her the way she thought it would. Instead, she let herself go, free to indulge in the waves of pleasure he gave her. The strokes turned heavy, frantic, and Andrew's groans filled the air, matching her own desperate sounds of passion and the slap of skin on skin. He kissed her passionately as he reached his climax.

"Thank you," he whispered, laying his head on the pillow next to her cheek, holding his weight off her. "Thank you for trusting me."

Michele nodded. Only Andrew could have made her feel so safe and cherished in his arms.

I love you, she thought.

But she didn't dare say it aloud.

* * * * *

Michele stood in front of the open refrigerator door in Andrew's kitchenette, luxuriating in the cool air that wafted over her from its chilly interior.

287

"I can't get over how amazing your new wig looks," he said, coming up behind her. "It looks natural."

"Thanks," she said, smiling. "Having a human hair wig really does make a difference."

Andrew reached around past her and grabbed a beer. "I hate to sound like my mom, but you're wasting energy standing there with the fridge open."

"Ugh. I know." She pulled her wig off and draped it over her purse on one of the high stools at the counter, which separated the "kitchen" corner of the apartment from the living room/dining area.

Blessed air cooled her overheated head and she sighed. "When is this summer ever going to end?" she asked, taking the beer out of Andrew's hand.

"Hey," he laughed, "get your own beer!"

She sipped deeply and handed it back to him. "Thanks."

His intercom buzzed by the front door.

"Are you expecting company?" Michele asked.

He looked at her as if she'd grown a third eyeball. "Seriously? You forgot Richard and John were coming in from Ohio?"

The names rang a bell but she didn't respond quickly enough to cover her memory lapse.

"My best friends from home. I told you about it."

Oh god. That was *this* weekend? The whole getting the new wig and tattoos thing had thrown her off. She didn't usually forget things like that.

Andrew pressed the button to speak to whoever was standing outside the building, waiting to be buzzed in. "Who's there?"

"Hey man," a voice came back, tinny-sounding through the old intercom system. "We're here!"

Andrew buzzed them up.

"I can't believe I forgot your friends were coming this weekend." Michele said, shaking her head.

Andrew looked at her and grinned. "You're still going out with us tonight, right?"

"Of course. Oh my god, my wig!" she said, suddenly realizing it was sitting on the kitchen stool when it really needed to be on her head, like, three minutes ago. "Shit." She threw it on, knowing it was lopsided and messy looking. How could she forget his friends were coming today?

"Don't worry about it," Andrew said, casually taking the wig back off her head. "You don't need to put the wig on, you were just saying about how sweaty it makes you feel."

She sighed, exasperated. "You still don't get it, do you? I'm barely comfortable bareheaded around you now—I can't have your friends seeing my naked scalp."

He raised his eyebrows and shrugged when she grabbed the wig back from him and put it back on her head.

"Don't let them in yet," she warned, rushing past him to the bathroom so she could make herself presentable.

"You don't need to do this," he repeated, calling after her. "They already know about the alopecia anyway."

"You didn't!" she gasped when he followed her into the bathroom.

"I did. And they're fine with it."

Okay. Inhale, one, two, three. Exhale, one, two, three, four, five. Michele quickly adjusted her wig, smoothing the wayward strands in front of the bathroom mirror. The breathing hadn't helped. She looked as upset as she felt.

"Andrew," she said quietly, forcing herself to sound calm. "You shouldn't have told them my personal business. What makes you think I want total strangers to know I'm wearing a wig? Especially now that I'm wearing a human hair wig that might mean they'd never have to even guess about it?"

There was a knock at the door. His friends had arrived.

Andrew looked visibly shaken. "I'm sorry, I didn't think about it that way. I'm really, really sorry."

She shook her head. Now he'd have to answer the door and his friends would come in and they'd know her secret right away. Forget trying to get to know them a bit before the truth came out. They'd immediately look at her head, no doubt, knowing it was a wig.

Damn it. *What had Andrew been thinking?*

"I have to let them in now," he said as he crossed the room to answer the door. "Are you okay? You look great."

Fuck you very much. "Thank you," she said, stepping out of the bathroom, taking a cleansing breath to compose herself. It wasn't working.

The door swung open and two grinning guys in T-shirts and jeans waltzed in. "You weren't kidding when you said you lived in a shoebox," one joked.

She wasn't sure if it was Richard or John. His friend looked at her and stuck out his hand.

"Richard," he said in answer to her unspoken question, pumping her hand enthusiastically.

The other guy also offered his hand, which she shook, trying to keep a genuine smile on her face even though tears threatened to spill onto her cheeks. Her hand disappeared in his big paw.

"Nice to meet you both." She smiled thinly, still upset. It was too weird, these strangers knowing her secret, despite the fact that she was wearing her fancy new wig. She felt cheated out of a normal introduction.

"Andrew said you'll be coming out with us tonight, right?" John asked.

"Unfortunately," she said, forcing the quaver to remain out of her voice, "something came up. I can't go tonight. But it was very nice meeting you."

"What the—" Andrew looked at her in confusion.

"I have to go," she mumbled, and stepped past the three men.

Michele sat on her couch and wiped her eyes again, still tender from the recent eyeliner tattooing. Strands of hair fell over her cheeks and she brushed them back angrily.

But she didn't take the wig off.

Damn him. Damn that fucking asshole for making her feel so safe and comfortable about herself that she could be bald around him—be completely open and vulnerable—and then for ruining it all in one fell swoop by assuming she could just be bald in front of everyone else as well.

He just didn't get it. He didn't understand how hard it was for her to open herself up to him and to be completely herself around him by taking the wig off. Why would he tell his friends about her alopecia?

Were they laughing at her behind her back? Oh god.

Fucking asshole. She burst into tears again, unable to control herself. Not only had he hurt her newly burgeoning sense of desirability, he'd damaged their relationship.

Because there was no way she'd be able to go out with him again. Not after this. If after all this time he still didn't understand how she felt, then he never would.

Andrew loaded his friends' bags in the corner of his small apartment. He felt as though someone had just punched him in the gut. When Michele walked out, half of him had wanted to chase after her.

The other half didn't want Rich and John to witness the huge fight they'd surely have if he'd done that.

He was an idiot. Why had he tried to make her keep the wig off around total strangers when it took her so long to get her comfortable not wearing it just around him? And telling them about the alopecia...at the time he told them he hadn't thought of it as her personal secret that he was sharing, but now it was pretty clear he'd overshared. Majorly.

But honestly, when he thought of Michele, he saw past the alopecia. Past the wig. The first thing he told his friends on the phone after he met her was how funny and cute she was. How they drank the same type of beer and were already finishing each other's sentences.

And he told them how beautiful she was, even without hair. Maybe even *because* she had no hair. Michele's baldness lent a certain exotic quality to her looks.

But she wanted Richard and John to meet her and get to know her first, just like Andrew had. And he'd ruined that for her.

Fuck. What an idiot.

Rich put his feet up on the coffee table and looked around. "Too bad Michele can't come out tonight, show us the town from a real New Yorker's perspective."

"That's my fault."

"What do you mean?"

Andrew shrugged. He may as well tell them, especially since there was a very good possibility that he'd already ruined his relationship with Michele permanently. "I shouldn't have told you guys about her alopecia. She was really embarrassed." Andrew sipped his beer.

"Really?" John said, raising his eyebrows. "Honestly, if you didn't tell me I never would have known. That was a damn good wig. She looked smokin' to me."

"When she's alone she likes to not wear it since it's kinda uncomfortable, especially in the summer. We'd finally gotten to a place in our relationship where she felt okay having me around with her wig off."

"Is that weird for you?" Rich asked.

"No," Andrew said truthfully. "She's beautiful either way. But I really screwed up by expecting her to just be fine with being bald around you guys too. She thinks I must not get what she's been going through this whole time."

Rich let out a low whistle. "Yup. You screwed up."

"What do I do?"

"Man, if I knew answers to shit like that I wouldn't still be single," Rich said.

John laughed and nodded in agreement. "Tell her you fucked up. Chicks like to hear that."

"Yeah, like you know what chicks like to hear," Andrew scoffed, but he knew the advice was sound. "Okay," he said, standing. "I'm going to go try and fix this."

Andrew pulled out his phone and texted Michele.

I need to see you.

She texted back immediately.

But I don't want to see you.

Shit. He had to go over there and make this right.

"Hey man—" Rich said as Andrew stepped out the front door of his apartment.

"Yeah?"

"Bring flowers. Chicks dig flowers."

Noted. "Wait," Andrew said, stopping in his tracks. "I have an idea. A grand gesture. But I'm going to need a big favor from both of you."

* * * * *

"You're not serious," John said nervously when Andrew emerged from his bathroom with his electric hair clippers.

Andrew and Richard grinned at John and Rich ruffled John's hair. "Oh, come on," Rich said. "Peer pressure."

"Well," John grunted. "When you put it that way."

Andrew turned the buzzer on and started going to town on his own head before he could talk himself out of it.

"You know," Rich said, eyeing Andrew's falling hair. "If all three of us shave our heads, people are going to think we're some kind of gang. KKK or something."

Andrew sighed. "It's not a political statement," he assured him. "Just a summer hair cut. And a way to show solidarity with Michele."

"Sounds like quite a statement to me," John said, shrugging. "Here, you missed a spot. He took the clippers from Andrew and went to work. Locks of brown and blond hair and Andrew's own shaggy dark hair fell to the hardwood floor.

When they were done, Andrew assessed their work objectively.

His friends looked different without any hair at all. Not bad, just...different. And he knew he did too. Andrew hadn't been without hair since he was born. Even then, actually, he'd had a lot of hair. Something about heartburn during pregnancy, if you asked his late great-grandmother how he managed to come out with a shock of dark hair.

"I hope this works," Andrew said, pulling on a baseball cap to protect his bare head from the sun.

He heard both Rich and John calling after him as he stepped out the door. "Don't forget the flowers!"

Andrew grinned. God, he hoped this worked. Because he wasn't willing to let Michele go.

Chapter Six

∞

Michele's stomach flip-flopped when her doorbell rang. She didn't need to peer through the peephole to know it was Andrew but she did anyway.

He had flowers. Sighing, she opened the door.

"Thanks for seeing me," he said, handing her the sparse bouquet.

"You can't just buy me some cheap flowers from a street vendor every time you screw up."

"I know."

"You know you can't just buy me off with carnations or you know that you screwed up?"

Andrew pulled her into his arms. "Both."

She wanted to melt into the warmth of his embrace and forget everything that had happened, but she couldn't. This was too big.

"I was finally feeling like I could be myself around you," she whispered.

"I know."

"You ruined it, Andrew. You ruined everything. I don't think I can ever be bald around you again, knowing how you really feel."

"How I really feel? What are you talking about? You don't know how I feel."

"Yes, I do. Because actions speak louder than words. You told me exactly how you feel about my alopecia when you went behind my back, told your buddies about me being bald, and then expected me to just be fine being bald around them."

Andrew shook his head. "My actions misspoke for me then."

"I worry you'll never get it. You'll never know what it's like to be bald."

"I told Rich and John it wasn't my place to tell them about your alopecia, and that you felt embarrassed."

"And?"

"And they agree I'm an idiot and I screwed up. And that you're smokin' hot."

Tears stung her eyes. "I don't think I'll be able to feel at home around someone who doesn't understand my feelings on this. It's not a big deal to you, but it's a huge deal to me. Maybe that sounds stupid, but that's how I feel."

Andrew took off his baseball cap, revealing a freshly shaved bald head, complete with a couple of missed areas. A messy, home-done job.

She gasped. God, that was sweet of him. "You didn't."

"I did. We all did."

"What?"

"Richard and John shaved their heads too. You know, like in solidarity."

Oh my god. She laughed, the bubble of tension that sat in her chest feeling as if it had popped and she could breathe again.

He gently tugged the ends of her wig, running his fingers through it. It fell to the floor in a mess of long blonde strands.

"Why?" she whispered. "Why me? Why do you want to be with a bald woman?"

"I don't particularly care if I'm with a bald woman or not. What I care about is being with you."

His words melted some of the ice that she'd let cover her feelings toward him. God, he was handsome. Even bald. Hell, *especially* bald. And even if he had bad taste in street vendor flowers, it was the thought that counted. Shaving his head and convincing his friends to shave their heads was a really big, nice thought.

"Let me prove to you how desirable I find you," he said, his breath hot on her ear.

She tilted her head, painfully aware that she no longer had her long blonde wig to sway across her shoulders. "How?"

"However you want."

"What if I told you I'd probably never go out with you and your buddies without my wig on? Would you still feel the same way?"

He didn't hesitate, and she loved him for it. "Yes. Whatever you want."

She loved him. She really did. Yeah, he'd acted like a bonehead, but he'd recognized the error of his ways pretty quickly.

"Good. Because I don't really want to go out without my wig on," she admitted, her shoulders sagging. "I'm just not there yet. Maybe in the future. But I'm glad I can at least feel comfortable alone with you without the wig."

"Absolutely," he said. "What can I do to make you feel better?"

She felt a small smile play across her lips. "Maybe— maybe you could distract me for a bit so I can stop thinking about how naked I feel now."

His mouth claimed hers, hot and hungry. He tasted like Andrew, sweet and salty and so very male.

I love you, she thought, but she didn't say it.

After everything that happened, she shouldn't even be thinking it, much less wanting to say it.

"You say you feel naked," he murmured against her mouth, "but I don't think you're nearly naked enough."

"Agreed," she nodded, fumbling with her zipper. He helped her tug her jeans down her thighs, her pussy throbbing with need. She gasped in surprise as he lifted her up, pulling her body against his chest so he had better access to her pants. The tough denim slid off her legs when he pulled one last time.

"Finally," he said, dropping her carefully on the carpet.

"What, am I too heavy?" she asked, feeling warmth creep back up over her cheeks.

He didn't answer, just shook his head, his mouth already on her belly, his hands lifting her shirt up over her head. No need to worry about the wig falling off, it lay next to her on the floor, the blonde strands spread out across the carpet, tickling her cheek.

He placed light, nipping kisses down her belly, licking across the expanse of her hips until his mouth finally came to rest right where she needed it most. She spread her legs, feeling his hot breath on her bare nether lips.

"Yes," she moaned, raking her fingernails across his back. His shirt got in her way and she clawed at the thick material until she managed to strip it off over his freshly shaved head. Hard muscles on his back rippled beneath her fingertips as he slowly licked her core.

"How's that for a distraction?" he asked, his words vibrating across her thrumming clit.

"Don't stop." Michele kneaded his shoulders, holding him in place as he sucked her clit full into his mouth, flicking it with his tongue over and over.

"You're beautiful, baby," he whispered, and she gasped at the vibrations of his mouth against her clit once more.

"More," she begged. "Talk more, it feels so good."

"Like this?" he asked, punctuating his words with his tongue. "You want me to move my mouth around your little pussy like this?"

Sensation rose within her and she cried out as it threatened to boil over and melt her completely. "Yes, god yes."

"You're so fucking hot, Michele."

She came, her muscles clenching, contracting tightly, her naked head snapping up off the carpet as she rode the waves of her climax.

"Fuck me, Andrew." Her pussy felt empty and she was aching for him now, needing him to fill her completely.

He stood over her and pulled his belt off, dropping it to the floor next to her wig. His unzipped his fly slowly, his hard cock bursting against the soft cotton of his black boxer-briefs as he stepped out of the pants.

She licked her lips in anticipation, admiring the way he deftly kicked his clothes out of his way before bringing his large body down onto hers. "Fuck me," she said again, unable to think clearly, not with his scent surrounding her and his cock so close to her hip.

He slicked a latex condom down the length of his shaft, inhaling sharply as his hand stroked his thick cock. "Spread your legs for me, baby," he whispered.

The carpet underneath her thighs seemed to heighten the sensitive nerve endings all along her skin. Moisture pooled in her core at his words, at the sight of him, ready for her.

Slowly, forcing herself to stop begging for it, she spread her thighs, giving him unlimited access to her cunt. He slid deep inside her, his cock pressing into her inch by inch, pushing into her wet heat.

"Yes," she moaned, rocking into his thrusts. "Just like that."

"You like that, baby?"

"I love it." She raked her fingers up his back and over his now mostly smooth head, running her fingers over it.

He responded by fucking her harder, more forcefully, driving himself deep within her as she wrapped her legs around his ass and urged him on with her moans.

His breath was hot on her ear, tickling the tender lobe, and she gasped when he nibbled her ear, sucking it into his mouth the way he'd sucked her clit.

"Let me get on top," she said, spurring him to roll over with a gentle nudge of her heel on his ass cheek. He grinned down at her and held on tightly, pulling her on top of him with his cock still buried inside her.

She liked the feeling of being on top, of taking both of their pleasure in her hands. In this position, she could put him exactly how she needed him.

"Touch my clit," she whispered and he reached forward, angling his thumb so it rubbed her in exactly the right way every time she gyrated her hips. His cock hit her G-spot perfectly. But Andrew still had a free hand.

Her nipples tightened, rosy peaks of sensation. She lifted his free hand and placed it on her breast, gasping as he pinched her nipple rhythmically, in time to the flickering on her clit.

She moved in excruciatingly slow circles on his thick cock, her eyes shut in ecstasy.

"I can do this all night," he said, flicking her clit, pinching her nipples, alternating one and then the other. He lifted his hips into hers, increasing the pressure on her G-spot. "You're fucking me so sweetly."

She exploded around him, the wave of pleasure crashing around her. He groaned and flipped her over onto her stomach, keeping his hand on her clit, trapped between her body and the carpet.

Michele gasped as he pounded into her from behind, her body spasming around his. His cock twitched inside her, pulsating, and he groaned in satisfaction.

She felt him carefully pull out and lie beside her, his breath coming hard and fast, matching hers.

Michele rolled over and lay on the carpet, panting, her body shivering with delicious aftershocks from her orgasm.

Andrew looked at her. "I'm sorry I hurt your feelings. I really am."

"I know," she said quietly. "Thank you."

"I love you, you know."

Excitement rushed through her, as powerful as any physical sensation he'd just given her. Did he really just say that, or was she dreaming?

He kissed her, his brow furrowed. "Please say something."

"Something."

He frowned. "Did I say it too soon?"

"Yes," she said, smiling. "But that's okay because I love you too."

I said it! And it's true. Oh my god.

Andrew laughed and pulled her into his arms, crushing her against his muscular torso. His heart thudded against the sensitive skin on her chest, and she knew her heart was fluttering against him as well.

"Would it be really cheesy," he asked, "if I said great minds think alike?"

"Totally cheesy, but that's okay too." She grinned and pressed a tiny kiss on his flat little nipple.

And she realized she hadn't thought about her hair, or lack of it, since he undressed her. She was able to have a thoroughly enjoyable sexual experience, and she hadn't even had to have a hair transplant.

Hell, she didn't even have to wear her fancy new wig.

"Will you come out with me and my friends tonight?" he asked. "Please?"

"Yeah, I'll go."

"Hope you don't mind being seen with three bald dudes."

She laughed at the image. "Nope, I don't mind a bit."

301

Epilogue
❧

Dear Durban Trust,

It's been a year since you first offered me a grant to have a hair transplant. I will forever be appreciative of your kindness and generosity, even though I ultimately wasn't a candidate for the surgery.

The custom human hair wig still looks fabulous. I know when I go out that no one but me knows it's not my real hair. The cosmetic tattoos are so natural looking too. I feel like I can wake up and go and still look good. Once again, thank you, thank you!

But the real reason I'm writing today is to let you know that I've achieved my dream. I've been dating an incredible man who loves me for who I am, inside and out — and he's shown me I don't need hair to have an amazing sexual experience.

He shows me that a lot... I can't believe I'm writing this, but did you know that the scalp is positively covered in sensitive nerve endings? When he runs his fingertips over my head, I start to wonder why I ever wanted hair in the first place, LOL!

But ultimately no man, not even Andrew, could show me how to feel good about myself and how to let go and lose myself in sensuality. I had to learn that for myself. This year has been a true learning experience, and I'm grateful I had a chance to grow as a person.

So that's it — I just wanted to let you know how things turned out.

Sincerely,
Michele Peterson

Michele smiled to herself as she reread her email one last time before hitting send.

She startled when Andrew sneaked up behind her and placed a tender kiss right on top of her bare head. They'd been living together for the past few months, and it was heaven. Seeing him every day felt so…right. She tilted her head back and he planted an upside-down kiss on her lips. His hair had grown back, and she insisted he keep it. No reason for them both to be bald if they didn't have to be.

"Whatcha working on?" he asked.

"Just sending off a thank you."

"It's too nice outside to spend all Saturday cooped up inside," Andrew said, helping her to her feet.

"Agreed." She grabbed a wide-brimmed hat that kept the sun off her head but still let her scalp breathe and followed him out the door. This summer, she'd decided not to torture herself under a hot wig if she didn't feel like it. Sure, she still wore the wig to work, but to the park? No need.

And she still felt beautiful.

Thinking of work brought a To Do list a mile long to mind, and she quickly forced herself to relax and enjoy her weekend off. Not that she didn't enjoy work, though. She was at the same company, still doing customer service, but her devotion to her customers had gotten her promoted to supervisor. With the pay raise came the ability to delve deeper into customer complaints so she could solve their problems. Some days it was grueling, but usually she felt a real sense of accomplishment. And she'd signed a contract that meant she didn't have to worry about her job being outsourced to India, at least for another year, anyway.

Andrew held her hand as they walked down the crowded Manhattan sidewalk.

"Let's get something to eat at the park. We'll picnic," Andrew suggested. They stepped into Mr. Patel's corner market. The cramped, overly bright convenience store brought a smile to her face every time she came by now.

She'd even managed to buy some condoms from behind the counter. Unfortunately, she hadn't quite been able not to blush like she'd planned. Baby steps.

"Hello lovebirds," Mr. Patel called as the bell above the door chimed their entrance.

"Hi, Mr. Patel," they replied in unison.

"Jinx," they said at the same time.

Michele laughed. "You realize we're ridiculous, right?"

Andrew kissed her, still chuckling. "Bet you can't guess what I'm going to say next."

"Um," she thought hard. "You want beer?"

He dropped to his knee on the worn linoleum shop floor. "No — well, maybe later."

She laughed. *Oh my god, is this happening?* And did she just interrupt her own marriage proposal?

"I want you to marry me," he said, looking up at her. "So I'm proposing in the same place where we first met. Will you marry me, Michele?"

Tears of happiness filled her eyes and she swiped them away with the back of her hand, no longer even thinking about accidentally rubbing off false eyelashes.

"Yes," she whispered, her voice breaking. "Oh my god. Yes!"

He stayed kneeling, a huge grin on his face. "I didn't pick out a ring, I thought it would be fun to go ring shopping together."

She tugged his hands, pulling him to standing. He knew her so well. "I love you," she said, and melted into his kiss.

The End

Also by Desiree Holt

৪০

eBooks:

1-800-DOM-help: Delight Me

Cougar Challenge 4: Hot to Trot

Cupid's Shaft

Dancing With Danger

Diamond Lady

Double Entry

Downstroke

Driven by Hunger

Ellora's Cavemen: Flavors of Ecstasy I *(anthology)*

Emerald Green

Erector Set 1: Erected

Erector Set 2: Hammered

Escape the Night

Hard Lovin'

Hot Moon Rising

Hot, Wicked and Wild

I Dare You

Journey to the Pearl

Just Say Yes

Kidnapping the Groom *(with Allie Standifer)*

Letting Go

Line of Sight

Mistletoe Magic 2: Touch of Magic

Mistletoe Magic 4: Elven Magic (*with Regina Carlysle & Cindy Spencer Pape*)

Nemesis 1: Until the Dawn (*with Cerise DeLand*)

Nemesis 2: Until Midnight (*with Cerise DeLand*)

Nemesis 3: Until Twilight (*with Cerise DeLand*)

Night Heat

Night Seekers 1: Lust Unleashed

Night Seekers 2: Lust by Moonlight

Night Seekers 3: Lust Undone

Once Burned

Once Upon a Wedding

Phoenix Agency 1: Jungle Inferno

Phoenix Agency 2: Extrasensory

Phoenix Agency 3: Delicious Danger

Phoenix Agency 4: F-Stop

Riding Out the Storm

Rodeo Heat

Seductive Illusion (*with Allie Standifer*)

Sequins, Saddles and Spurs 1: Trouble in Cowboy Boots

Skin Deep: Bedroom Eyes

Something Wicked This Way Comes, Volume 1 (*anthology*)

Switched

Teaching Molly

Texas Passions 1: Eagle's Run

Training Amber

Turn Up the Heat 1: Scorched (*with Allie Standifer*)

Turn Up the Heat 2: Scalded (*with Allie Standifer*)

Turn Up the Heat 3: Singed (*with Allie Standifer*)

Turn Up the Heat 4: Steamed (*with Allie Standifer*)

Wedding Belles 3: Something Borrowed

Wedding Belles 4: Something Blue *(with Cerise DeLand & Allie Standifer)*

Where Danger Hides

Print Books:
Candy Caresses *(anthology)*
Cougar Challenge: Tease the Cougar *(anthology)*
Downstroke
Ellora's Cavemen: Flavors of Ecstasy I *(anthology)*
Erotic Emerald *(anthology)*
Mistletoe Magic *(anthology)*
Naughty Nuptials *(anthology)*
Night Heat
Night Seekers 1: Lust Unleashed
Night Seekers 2: Lust by Moonlight
Once Burned
Rodeo Heat
Sequins, Saddles and Spurs *(anthology)*
Something Wicked This Way Comes, Volume 1 *(anthology)*
Texas Passions *(anthology)*
Turn Up the Heat *(anthology)*
Wedding Belles *(anthology)*
Where Danger Hides

About Desiree Holt

ൠ

I always wonder what readers really want to know when I write one of these things. Getting to this point in my career has been an interesting journey. I've managed rock and roll bands and organized concerts. Been the only female on the sports staff of a university newspaper. Immersed myself in Nashville peddling a country singer. Lived in five different states. Married two very interesting but totally different men.

I think I must have lived in Texas in another life, because the minute I set foot on Texas soil I knew I was home. Living in Texas Hill Country gives me inspiration for more stories than I'll probably ever be able to tell, what with all the sexy cowboys who surround me and the gorgeous scenery that provides a great setting.

Each day is a new adventure for me, as my characters come to life on the pages of my current work in progress. I'm absolutely compulsive about it when I'm writing and thank all the gods and goddesses that I have such a terrific husband who encourages my writing and puts up with my obsession. As a multi-published author, I love to hear from my readers. Their input keeps my mind fresh and always hunting for new ideas.

Also by Lynne Connolly

୫

eBooks:
Cougar Challenge: Seychelles Sunset
Cougar Challenge: Sunshine on Chrome
Cougar Challenge 2: Beauty of Sunset
Ecstasy in Red 1: Red Alert
Ecstasy in Red 2: Red Heat
Ecstasy in Red 3: Red Shadow
Ecstasy in Red 4: Red Inferno
Emotion in Motion
Nightstar 1: In the Mood
Pure Wildfire 1: Sunfire
Pure Wildfire 2: Icefire
Pure Wildfire 3: Moonfire
Pure Wildfire 4: Thunderfire
Skin Deep: Strangers No More
Storm: Shifting Heat

Print Books:
Cougar Challenge: Tempt the Cougar *(anthology)*
Ecstasy in Red 1: Red Alert
Ecstasy in Red 2: Red Heat
Ecstasy in Red 3: Red Shadow
Pure Wildfire 1: Sunfire
Pure Wildfire 2: Icefire
Pure Wildfire 3: Moonfire

About Lynne Connolly

ᏠᏩ

Lynne Connolly writes for a number of online publishers. She writes paranormal romance, contemporary romance and historical romance. She is the winner of two Eppies (now retitled the EPIC ebook awards) and a goodly number of Recommended Reads etc from review sites.

While these are very gratifying, that isn't why she writes. She wants to bring the stories in her head to life and share them with others, in the hope that they might give her some peace.

She lives in the UK with her family, cat and doll's houses. Creating worlds on paper or in miniature seems to be her specialty!

Also by Shoshanna Evers

℘

eBooks:

Chastity Belt

Ginger Snap

Hollywood Spank

Punishing the Art Thief

Skin Deep: Bedhead

Print Books:

Bound to be Naughty *(anthology)*

About Shoshanna Evers

ஐ

Shoshanna Evers is an Amazon Erotica Bestselling multi-published romance author. When she's not writing hot sex, she's a newspaper advice columnist, a registered nurse, and a stay-at-home mom. Shoshanna lives with her family and three big dogs in Port Saint Lucie, Florida. Her favorite thing to do is cuddle up with a good book...and her husband. She welcomes emails from readers and writers. *Sexily *Evers* After...*

ஐ

The authors welcome comments from readers. You can find their websites and email addresses on their author bio pages at www.ellorascave.com.

Tell Us What You Think

We appreciate hearing reader opinions about our books. You can email us at Comments@EllorasCave.com.

Why an electronic book?

We live in the Information Age—an exciting time in the history of human civilization, in which technology rules supreme and continues to progress in leaps and bounds every minute of every day. For a multitude of reasons, more and more avid literary fans are opting to purchase e-books instead of paper books. The question from those not yet initiated into the world of electronic reading is simply: *Why?*

1. *Price.* An electronic title at Ellora's Cave Publishing runs anywhere from 40% to 75% less than the cover price of the exact same title in paperback format. Why? Basic mathematics and cost. It is less expensive to publish an e-book (no paper and printing, no warehousing and shipping) than it is to publish a paperback, so the savings are passed along to the consumer.

2. *Space.* Running out of room in your house for your books? That is one worry you will never have with electronic books. For a low one-time cost, you can purchase a handheld device specifically designed for e-reading. Many e-readers have large, convenient screens for viewing. Better yet, hundreds of titles can be stored within your new library—on a single microchip. There are a variety of e-readers from different manufacturers. You can also read e-books on your PC or laptop computer. (Please note that Ellora's Cave does not endorse any specific brands.

You can check our website at www.ellorascave.com for information we make available to new consumers.)

3. *Mobility.* Because your new e-library consists of only a microchip within a small, easily transportable e-reader, your entire cache of books can be taken with you wherever you go.

4. *Personal Viewing Preferences.* Are the words you are currently reading too small? Too large? Too… ANNOYING? Paperback books cannot be modified according to personal preferences, but e-books can.

5. *Instant Gratification.* Is it the middle of the night and all the bookstores near you are closed? Are you tired of waiting days, sometimes weeks, for bookstores to ship the novels you bought? Ellora's Cave Publishing sells instantaneous downloads twenty-four hours a day, seven days a week, every day of the year. Our webstore is never closed. Our e-book delivery system is 100% automated, meaning your order is filled as soon as you pay for it.

Those are a few of the top reasons why electronic books are replacing paperbacks for many avid readers.

As always, Ellora's Cave welcomes your questions and comments. We invite you to email us at Comments@ellorascave.com or write to us directly at Ellora's Cave Publishing Inc., 1056 Home Avenue, Akron, OH 44310-3502.

MAKE EACH DAY MORE *EXCITING* WITH OUR

ELLORA'S CAVEMEN
CALENDAR

WWW.ELLORASCAVE.COM

ELLORA'S CAVE

Romanticon

Annual convention
for women who
refuse to behave

Discover for yourself why readers can't get enough
of the multiple award-winning publisher

Ellora's Cave.

Whether you prefer e-books or paperbacks,

be sure to visit EC on the web at
www.ellorascave.com

for an erotic reading experience that will leave you
breathless.

CPSIA information can be obtained at www.ICGtesting.com
Printed in the USA
BVOW040245270812

298756BV00002B/3/P

9 781419 966484